Mozart's Fugue

Foxrock Books: London

MOZART'S FUGUE

Jay Raymond

FOXROCK BOOKS : LONDON AND TORONTO

Foxrock Books
17 Sovereign Court
Northwood, Middlesex
Foxrock Books
21 McGillivray Avenue
Toronto, Ontario, Canada

First published 2000 in electronic form
on the Internet by Online Originals.com.
First published in printed form 2002

Cataloguing-in-Publication Data. A
catalogue record of this book is available
from the British Library

ISBN: 09514368 9 9

Mozart's Fugue

ONE

Antique dealers, Tom and Gwen Bateson, were hopelessly outbid when they attended an auction, intending to buy a violin for their daughter, a student at the Royal College of Music. Out of desperation, Gwen recklessly bid for the last item in the catalogue, an eighteenth-century German piano-stool, ignoring her husband's warning that it might be a late nineteenth-century fake. She paid with her credit card and returned with her husband to Camden Passage, North London. Tom placed the piano stool in a dark corner of the shop, grumbling that she had paid far too much for it. The following day, when a customer idly lifted the lid, Gwen noticed some buff-coloured music sheets in the torn yellow satin lining at the base of the piano stool. She said to the man, half in jest: 'The contents are included.'

He shook his head and walked out.

When Tom returned from a buying expedition the following evening, Gwen showed him a thick wad of documents she had recovered carrying the signature: Johann Wunder. Tom, after giving them a cursory glance, suggested that their daughter Carla show them to Professor Bernard Beinmender, who taught music history at the college. A few days later Beinmender telephoned to say that the manuscripts consisted of an unknown opera, a flute concerto and a violin concerto of the early classical period. There was also a fugue entitled *Sieben* and a journal written in old-fashioned Gothic script. The music had a compelling likeness to some of

1

Mozart's compositions but the dates clearly indicated that the works had been composed subsequent to his death.

Beinmender made an extensive search on the Internet for the name Johann Wunder and was eventually rewarded by the discovery of a letter in the archives of a small commercial museum in Vienna:

March 23rd 1792

To the proprietor of the Stilvoll Outfitters in Reitterstrasse, Vienna.

Esteemed Sir,

Some months ago I was found suffering from a serious illness which has robbed me of my memory. The items of clothing I was wearing at the time may have been purchased in your excellent emporium. They include a waistcoat of blue satin with six matching blue buttons. I am five-feet three-inches tall, of medium build. The garment is badly stained but otherwise in good order.
When I have recovered from my present sickness, I shall travel to Vienna from the remote village in Galicia where I am presently living, and hope that with your invaluable assistance the garment in question may help to ascertain my true identity.
I sign below the name which has been temporarily assigned to me by Shmul Perlman, a kind benefactor to whom I owe my life.

Johann Wunder, 12 Brocher Street
Korlyshev, Province of Galicia.

Colleagues of Beinmender agreed that the works found in the piano stool were strongly reminiscent of Wolfgang Amadeus Mozart.. There was no mention of any of the works in the Ludvig Von Köchel listings. Whoever had written them had reproduced Mozart's sparkling musical wit and intellectual grace with uncanny accuracy. Beinmender's first assumption was that the documents were forgeries deliberately designed to give the impression that Mozart had survived his last illness.

Gwen Bateson answered when he telephoned.

'Hi, Mrs Bateson. I've taken another good look at the manuscripts Carla showed me. Johann Wunder writes and sounds like Mozart. I should like to hang on to them for a while longer.'

'Do you think they might be valuable?'

'The music is clearly the work of a highly talented musician. But there were thousands of very gifted musical wannabes in the eighteenth-century, just as there are thousands of would-be Pop stars today.'

'Why should the music resemble Mozart's, if he didn't write it?'

'The history of music is full of attempts by frustrated musicians to copy the works of other, more successful, musicians.'

'Do you think someone might be interested in publishing it.'

'Possibly. But you could spend years hawking it around with no guarantee of success.'

'Would you care to come for dinner tomorrow. I'm desperately anxious to know more.'

'Yes. Thank you. I have translated part of the journal. I'll bring it along to give you something of its flavour.'

*

Gwen had met Bernard Beinmender, a teacher of music history, the previous year when she and her husband had attended a concert in the Royal College of Music. Their daughter, Carla, had praised him enthusiastically, pointing out that as well as being a brilliant pianist he was also an excellent

3

teacher. The possibility that Carla might be in love with him had not even remotely entered Gwen's mind.

The Batesons had recently moved from a large house in Hampstead to a small flat in Highbury. Beinmender presented his hostess with a bottle of wine and a folder containing a translation of part of the journal. Gwen led him into a pleasantly-furnished dining-room and apologized for her husband's absence, explaining that he was attending an executors' sale in Birmingham. Scarcely able to keep the excitement out of her voice, she enquired: as they sat down, 'Do you think I have made an important musical discovery?'

'Mrs Bateson, people are going to take an awful lot of convincing that Mozart rose from the dead and then went on to write an opera, a fugue and two concertos.'

'Do call me Gwen. May I remind you that you said that the music is beautiful.'

'It certainly is — I'm Bernard, by the way. But just because the music is beautiful it doesn't necessarily follow that Mozart wrote it.'

'Then who did?'

'We don't know. Whoever did was undoubtedly an accomplished musician. But the manuscripts may not be worth much.'

'Really.' Gwen replied, trying hard to swallow her disappointment.

Beinmender said soothingly: 'Other people more expert than myself might take a different view. The good news is that tests have shown that the paper is of the correct type for the period. At least, if they are forgeries, they are very old ones. The watermark shows that it is not the same paper as Mozart customarily used in Vienna. But the method of writing is the same — he uses, for example, twelve staves to the page. It fits in with the supposition that the person who wrote it was taken to Galicia, which is now part of Poland.'

He sipped the wine she had just poured and commented: 'But you must try not to get too excited about it.'

4

'Tom isn't very optimistic, either He never is these days.'

She refilled his glass and said: 'But you did say that the music is of the highest quality.'

'I'm sorry if I raised your hopes.'

She poured out more wine and asked if he had ever been questioned about other manuscripts.

'Somebody once showed me what he thought was an unknown piece by Chopin. But I am afraid it wasn't.'

.   'Just supposing the manuscripts were genuinely by Mozart, how much would they be worth?'

'A king's ransom. An envelope he had written was once auctioned for twelve-thousand pounds. By the way, where's Carla this evening?'

'She's staying at a friend's house.'

Quite awed by the possibility of becoming extremely rich, Gwen poured out more wine. Under its influence, Beinmender, commented: 'That lovely titian hair of yours reminds me of a red-haired opera singer of whom Mozart is supposed to have been very fond.'

'I wonder if he would have taken a fancy to me — I trained as an opera singer. I think I might have excelled as Carmen.'

'Really?'

'Unfortunately, I met Tom and gave up my career.'

'I'm sure Mozart would have made a pass at you.'

'You did say that Johann Wunder writes and sounds exactly like him.'

'He may simply have copied his style. He would have known all about his idiosyncrasies, just as we all know about those of modern Pop stars.'

Gwen declared: 'I still have a hunch that the music will turn out to be genuine. Tom says I have an uncanny instinct for spotting the real thing.'

'Can you honestly and seriously believe that Wolfgang Mozart survived, when all the records agree that he was buried in St. Marks graveyard on December 5 1791.'

'Miracles do happen'

'I think it would be a mistake to be too optimistic.'

'Would you like coffee?'

'Yes, please.'

Later, Gwen said quietly: 'You must think I'm very obstinate.'

'A little unrealistic perhaps. But I have only translated part of the journal. The rest of it may provide some insight as to how the manuscripts came into being.'

'What would be required to get them accepted as the works of Mozart?'

'It would need a consensus among reputable scholars and musicologists all over the world that the music was produced by Wolfgang Amadeus Mozart and by no one else. Your husband, Tom, is right to be sceptical.'

'The reason that I am so keen to make some money is that I want to open a new business.'

'Does Tom like the idea?'

'It has nothing to do with him. We don't get on all that well these days.'

'To be frank there's about as much chance of Johann Wunder turning out to be Wolfgang Amadeus Mozart as there is of him walking through the door.'

'Do you mean Mozart or my husband?'

'Mozart.'

'If it was my husband, he would probably jump to the conclusion that we were having an affair.'

Beinmender laughed and said: 'The chances of the manuscripts turning out to be genuine are so remote that I would be prepared to justify his suspicions.'

He took a piece of paper and scribbled on it: 'If Johann Wunder is Wolfgang Mozart, we'll have an affair. Sign there.'

Gwen, smiling playfully, scribbled her signature and said: 'You are now fully and absolutely committed to proving that Wunder and Mozart were one and the same person.'

'Let's hope for the best. But I'm afraid the chances are not very great.'

As he was about to leave, Gwen said archly: 'Don't forget our little bargain.'

The following morning, Beinmender, remembering the conversation, assured himself that Gwen had fully understood that he had merely been trying to warn her against entertaining false hopes.

TWO

Johann Wunder's Journal

My head ached terribly, was heavy beyond belief and seemed full of angry, buzzing insects. I shivered uncontrollably. Every now and again the lurching of the vehicle in which I was travelling caused unbearable pain in my side. I slept for long periods. During brief waking interludes snow flakes fell out of a leaden sky and danced crazily in front of my eyes. A burly, white-bearded man with a red complexion and a bulbous red nose loomed above me. I closed my eyes He knelt down, attacked my nostrils with a piece of straw and said with a puzzled expression, in a strange kind of German: 'It's a miracle.'

I opened my eyes.

A wooden spoon brushed against my lips.

'You must take nourishment,' the bearded face declared. '*Gott in Himmel*, you must eat. We've been travelling three days.'

I tried to escape into a dark, pleasant haven of dreams but was rudely awakened and forced to swallow spoonfuls of hot broth.

I slept again for a long period of time, until I was wakened by the noise of the wagon wheels trundling over marbled, hard, rutted snow. Reb Perlman later told me what had happened. I shall never know for certain whether he was telling the truth.

'Your escape from death must have been *bershert*. He spoke in Yiddish, a strange language I was barely able to understand. I learned later the word means predestined. I was sitting muffled in furs, having regained sufficient strength to sit on the seat beside him. He went on, almost as though he was talking to himself: 'I invariably avoid St. Marks church graveyard when I am working in Vienna — graveyards remind me that my own time must come soon. But drunken hooligans were throwing bottles on my usual route, so I made a detour. Approaching the graveyard, I gave Shlotkin my horse a tap with my whip to make him hurry. As he increased his pace, I saw a corpse lying half in and half out of the ground. 'Those devils of gravediggers!' I said to myself. 'They get drunk and don't do their job.

'As we passed by, I noticed the half-buried corpse was wearing an expensive waistcoat and an embroidered shirt. The shirt took my attention, because my dear departed wife, God rest her soul, had been an expert embroiderer.

'I called out to Shlotkin to halt — it seemed a sin to waste such an expensive garment. But I threw off the evil inclination and decided that grave-robbing was not for me. I urged Shlotkin forward. But his attention was distracted by a magpie that swooped past his head and he didn't hear me. You owe your life to that magpie. Again, I called out to Shlotkin to move and as I cast my eye back, I saw the ruffled sleeve the corpse was wearing stir slightly. Shlotkin began to move forward again. But I shouted: 'Whoa!'

He stopped so suddenly that I was nearly thrown off my seat.

'I jumped down, came closer to the body and cursed the reprobates of grave-diggers for not doing their job properly. Then came another shock your arm moved again. I decided it was caused by a mud slide — there had been heavy rain the night before. But in spite of the dread I felt in my heart, I came closer. Life is precious — we Jews say the toast, *l'chaym,* which means to life. One has a duty to preserve life, however faintly the flame burns. Who knows what lies beyond the grave. Indeed, it is forbidden to ask.

'I looked down again and saw your fingers clutch at the mud.

'What was I to do? I am not a doctor and know nothing of such things.

9

'I went back to my wagon and found a mirror. Holding it to your face, I detected a faint condensation. My conscience would not allow me to leave you. So using a spade that I always carry on my wagon, I dug away the wet soil surrounding your lower limbs, placed you among my merchandise, covered you with blankets and urged Shlotkin forward. I intended to find someone who would take care of you. But things are never simple.

'I called at a house. The occupant said: 'Go away you dirty vagabond.'

'At the next house, the owner spat at me and said: 'I can see through your trick you're just trying to extort money from me.'

'When I told my story at the third one, the occupant told me scornfully: 'Lazarus rose from the dead. That kind of miracle doesn't happen nowadays.'

'I was in a terrible dilemma. If I let you die, I would be a murderer. If I was found with a corpse on my wagon I would be accused of grave-robbing.'

Shmul made a helpless gesture and continued: 'I had no alternative but to take you with me. If you died on the way home, I would have hidden your body in a ditch. But I kept you warm and gave you nourishment. It seemed like a miracle when you finally opened your eyes. Still, miracles happen all the time... The world itself is a miracle... Who are you? What happened?'

I shook my head, too exhausted to talk.

In the days that followed, I tried very hard to remember my past. But I couldn't even remember my own name. Shadowy faces returned and then faded. I could not put names to them.

I murmured: 'I don't know who I am.'

'Well, at least you can speak. That's a good sign. When your memory comes back, I will take you back to Vienna. I am a widower, a Jew, a merchant. More a pedlar than a merchant. What's the difference? A merchant is someone who lends

10

money to a poor pedlar. A pedlar is someone who is lucky if he earns enough to pay back the merchant.

'I have two sons and two daughters. One daughter is married and lives in Warsaw. My sons have gone to Paris. Since the Revolution I haven't heard from them. So now all I have to keep me company is my daughter, Leah.'

Shmul paused, as we descended into a snow-covered gully. Shlotkin ploughed into the deep snow, shuddered and snorted, then pulled the wagon through with a gallant effort, before resuming his slow steady plodding.

Shmul went on: 'You don't answer. But don't worry. I am used to silence. I talk all the while to Shlotkin. He understands every word. I speak Yiddish but when I talk to him in Hebrew, the holy language, he understands even better!'

Shmul gave a great guffaw and went on: 'The rabbis tell us that language is more than something that the tongue wraps itself around. Everything speaks a language — the flowers, the stones even. You hum a tune that's a language. You dance a few steps that's a language. You can translate one into the other. When you say something in German, I change it into Yiddish, although they are very similar. God spoke a word in his language and the world sprang into being. Maybe He shouldn't have bothered. Understanding God's language is very difficult, if not impossible. Our rabbi tries very hard but doesn't succeed. When my wife, Zeta, *alev a sholem*, died, he was unable to translate God's language into mine and explain why she had to die. But it does him credit that he tries. Sometimes it makes him look like a fool, although I shouldn't say that about a man who has studied the Talmud, the Mishnah Torah, the Gemara and the Guide of the Perplexed.'

We mounted a ridge.

Below me I could see against a darkening sky the outline of a small town. The road leading towards it was unpaved and full of frozen puddles. Rangy dogs barked at us as we went by. We passed houses with shingled roofs and some covered with rushes that looked as though they might collapse any minute.

11

Shmul pointed with his whip to a crook-backed building and said: 'That's our synagogue.'

I was feeling faint and exhausted and did not care whether I lived or died. A young woman came out to greet us as the wagon rumbled towards a small wooden house with a stable alongside and an outhouse, where I later learned Shmul kept his merchandise.

'I've brought home someone who was nearly a corpse,' Shmul remarked to the woman.

She asked what was wrong with me and gave me a strange look. That is all I remember of that day. As I attempted to step down from the driving seat of the wagon, I fell and lost consciousness.

THREE

The sun's dying rays were reddening the walls of the wooden house opposite when I awoke. I was lying under bundles of furs on a straw pallet. All around me were pots and pans, oil lamps, spittoons, bales of cloth, cheap Turkish rugs and boxes of candles — one of which had spilled its contents over the rush mats covering the clay floor Outside, hens were squawking.

Feeling an urgent need to urinate, I tried to stand up but my legs were wobbly and I immediately collapsed. I lay for a while fighting to contain myself. The young woman I had seen on my arrival entered the room and enquired how I was feeling. She spoke in Yiddish, a language to which I had become attuned while travelling. I told her of my predicament. She withdrew. Soon a stockily-built, bald hunchback with hollow cheeks and large, protruding ears appeared. His hooked nose matched the crooked angle of his spine.

'Come on, young man.'

Exposing yellowing teeth in a friendly smile, he levered me upright. With his strong hands supporting me, I stumbled to a privy at the back of Reb Perlman's house. On the way, we passed a stable from which a warm smell emerged, giving me the impression that Shlotkin was better housed than I was. The hunchback whose name was Yankel handed me an old newspaper and waited outside. I urinated strong-smelling urine. My bowels rushed open. When I emerged, shivering, scarcely able to stand, he helped me back into my makeshift bed.

I muttered thanks and huddled again under the animal skins. Soon afterwards, the daughter, Leah, arrived with a cup of soup filled with noodles.

'Where am I?' I asked.

She told me I was in a small town called Korlyshev. Half the population were Jews; the other half Christians. They lived together in amity. She asked if I would like the local priest to call on me. The word priest brought back a faint recollection of a man wearing a black hat and a long black soutane.

'I am beyond the help of a priest,' I replied. 'I feel as though I have already died.'

'You should be grateful that God in his mercy has preserved you. My father has gone into town to buy more food. As she held the cup to my lips, she said soothingly: 'I have a boiled chicken stew for you.'

'How can I ever thank you?' I murmured.

'A good deed is its own reward.'

Leah was about thirty, her nose short and slightly bent. There was a wart on the right-hand side of her chin. Her shining, light brown hair came down almost to her waist. She had a gentle, kind personality. I discovered later that she was well versed in the Torah, the holy book of the Jews.

She returned shortly afterwards with the chicken stew and a crust of bread, of which I ate a small amount. When I thanked her again, she smiled and assured me that I would soon be on the road to recovery. The effort of eating and talking, however, had tired me. I lay down and slept for a long time.

A crescent moon was shining through the window against a background of dark sky, when I awoke. A dog howled in the distance. I tried to remember who I was but my mind refused to cooperate. Words came into my mind which did not make sense. It was as if I was throwing stones into a well from which no echo returns. The experience left me feeling frightened, frustrated and miserable. Leah's kindness, however, saved me from plumbing the utter depths of despair and gave me the will to live.

I asked myself how I could repay these strange people who sheltered and fed me. Even at that early stage in my recovery my pride was such that I could not help fretting over my total

14

dependency. Somewhere in the world outside I knew I had friends, family, colleagues and acquaintances. But I could recall only faceless, shapeless phantoms. One face stood out, which I recognised as that of my mother. Her expression of sad resentment caused me to burst into tears.

There seemed nothing to look forward to. Shmul Perlman's assurance during our journey that my clothes were those of a gentleman suggested that I must once have been a person of some means and consequence. But now I was nameless, poverty-stricken and without a past. It appeared I had come from Vienna.

The names of other cities Prague, Salzburg, Paris came to me. Cloudy pictures of buildings floated through my mind. I saw richly-clad figures, disdainful faces and heard the sound of applause. But I did not know why the people were clapping.

I had no idea of my present location. At some time during our seemingly endless journey Shmul had told me that we were travelling north-eastwards. But I knew nothing of this region, which seemed backwards, poverty-stricken and possessed few buildings of merit or substance.

Words of reproach came to me, as I lay in the darkness, 'Seven of your brothers and sisters died so that you could live and make music!'

My mother had once spoken these words to me. How unworthy I must have been to earn this rebuke. How much more so was I now!

*

An apothecary in the town prescribed medicine, which Leah conscientiously administered to me. One day a priest, Father Pacek, called to see me. Outside, a blizzard was blowing — his wide-brimmed hat and fur coat were white with snow flakes.

He asked if I could remember my name.

'I cannot remember my birth name. Nor can I remember anything of my former life.'

15

'Would you prefer to live among Christians than among Jews?'

I shook my head. The thought of moving to another house distressed me.

'You will return to a state of grace more swiftly if you live among Christians than among these heathens.'

'I am perfectly happy here.'

'Christ has saved you from Eternal Damnation. Be grateful for that act of sublime mercy. I will come in a few weeks to see if your memory has returned.'

He handed me a missal, opened the door and disappeared into a cloud of swirling snowflakes,

A few days later, an old man with a long white beard and yellowing sidelocks shuffled into the room and introduced himself as the local rabbi. He stared down at me for a long time as if I was a wild, captive animal and then asked if I was circumcised. The fact that I had grown a beard and was reluctant to move to the Christian side of the town seemed to have persuaded him that I was a Jew.

I replied: 'No.'

'Do you wish to move to a Christian household?'

'I am not well enough.'

'How are you feeling?'

'Much improved, thank you, sir. But not yet ready to face the world.'

He said with a faint smile: 'Reb Perlman told me you have seen what lies beyond the grave. That is a rare privilege.'

'I can remember nothing of my experience. My memory has been almost totally destroyed.'

'Be thankful that you are alive.'

He stared at me closely as if seeking some inspiration, muttered goodbye and left me alone with my thoughts. The two meetings increased my sense of confusion. I resolved to tell Shmul that I must return to Vienna as soon as possible to establish my identity.

Weeks passed. Strength returned to my limbs. Leah continued to bring me food but I no longer needed the assistance of the hunchback to go to the privy. Shmul occasionally entered the room to remove items of merchandise. His absences sometimes lasted several days. I asked him on one occasion when I could return to Vienna. He replied not for some time — apparently his dealings there on his last visit had not been very successful.

One day when I was feeling better, I left my bed, stood by the door and looked past Shlotkin's stable at the entrance to Perlman's small wooden house. Tempting cooking smells were coming from it. But I yearned as much for Leah's company as food.

I had told her that a total blankness greeted all my efforts to remember my past. I could not remember whether I had a wife and children. Leah usually came early in the day with food, a basin of hot water and a towel and rearranged the hides and pelts on my mattress. As dusk fell, she brought an oil lamp to provide light and warmth in the room. She assured me that my memory would one day return, enabling me to take my rightful place in the world.

'No money can ever repay you and your father for the kindness you have both shown.'

'Any human being would do the same.'

She tried to jog my memory.

'Do you know the name of the King of Prussia?'

I frowned and shook my head.

'Have you heard of Louis 16th of France...of the Emperor Leopold?'

'No.'

'Empress Catherine of Russia?'

She mentioned musicians: Haydn, Mozart, Salieri, Anfossi. These names evoked what I can only describe as a dull, thudding resonance in my head. Some impediment in my brain prevented further information from coming through.

I began to feel that I was a completely useless being. I hated existing on the charity of others. Leah's gentle warmth

17

and constant kindness, however, prevented me from falling into total despair.

For several more weeks I lay among the pelts of long-dead animals, breathing in their stale odour, intensely frustrated by the thick fog that had obliterated all recollections of my previous existence. Trying to recall them made me like a dog chasing his tail. The dog knows that it is there, even though at times it remains tantalisingly out of view. Faint images occasionally appeared but vanished when I tried to focus on them.

I spent much of the time asleep, waking to sip the warm broth that Leah brought me and then relapsing again into unconsciousness for long periods. I dreamed of wolves and wild animals caught in traps. Their cries of pain reflected my own distress at being caught in a dreadful snare that had robbed me of my past.

Soon, however, a surprising event occurred that gave me hope for the future.

FOUR

Smul came into the store room one day after one of his long journeys and said heartily: 'I have had a good trip. I disposed of almost all my merchandise.'

I tried to raise myself. But he thrust me back with a large hand onto the mattress.

'Stay still, young man. Conserve your strength. You're getting better all the time. I sold everything except an old firescreen, which I exchanged for this.' He showed me an ancient flute. 'It's not worth much, but then neither was the firescreen.'

He placed the battered instrument to his lips and produced a shrill whistling sound. Seeing the pained expression on my face, he handed it to me and said sarcastically: 'See if you can do any better.'

I put the instrument to my lips and forming an embouchure, managed to produce a few notes. The effort, however, exhausted me.

Shmul then announced that he was going to feed his horse — loud neighs of protest were coming from the stable next door. I slept. When I woke, it was dark. I was clutching the musical instrument to my chest like a long lost lover. I resisted the temptation to play it, out of consideration for Shmul Perlman and his daughter in the house nearby.

A few days later, when Shmul visited me, I surprised him by producing a simple tune. He performed a little jig with surprising agility for a man of his age and then said: 'You have talent, no doubt about it. Keep practising until I find a buyer for it.'

I fell asleep again.

It was still dark when I woke, feeling excited by the prospect of making more music. I decided to wait until it was

19

light before playing. The instrument had evoked a thousand memories of orchestral sounds. Images of musical notations appeared in my mind and danced and tumbled to the music.

I occupied the time by dwelling on my present unsatisfactory circumstances. It was demeaning having to accept the hospitality of a poor working man. Better perhaps to have been left to die. I knew that it was wrong to harbour such thoughts. But I believe in retrospect that this keen resentment at having to accept charity marked the beginning of my recovery.

Leah and her father came to see me one day, Leah carrying a tray of food. Shmul said joshingly to her: 'How should we address this high-ranking nobleman from Vienna?'

Leah handing me a bowl of chicken broth, said softly: Let's call him Herr Wunder; it's a wonder that he survived.'

'And for a forename — Mordecai, Chaim, Ozer?'

'No, they're Jewish names. Let's call him Rudolph or Franz or Johann. Yes, we'll call him Johann.' She turned to me and said: 'Would you like a middle name?'

I muttered: 'I don't really care.'

'God was looking after you when my father found you. We'll also call you Theophilius.'

So it was that I became Johann Theophilius Wunder.

The snows began to clear from around the house. As my body recovered its strength, shadowy memories came back to me of my early childhood. None, however, provided a clue as to my identity. Nevertheless, about this time I began to take an interest in the world around me. The passing of time, which hitherto I had ignored, suddenly assumed significance. Formerly, when Shmul announced that he was going on one of his journeys and would be back for the Sabbath I hardly understood what he was saying. Now, as I stood at my door on legs that were still weak and watched as he loaded his wagon with hay, food, canisters of water and merchandise and filled his huge pockets with money, letters, invoices and documents of various kinds, his activity engaged my interest. A world formerly blurred suddenly came into focus.

Reb Shmul confided to me one day that he had fallen far from the pious ways of his Jewish parents. He said almost proudly: 'The Ten Commandments is enough for an old pedlar like me. The Shalchun Arach lists six-hundred and thirteen laws a Jew must observe. No man who has to sweat for his daily bread can remember them all, let alone the six-hundred-thousand reasons why they must be kept. I say to myself the First Law of Life is to survive. I have helped you to obey that law, isn't that right, Johann?'

He slapped me on the back so hard that it gave me a fit of coughing.

'Rich merchants,' he went on, 'love to show off their piety. They flaunt their knowledge of the Torah but with the Almighty it's actions that count, not hair-splitting disputations about mixing cotton and wool and suchlike. Take old Abraham Koch for example ...'

Shmuel's weather-beaten face looked grim as he listed his complaints against his main creditor, a rich merchant who was a pillar of the study house and synagogue. Shmul owed him a great deal of money.

As the days went by my hunger to know my true identity grew stronger. Shmul again assured me that the expensive clothes in which I had been buried indicated that I had been a man of consequence. The grave-digger must have been very drunk, he told me, otherwise he would have stripped me before throwing me into a half-dug grave. His over-indulgence in liquor had been my saviour. I wondered briefly whether Shmul hoped to earn a reward by saving me. But I thrust aside that unworthy thought and promised myself that one day, when I returned to my rightful place in society, I would repay him handsomely for his kindness.

I informed Leah of my wish to return to Vienna, in order to reclaim my possessions. She suggested that in the meantime I should write to owners of men's clothing stores in that town asking them if they could identify the person who had purchased the waistcoat I had been wearing when Shmul found me.

I continued to practise diligently on the flute.

Leah asked me one day, when I grumbled about having to exist on charity: 'Can you read and write?'

'I believe so,' I replied.

She brought a quill pen and ink and some paper and I made some marks.

She pointed out politely that I had written musical notations and suggested that in my former life I might have been a musician.

I told her that music had the power to move me deeply and there might be some truth in what she had said.

'Can you remember who taught you music?'

A picture of a small, slightly wrinkled hand came into my mind and I uttered the word "Lion", which sprang for no reason into my mind.

'Was that the name of your school or your teacher?' Leah enquired.

'I can't remember. But I'm sure I can write letters as well as music.'

'If you can write a clear hand, we may be able to find you employment as a clerk.'

Leah then invited me to accompany her into Reb Shmul's house next door, so that I could sit at a table and practise writing. I threw on an old woollen overcoat of Shmul's that was hanging on the wall. A cold wind attacked our faces and bodies, as we made our way past Shlotkin's wooden stable.

This was the first time I had left the storehouse. Opposite, was a rickety wooden dwelling, which belonged to Yankel the hunchback. Alongside were half a dozen chicken shacks. The heavily-rutted road with wooden houses on either side ran for half a mile before entering the town of Korlyshev. In the distance were more substantial houses with tiled roofs and a church with a wooden steeple. The winding road continued through the town towards some distant mountains, which were still snow-covered.

A castle standing on a hill dominated the town.

Leah led me into her home. The tattered curtains were drawn to conserve heat from a wood fire, which also served as a cooking range. The walls were smoke-blackened. A pestle and mortar stood on the floor next to a dresser with cups, saucers and plates in the upper section; basins and colanders in the lower. A chest of drawers stood in one corner of the room, a large oak table occupied the centre.

Obeying Leah's instructions, I sat down at the table and wrote the Roman alphabet in its entirety, as well as Arabic numerals up to one hundred. When I had shown myself competent, she promised to make enquiries about finding me employment in the town. She had high hopes that a property manager called Reb Chaim Ben-Levi might employ me, because he had recently lost his assistant. Ben-Levi was employed by Count Poceski, who owned the land for miles around. A leather merchant called Reb Itzak Feldman was also a possible employer. She would not apply to Reb Abraham Koch, because of the enmity her father felt towards him.

Leah's calm, dignified demeanour was in marked contrast to that of her unruly father. She apologised for his occasional outbursts, saying that he was sorely tried by his attempts to struggle out of debt.

I asked her if she had ever thought to marry. She replied: 'My father borrowed heavily to pay for my sister's dowry and there is nothing left over for me. Fate has decreed that I should look after him. He is a good man and deserves some comfort in his old age.'

'You're too young and good-looking to become an old maid. Would you not like children?'

'Children have to be looked after and that requires money.'

'Your father says I must at one time have had money. Alas, it did not save me from being buried alive in St. Mark's churchyard.'

She interjected excitedly: 'Your memory it's beginning to return. You just mentioned the name, St. Marks.'

'Only because your father has told me a hundred times that that was where he found me.'

'Never mind. Your memory will eventually come back. When it does, it will be like the bursting of a dam.'

'How do you know? You have never suffered from such an illness.'

'Some things one knows by instinct.'

'What else does your instinct tell you about me?' I enquired.

Leah pursed her lips thoughtfully. The disfiguring wart on her chin faded into insignificance and I thought she looked quite beautiful.

'It tells me you must have led a very busy life.'

'Why do you say that?'

'You speak a high German — very grammatical. You can also write music, which suggests that you have had an excellent education. People of that class who live in Vienna need to be busy to retain their place in society.'

'For a country girl you are remarkably well informed.'

'I am not ignorant. I have visited Bratislava and I once visited an uncle in Vienna — my late mother's brother. I stayed only two days but I had a wonderful time.'

There was a pair of elaborate brass candle-sticks on the varnished chest of drawers. Beside them were two large tomes with unfamiliar characters on their spines. I enquired: 'What kind of writing is that?'

'It is the Hebraic language we Jews use in our prayer houses.'

'Why do Jews have their own language?'

'Poles have their own language. So do the French, the Germans and the Czechs.'

'The Jews don't have a country, so why do they need their own language?'

'We hope one day to have one. In the meantime, we keep our language alive by using it in our prayer houses.'

'But you also speak Yiddish, which is so much like German that I can now understand it though it still sounds odd.'

'It is our *mamaloschen*. God must have intended it. '

'Do you believe in God?

'You of all people should know better than to ask such a question!'

'I'm sorry,' I replied contritely. 'I just wondered if your vision of God is similar to my own.'

Leah said crossly: 'You had better leave now. It is improper for us to be alone in this house together.'

'What would your father say?'

'I don't think he would be angry. He is full of praise for you. But I should warn you this town is full of wicked gossips. Already there are rumours that my father found you drunk and unconscious in a Viennese brothel and rescued you in the hope of obtaining a rich reward.'

I replied angrily: 'I'll put a curb on their wicked tongues.'

'How would you know whether the rumours are true or false?' Leah said mockingly. 'You were unconscious at the time.'

'How could they possibly think that a man like your father would go into a brothel!'

'My father would venture into Hell itself, if he thought he could make a sale. You must go now.'

We both stood up.

I said: 'Thank you for all you have done. Whenever you hear me playing the flute you will know I am playing it for you.'

Spoken like a true Viennese gallant,' Leah said. 'Out you go!' And she gave me a playful push to help me on my way.

I drew the old woollen coat around me and returned to the storehouse, humming a tune and feeling so unaccountably cheerful that I hardly noticed the freezing wind that was giving me goose-pimples.

FIVE

Several months have passed since Reb Shmul Perlman rescued me from St Marks graveyard .I have tried hard during all this time to remember incidents from my previous life but with little success. I believe that returning to where I was found is the only sure way of recovering my lost memory. Leah is of the opinion that remembering my past will not necessarily make me any happier and begs me to remain here in Korlishev. I lack both the money and the confidence at present to make the journey.

Reb Perlman has promised that one day when he has business in Vienna he will take me there on his wagon. Leah declares there is little point in my returning, because those who have inherited my possessions and estate will resist any claim to have them returned and pleads with me to settle down in this town where God in his infinite mercy has placed me. She tries to console me by pointing out that memories can be a burden. I assure her that having one's past obliterated is infinitely worse.

I am angry with the doctors who declared me dead. Shmul recommends that when I do go back I should seek compensation for their negligence. I am, however, much more concerned with achieving a loving reunion with friends and relations who are now lost to me. There must be many good citizens in Vienna who will be eager to help me re-establish myself in society. Leah frequently enquires whether I have any recollection of being married. The names Aloysia and Constanze sometimes come to my mind in this regard. Constanze I associate with a deep, resonant cello, Aloysia sounds like a plaintive harp in the distance.

I now live in the Bear Tavern in the centre of the town — Leah has found me employment with Count Poceski's business agent, Reb Chaim Ben-Levi. I easily passed the tests of my mathematical and writing skills. I work as his clerk, calculating how many cubic measures of lumber a forest will produce and how much profit it will make after paying for the labour of the tree-cutters and the cost of transportation. I also draw up invoices and other documents.

Reb Chaim Ben-Levi is a short, spare man with a small spade-shaped white beard that is going yellow in places. His sharp black eyes nestle in wrinkles behind his pince-nez. Having learned about my miraculous return from the dead, he says it is a privilege to employ me. He is a famous chessplayer and needs someone to keep the books while he is away answering the many challenges he receives from noblemen all over Europe. My predecessor in the job married recently and has gone to live with his father-in-law in Lodz. Nobody has beaten Reb Chaim Ben-Levi at chess during the past thirty years. Count Poceski sometimes invites him to his castle and after discussing business affairs, they settle down to a game which Reb Chaim invariably wins. The Count has said that he will throw a feast in the town if ever he succeeds in beating him.

My departure from the Perlman household was brought about by another visit from Father Pacik. He informed me that I must move to the Christian part of the town, because my continued presence in a Jewish household might disturb the good relations that presently exist between the two communities. His point of view was upheld by the rabbi, who hinted that Leah's reputation would be in jeopardy if I declined. I was left with little choice in the matter.

My new employer, although he is called, Reb, a courtesy title indicating that he is upright and Godfearing, is also shrewd, worldly and understanding. Rumours must have reached him about my relationship with Leah. Soon after I started work, he stroked his beard and whispered: 'Just make sure that if anything is going on between you and Shmul's daughter it is done discreetly.' Apparently, Count Poceski, who hears of everything that goes on in the town, backed the religious leaders' demands that I should leave Shmul Perlman's house. When the Count was told by Ben-Levi of my reluctance to move he replied ominously: 'Tell him a parting is less trouble than a pogrom.'

I now realise that Count Poceski took an interest in this trivial matter in order to throw a smokescreen over his own misdemeanour. I found out that he had had an affair with a Jewish girl. More of that later. He has a wife, seven children and numerous other mistresses. Reb Chaim doesn't know that I know. There are notes in ledgers in coded form, which I easily decyphered, detailing various sums of money which Reb Chaim has paid to women on his master's behalf. I also came across a very moving letter.

Reb Chaim Ben-Levi is a widower. He has studied the Torah and all the manifold books and commentaries on it. He is also a cabbalist. Because of his passion for playing chess he is fond of saying: 'Lives are like games of chess. If you play an honest and true game against the Ultimate Chess Master, rest assured that after you are finally checkmated, you will be granted your eternal reward.'

Irritated by his pronouncement, I replied: 'How can you claim there is a reward? As soon as the game is over you are thrown into a box among all the other discarded pieces!'

'The Ultimate Chess Master allowed *you* to come back to play another game, did he not?' Reb Chaim commented dryly.

I fumed at this pointed reference to my unusual situation.

Father Pacik came to visit me again after I had taken a room in the Bear Tavern. He informed me that a debate was going on in Church circles. Someone had suggested that since my mind was a tabula rasa, robbed of all its former knowledge, I should undergo another baptism. He said he was in consultation with his archbishop and urged me in the meantime to be zealous in my religious duties. I assured him of my good

28

intentions in that respect and heaved a huge sigh of relief when he had gone. The truth of the matter is that, having been so close to death, I feel that from now on I should concentrate on enjoying as many of life's blessings as possible.

I have regained my interest in women. Leah is, of course, the closest to my heart. I even consider marrying her, although such a union would be frowned upon by both sides of the community.

I was so weak when first delivered into her care that Shmul, during his long sojourns away from home, must have assumed that nothing of an amatory nature was likely to develop. Indeed, I had thought that attending to all my bodily needs when I was ill would make me abhorrent to his daughter.

This was far from the truth.

I hear music in my head all the time and have started to write it down. Leah has been hard put to satisfy my demands for paper. I hope that eventually some clue as to my identity will come to me from the music.

One bright, sunny day, as I sat on a chair in Reb Schmul's house, a trick of the light gave the impression that dozens of golden cherubs were fluttering and dancing around the room. I put my flute to my lips and played a melody that synchronised with their movements. Suddenly, I was aware of Leah's soft weight on my lap, I continued to play until she took the instrument out of my hands and kissed me.

We embraced.

I murmured: 'Leah, you are a wonderful girl.'

'No, Johann Wunder, your tunes are so beautiful they take my breath away. Tell me how they come into your head?'

'Doesn't everyone have tunes in their head?'

'No, Johann. You are unique. You must once have been a musician.'

'I do occasionally hear an orchestra playing. I remember...

'What do you remember?'

'I can remember it is a name that begins with an H. No, I cannot remember.'

'You must remember!' Leah said vehemently.

'I shook my head, pulled her face down to mine again and caressed her bosom.

'You mustn't, you mustn't,' Leah exclaimed, pulling my hands away. 'Just as we are about to make an important discovery about your former life, you start to behave naughtily.'

'Who would be born, if it wasn't for naughtiness?'

'What you are doing is for people who are married. We can never be married.'

'Why not?'

'Christians and Jews do not marry.'

'Some human beings are alive and some are dead — that is the only distinction one should make.

'There is a distinction between male and female.'

'Thank Heavens for that!'

I kissed her again. She responded with a deep sigh, pressing her lips to mine.

Then she stood up suddenly, her face very flushed. Patting her hair with her hands, she said in a quivering voice: 'I intend to write to all the musical academies in Europe giving a description of you. Someone somewhere is bound to recognise you.

'You will tell them that I am handsome, talented and of good report?'

'Yes,' she replied: 'Also that you are very conceited.'

With that, she brusquely ordered me to return to the store room where I slept.

SIX

The walls of the tiny attic room I occupy in the Bear Inn incline so steeply that I have to bend down to move around the straw mattress. Salka, the maid, told me that the room was until recently an alcove used for cleaning boots, but a door was added so that it could accommodate an extra guest. A wooden shelf holds my sole possessions: a razor, a spare shirt, a pair of trousers. The flute, which I suppose must one day be returned to Shmul Perlman, rests alongside the mattress. Standing on tiptoe and craning my neck, I can see out of the tiny window the remains of a stork's nest at the foot of one of the tall chimneys. The inn sign creaks alarmingly. At night mice squeak and scuffle. But I sleep soundly enough. Celestial music comes to me in my dreams, filling my heart with a joy beyond description.

Herr Müller, the proprietor of the inn, is a great barrel of a man with a vacant expression on his red-veined face that belies a shrewd business sense. He sits by the bar with a jug of beer in his hand most of the day, grumbling in a deep, loud voice about the injustices of the world. He is fond of talking about his imaginary affair with the Empress Catherine of Russia, a coloured picture of whom hangs on the wall behind the bar. He complains that she has been unfaithful to him and adds, shaking his head dolefully, that he is in deep despair over her infidelity. It is, of course, an act put on to amuse the guests.

He was sprawled in his usual place on a chair by the bar when I first entered the inn.

'Who are you?' he asked, with a surly expression.

'I am Johann Wunder, sire. I wish to rent a room.'

'So you're the man who came back from Heaven. I bet the schnapps up there is not as good as ours.'

31

He shouted out to his wife, who came bustling in, wearing a stained calico apron over a long-sleeved brown dress.

'Herr Wunder has honoured us with his presence and desires a room. Place him in the Sky and charge him the earth.' The Sky is his pet name for the room in the attic I now occupy.

I entered into negotiations with Frau Müller, during the course of which she extracted a promise that whenever possible I would take my meals at the inn. She is a slim woman, pale-faced, with a beaky nose and a passion for money. She asked me to pay extra for the privilege of keeping a musical instrument in the room. I countered by offering to entertain the customers with it. She relented and said that in that case I could keep it without extra charge.

I hug the ancient instrument to my bosom when I go to bed at night — it is a poor substitute for Leah. Her kindness has not only restored my bodily vigour but has even given me back that sense of striving which keeps a man alert and working hard. I practise assiduously on the flute in my spare time. Word has spread around the town concerning my musical ability. Elsa Müller's bargain with me has proved a shrewd one.

I was deeply upset at having to leave the Perlman's household, which I had come to regard as my home. But it is not acceptable for a Christian to live in a Jewish household — it was assumed, apparently, that since I am not a Jew, I must be a Christian. I remarked to Leah before I left that if all the citizens of this town suffered the kind of total forgetfulness which has afflicted me they would no longer bother to argue about arcane differences in religious doctrine. Not that I have anything against religion, which points to the existence of a world beyond our own. I sometimes hear in my head a pizzicato of massed cellos like angels beating their wings in unison which must come from some ethereal region.

Reb Chaim Ben-Levi's house where I now work is larger and better built than most of the surrounding houses; it has a tiled roof and a highly-ornamented porch. He lives there with his old mother, who cooks and cleans for him. She occasionally peeps in when I am working in his office, which is furnished with a desk, a wardrobe full of files and a large safe. The latter contains the secrets of Count Poceski's business interests and of his amatory affairs, which are equally complicated. Reb Chaim went out recently and left his keys behind. Out of curiosity, I opened the safe and found documents recording the villages, houses, forests and farms that the Count owns. There was also a great deal of money in different currencies. In one corner of the safe were letters to the Count from his mistresses, including demands for money to pay for the upkeep of his bastards. At the top of the pile was a letter from a girl called Riva Gerschon.

It read:

To Count Poceski, my Master,

Now that you have taken my most cherished possession, I must throw myself on your mercy. If the loss of my virginity should ever be discovered by my family and my fellow Jews I would be shamed beyond redemption. My hopes of ever making a respectable marriage have been utterly destroyed.

Your love-making took my breath away, along with my powers of resistance. I must plead with you now to make restitution for the loss of that which was most precious to me. Because of what has happened I must soon leave Korlishev, my home town, for ever. I beg you to grant me the means to do so.

Henceforth, I must be a wandering exile, with no hope of entering decent society.

I throw myself on your mercy and trust that your noble heart will have sympathy for my desperate plight.

Your devoted,

Riva

Jews prize virtue and chastity above all else in their womenfolk. I have taken Leah's virginity. This occurred by mutual consent while we were thrown together in unusual circumstances. As far as I know, I have no other commitments.

Why, one must ask, has the Count with a wife and seven children and innumerable mistresses, seduced a young, vulnerable Jewish girl? The question exercised my mind while I was doing calculations concerning a forest some twenty miles away. The only conclusion I could come to is that forbidden fruits are the sweetest.

I took pains to leave Reb Chaims's keys in exactly the same position as he had left them. However, when I returned from a meal of bread and cheese and a glass of ale at the Bear Inn I found Reb Chaim pacing up and down the study, looking agitated.

I said: 'What ails you, sir?'

Reb Chaim responded, sharply: 'You have opened the safe.'

I stuttered: 'I — I'm afraid that my curiosity got the better of me. You will find that nothing has been taken or disturbed. Its secrets are secure with me.'

Reb Chaim gazed at my worried face for a while and then suddenly said disarmingly: 'No need to be afraid. As a matter of fact, I guessed that an intelligent man like you would not miss such an opportunity. If you had not looked inside, I would have thought you a fool.'

I felt an immediate sense of relief.

Reb Chaim resumed pacing up and down and after a while said: 'You must understand that Count Poceski trusts me down to the last groschen and I must never allow him to doubt my loyalty. If I did, it would not only affect my well being but also that of my fellow Jews. New laws have been enacted recently intended to ease the position of Jews. But laws do not change the human heart. Hatred can spring up at any time between the Jewish and gentile communities and for the most trifling of reasons.'

He paused and then went on: 'I want you to take to heart my solemn warning. You are employed by a Jew, which means that if any trouble ever occurred, you would also be in danger. Now that I have said that, we come to another matter. You saw Riva Gerschon's letter?'

'Yes, sir.'

'You may like to know the circumstances. A few months ago Count Poceski took a fancy to hallah bread cooked by a Jewish baker, Eli Gerschon, and ordered loaves to be delivered to his castle. This went on for several months. The count never paid for the deliveries. Gerschon, although he needed the money, was too frightened to ask for it and felt obliged to continue making deliveries. He foolishly asked his daughter to call on the Count with a request for payment. Count Poceski invited the girl into his library, plied her with liquor and seduced her. Soon afterwards, Eli Gerschon was paid what he was owed. Being both naive and stupid, he hadn't realised that his action had resulted in the loss of his daughter's virginity. In fact, he advised other tradesmen: "You should send your daughter to ask the Count for payment. He will always be nice to a good-looking girl."

'I have dealt with many of Count Poceski's women. He trusts me to pay them off and keep them in order. They live in fear and suspicion that he has formed yet another liaison but I usually manage to calm their fears. I don't condone what he does. But it is better I should make peace than otherwise. He always says he admires and respects Jews, which is a tribute to the way I run his business affairs. I apply myself to them with as much zeal as he applies to his love affairs.

'Since you are working for me you might as well understand the true state of affairs here in Korlishev. Maintaining harmony and keeping the balance between the two communities is my chief purpose in life. I have to go away occasionally to play chess, but apart from that small weakness, I feel that I am doing God's will in this small town where I have lived all my life and where I hope to die in peace.'

He took a pinch of snuff and paused for a while. I took the opportunity to ask a question which was still bothering me: 'Why does the fact that I work for a Jew put me in danger?'

'Because if any trouble should occur, which God forbid, you would be regarded as an apostate and a traitor. There are other reasons, of course.'

'What are they?' I enquired.

'No need to discuss that now. What I want you to do is to undertake a mission of the utmost delicacy.'

'What exactly do you require of me?'

'I have to leave this afternoon for Prague to play in a chess tournament and I shall be away for two weeks. In my absence you must handle the case of Riva Gerschon.'

I protested. 'But I don't understand what goes on here in this town. I don't even understand Polish.'

'The Count is fluent in several languages. The fact that you are a stranger might help rather than hinder your diplomatic mission.'

'But what am I supposed to do? The girl needs money to start a new life somewhere. Do you want me to ask him for it?'

'Exactly. She must have enough to go to Warsaw and live there for a year. She is not the first, incidentally, to whom this tragedy has happened.'

'What about her parents?'

'They need not know about the seduction. Riva will leave a note to say that she has been offered a position as a children's nurse with a Jewish family in Warsaw. Later, when the child is due, she will write back to say that she didn't like the family in question and has found other employment.'

'All this because she lost her virginity!'

Reb Chaim looked at me steadily for a while and then said: 'You must try to see this through the girl's eyes. For her it is a calamity. You may possibly one day, with God's help, recover your memory. She will never recover her virginity. The scandal, if the matter is left unattended, could cause great trouble in the town.' He paused and went on: 'Prince Poniotowski — he whispered the name — has paid all the expenses involved in my journey to Prague. We are playing a series of games in a hotel. Several of his fellow officers will be present. It will not be easy for me. That is why I have to entrust this mission to you. Keep in mind all the time that it is the girl's interests that are paramount and you cannot go far wrong.'

I promised to do my best.

But as I walked back that evening through the darkened streets to the Bear Inn, I felt heavy-hearted. The task seemed well beyond my capacity. I was angry, too, because Ben-Levi had hired me to do clerical work, not act as an emissary to a philandering, unscrupulous nobleman. The girl's father was a fool. She was an even greater fool. Why must I waste precious time, which would be better spent practising on my flute?

But I became more cheerful as I drew nearer the Bear Inn, reflecting that I had been granted the opportunity to ease the burden of another human being. If you act for this victim of a stupid father and a libidinous nobleman, it will make a better man of you. It might even persuade you to alleviate through your music the unhappiness which afflicts all of mankind.

SEVEN

I dined frugally in the eating-house which adjoins the coaching stables and then ran up the stairs to collect my flute, which lay on the floor next to the mattress. As I straightened up, I banged my head heavily on a wooden beam in the ceiling. Feeling giddy from the blow, I descended the stairs quickly in haste to start my performance, and informed Herr Müller that I was ready to entertain his customers. There were fifty or so men present, smoking, drinking and talking in a variety of languages - they included Pomeranians, Ruthenians, Ukranians, Carpathians and Bohemians, as well as Poles and Russians.

Herr Müller instructed me to go ahead and resumed his conversation with a small, swarthy man, who I learned later, was Count Poceski's head stableman. I blew a short, preliminary note. A bald-headed man smoking a pipe by the log-fire shouted good-naturedly: 'Stop farting, mate.' I ignored him and played some local folk songs I had heard Salka sing as she went about her duties. I then improvised a lively melody of my own. A man wearing a tyrolean hat began to tap his feet in time to the music. Someone started humming. Soon, I had the attention of the entire audience.

I played a minuet and then a bravura waltz, whose rhythm caused Salka, who was serving drinks on a tray, to sway charmingly on her way to each customer. I followed this with some jigs and reels that brought cheerful smiles to everyone's faces.

Passers-by began to trickle in from outside. Soon the room was full to overflowing. Elsa Müller peeped in from the side door, smiling at the prospect of increased trade.

I paused when someone thrust a glass of schnapps into my hand, tossed back the fiery liquid in a single gulp, and resumed playing. Shortly afterwards something strange happened: a harp seemed to float towards me, its phantom notes complementing those of the flute. A musical score appeared in front of my eyes and I fainted.

Herr Müller held out his burly arm, but was too late to prevent me from sliding onto the stone floor.

When I opened my eyes, the swarthy stableman was bending over me. He helped me to my feet. I thanked him, explaining that my blackout was due to a blow on the head I had suffered upstairs. However, in my heart I knew that it was the vivid glimpse of a musical composition that had caused the syncope.

Herr Müller urged me to resume playing.

I put the flute to my lips and improvised a tune. It described a vision of Leah standing by the front-door of Reb Shmul Perlman's house. As she walked swiftly towards me, I quickened the rhythm, imagining her dancing. The drinkers slapped their thighs and tapped their feet. Then, as the image faded, I slowed down. The expressions on the faces of my audience immediately became dreamily contemplative, reflecting the change in tempo.

My audience and I appeared to be in perfect accord.

Loud clapping followed. I bowed and retired, perspiring heavily, to an unoccupied bench. Salka handed me a mug of ale. I wiped my brow, resisting an impulse to bury my head in her generous bosom. She bent down and whispered: 'If the boss goes on about Catherine the Great, shall I do what we agreed?'

We had conspired to play a trick on Herr Müller when he began his usual boasting about his supposed love affair with Catherine the Great. The wall between the pantry in the kitchen and the bar being very thin, I had punctured the right eye of the Empress's portrait with a knife, opening a small flap in the picture. Salka had promised that standing on a chair she would substitute her own eye for that of the Empress of all the Russias.

I reminded her: 'Don't forget to wait until he gets into full flow.'

Ten or fifteen minutes later the publican began his highly-coloured account of his affair with the Empress, during which he spared no anatomical details about their lovemaking. "Her breasts burst out of her corset like two enormous pig's bladders. I struggled to pull down her drawers and slapped her fat arse."

At that precise moment I pointed to the picture and a great howl of laughter rang out as the portrait of Catherine winked.

Herr Müller, believing he was solely responsible for the applause, smirked and continued his mock confession. Salka contrived to wink at key moments during his discourse, causing further loud outbursts of laughter. I was relieved that she reappeared in the saloon before Herr Müller had finished. I don't know to this day whether he realised how much our little trick had amused his audience.

Delighted with the way the evening had gone and the success of his storytelling, Herr Müller said to me: 'Excellent. You play the flute like our late, lamented King Frederick of Prussia. You shall have free meals every day you give a performance.'

Soon after I had gone to bed, I heard a gentle knock. I stood up, taking care not to hit my head on the beam this time, and opened the door. Salka was standing outside in her flimsy night attire.

She said shyly: 'I have just come to report that the boss has said your playing was as if a fine wine suddenly appeared in an earthenware jug.'

'Splendid, Salka. It was your winking that brought the house down. We'll think up something else tomorrow night.'

Salka whispered with downcast eyes: 'Would you like me to be your Empress Catherine?'

Because my head was still aching from the blow it had received, I failed to take the obvious hint and shut the door.

*

The following morning I walked to Reb Shmul's house. The wagon was not there, which indicated that he was away on his travels. I knocked on the door. Leah appeared, flung her arms round my neck and drew me inside.

We kissed and embraced. She held me at arm's length and rebuked me for not coming sooner.

I sat on a chair and pulled her onto my lap. Hugging her tightly, I explained: 'I'm kept busy morn till night attending to Reb Chaim's business. Last night, I played the flute in the Bear Inn with great success. When does you father require it to be returned?'

'He wants you to keep it. Do they pay you for playing?'

'I get free meals, which is almost as good. While I was playing, I saw a vision of a musical score which seemed intensely familiar. The experience caused me to faint.'

'Don't worry, Johann. The mists will clear one day and then you will know everything about yourself.' She added: 'But perhaps you may not be the happier for knowing.'

'Even animals are entitled to know who they are.'

'Are you quite free from pain now?' Leah suddenly asked, anxiously.

I frowned, not liking to be reminded of my physical frailty.

'I am well enough for a man of my years...How old do you think I am, Leah?'

Leah studied my face for a moment.

'Middle-thirties. Perhaps even forty. Does it matter?'

'Of course it matters. You were right when you suggested that I must have been a professional musician. Playing the flute has knocked a tiny hole in the wall that separates me from my past. Perhaps playing other instruments will enable it to enlarge, until my memory is fully restored.'

41

'Johann, it's a miracle that you survived what happened to you. Your present life is all that matters. Please stay here in Korlishev and find happiness with me.'

'I feel I have abused your father's kindness and hospitality.'

Leah said angrily. 'I am not his slave and possession. I made love because I love you and wanted to heal your wounds. I shall never regret it, even though we shall never marry.'

'Don't say that, Leah.'

'I won't delude myself. Your music weaves a magic spell to which many women will succumb. I don't mind you having other women as long as you remember that I have given my heart to you and you alone.'

'Of course I shall remember always,' I added, drawing her into my arms and kissing her. Leah took my hand and led me into her bedroom.

She wept afterwards, saying it had been nearly as painful as the first time. But she recovered her spirits when I promised to write a ballad in her honour. She then set about cooking a meal consisting of flour balls and chicken in a delicious barley soup.

While we were eating I told her about Riva Gerschon and the task with which I had been entrusted by Reb Chaim. I asked: 'Why all this fuss just because the girl has lost her virginity. Not every girl can be a virgin when she marries.'

Leah responded: 'We are talking of very young girls who vow to be faithful to their husbands for the rest of their lives. It doesn't matter that you have taken my virginity. I shall never marry.'

'I shall marry you one day,' I interjected.

Leah shook her head impatiently and went on: 'Marrying a virgin is the only means a man has of knowing that he is raising his own children. It is bound very deeply into the social customs of Jews and, for that matter, other communities. Did you not want your wife to be a virgin?'

'I have no recollection of being married.'

Leah enquired: 'What exactly does Reb Ben-Levi want you to do about Riva Gerschon?'

'I am to ask the Count to provide enough money to enable her to go to Warsaw and live there for a year.'

'Reb Chaim handles all the Count's money. Why doesn't he just give her the amount she demands?'

'He daren't do that without his permission.'

'Then I suggest you do what I am about to propose. Ask the Count to pay Eli Gerschon for a year's supply of loaves in advance. He won't see that as a threat to his seigniorial rights. Tell Gerschon by way of explanation that the Count appreciates his baking so much that he wishes to guarantee his supply in this way.'

'And if Gerschon subsequently learns what has happened and refuses to keep up the supply?'

'That is a problem for another day. But I have a feeling that the Count, knowing in his heart of hearts that he has wronged the man, will not press the matter further.'

I decided to follow Leah's advice.

EIGHT

The following morning, on entering the Bear Inn restaurant, I picked up a newspaper which a customer had left on a chair. It contained an article denouncing Prince Poniatowski, a high-ranking general, who it was rumoured, had paid a secret visit to Prague in order to play a series of chess matches against Ben-Levi. I was astonished to find out that Ben-Levi mixed in such exalted circles, although I could well understand that a general might find it useful to sharpen his strategic wits against my employer's famous skills,

I ordered gruel, bread and a pot of ale, feeling grateful to Providence for the opportunity that had been granted me to lead an independent life. The garments Shmul Perlman gave me are hardly fit for a beggar. But thanks to my flute-playing, I can now save a little money towards the purchase of new clothes. How long this improvement in my affairs will last I do not know, but I am grateful for the improvement in my circumstances.

In spite of the religious differences which plague this small town, I have not lost my faith in the Deity. Bird songs which I hear outside my room every morning seem part of a great symphony of sound which pulsates through the universe under the command of a great orchestral Conductor. Even the lowliest human beings understand music, which by its very nature formulates ideas beyond the powers of mathematicians and philosophers to express. Dogs and horses respond to music, as indeed, do cats — I make this concession grudgingly because the latter make me sneeze. I draw a lesson also from my flute, which bears witness to the fact that there are more tunes to be played on it than there are grains of sand on the beach. An infinite number of consequences flow from a Single Cause. Not the least of which has been the miracle of my survival.

The thin, whey-faced serving maid called Bertha came to my table as these thoughts entered my mind and handed me a note written in Polish. I asked her to translate it for me. She blushed and read out the words: 'Johann, come to my room before you go to bed tonight. Your loving Salka.'

I thought to myself: if women can be so charmed by a humble flautist, how does a famous operatic tenor ever find time to sing! On my way through the town to the Castle, I stopped at Reb Ben-Levi's house and asked his mother if I might borrow clothing suitable for my meeting with the Count. She lent me a long, black woollen coat. It is rather tight about my person but will hide my tattered clothing.

I walked out of town at a brisk pace through dirt roads, passing dilapidated, unpainted shacks with roofs made of woven rushes. Moss was stuffed between the planks of their wooden walls to keep out winter winds. Ragged children were playing amid piles of rubbish. The poverty I saw reinforced my resolve to earn more money.

Once out of town, I walked through green pleasant meadows. On my right were the foothills of the Carpathian Mountains through which I had passed in Reb Shmul's wagon. They had been snowbound then.

Although I had given my heart to the charming, intelligent Leah who had nursed me back to health, I could not deny that Salka's invitation gave me some satisfaction.

Poceski's castle occupied a commanding position overlooking Korlishev. From this point he could see a great deal of what went on in the chief town in his province. The extensive grounds of the castle were surrounded by a stout, buttressed wall topped with iron spikes.

I was challenged in Polish at the sentry house by a soldier in a blue uniform armed with a flintlock musket. I spoke in Italian, French and German, the last of which he understood, and eventually succeeded in conveying that I wished to see the Count. The discovery that I could speak foreign languages raised my spirits because it seemed to indicate that I was well on my way to recovering my memory.

The sentinel led me at a brisk pace up a steep hill towards the studded double oak entrance-door, above which was a lead canopy surmounted by a large stone eagle. He tugged vigorously at a bell-pull. I informed the bewigged, uniformed servant who then opened the door that I had come on behalf of Reb Ben-Levi. He invited me to enter a large marble-floored hall surrounded by busts of Roman emperors. A statue of Aphrodite stood in the centre. The footman, after examining me from head to toe with an expression of ineffable disdain, turned abruptly on his heels and departed at a fast, swaying trot down a corridor.

Five minutes later, as I was examining some faded ancestral portraits hanging on the walls, he reappeared. Speaking to a point just above my head, he declared that Count Poceski had consented to see me. I followed him through a series of dark corridors to a library containing several thousand leather-bound volumes. Remembering the Count's reputation for philandering, I wondered how he had ever found time to read any of them. The footman urged me forward until I saw the Count sitting by a window in an armchair, idly flicking through a Russian magazine.

'*Le serviteur de Monsieur Ben-Levi,*' the footman announced. Count Poceski languidly invited me to sit on an elaborately-carved upright chair by his side. He was in his middle-forties with a lean, impassive face and a mass of gray, pomaded hair, which, I assumed, incorrectly as it later turned out, to be his own. There were deep lines on either side of his prominent roman nose. He continued reading for several minutes and then, looking up from the magazine, said: 'Ah, so you are the flautist.'

'I did not think my fame had spread this far, your Honour.'

'My stableman informed me of your skill. Little goes on in Korlishev with which I am not acquainted.'

Wrapping my coat around me a little more closely to hide my threadbare garments, I said: 'Sire, I have come to discuss a rather delicate matter. It concerns the daughter of a Jewish baker in the town. She desires to visit an aunt in Warsaw for a year. But her father does not possess the means to pay for the journey. He humbly asks if you would consider paying for a year's supply of loaves in advance, so that he can grant his daughter's wish.'

'Why does she want to leave?'

'It appears that she is embarrassed about rumours concerning her immoral behaviour.'

The Count gave a slight shrug and said: 'How absurd that the world should be governed by idle gossip. But never mind. Instruct Reb Ben-Levi to supply the baker with the money when he returns home.'

'Certainly, Count,' I replied, thankful that my task had been completed with such ease.

I stood up, expecting to be dismissed. But the Count asked me to sit down again. He waved his hand and a servant appeared from out of the shadows and handed me a glass of delicious French wine. The Count then looked at me curiously and said: 'I have heard of your strange history, Johann Wunder. You were given up for dead I believe.'

'That is correct, sire. And I have suffered a complete loss of memory.'

'But you remembered how to play the flute.'

'Yes, sir. Music comes to me very naturally.'

'Could you play that?' He pointed to a pianoforte which lay under dust sheets in the far corner of the room.

'I don't know.'

He waved his hand again and instructed a footman to remove the dust covers.

'Play something,' he commanded.

I stood by the piano and as I looked down at the keyboard, my whole body began to shake. Suddenly I gave vent to incoherent, racking sobs, which issued from the very depths of my being.

The Count looked at me sternly and said: 'You appear to be sick, Johann Wunder.'

When I had managed to compose myself, I said: 'I don't know what has come over me. I apologise deeply.'

'Can you play the piano?'

'If you will forgive me, Count, I would prefer to test my skill on some other occasion.'

He shook his head, looked displeased, and rang for his servant to conduct me out of the castle.

In spite of my humiliating experience, I felt relieved as I walked back to the town. My mission had been successfully accomplished, Leah's idea had worked beautifully. I could report to Ben-Levi when he returned that the Count had gone some little way towards repairing the damage he had inflicted on Riva Gerschon.

Gerschon's bakery lay in the Jewish quarter of the town. Its proprietor, wearing a flour-covered coat and a black skull cap spattered with white, was bending over a basket of loaves as I entered the shop. He looked up as I came in and said in Yiddish: 'You're too late for today's bread.'

I replied: 'I am Reb Ben-Levi's assistant. I have a message for you. Count Poceski wishes to order a year's supply of loaves. He is prepared to pay you in advance.'

He stood up and answered with a complacent smile: 'He doesn't have to do that. It is an honour to have such a generous order. You must be the Johann Wunder Reb Perlman brought back from Vienna.'

After examining my face, he added: 'You look quite human, in spite of your experience. Tell the Count there's no need to pay in advance.'

'Doesn't your daughter wish to go to Warsaw to stay with a relative?'

'What has that got to do with it?'

'I understood from Reb Ben-Levi that you needed to provide your daughter with some money. The Count has made this generous offer to help with her fare.'

'She's a young girl. She's only fifteen. She doesn't know her own mind.'

'Girls of fifteen can be more mature than men four times their age. I would recommend that you give her what her heart desires. She will bless you, if you allow her to do so.'

'And who are you to know about such things?' Eli Gerschon asked, suspiciously.

'I am only repeating Reb Chaim Ben-Levi's words of advice. I suggest you tell your daughter to prepare for her journey.'

Gerschon brushed flour off his hands and said peevishly: 'I'll do your bidding. But only because people in the town say you have the power to see into the future.'

'Why should anyone think that?'

'I don't know. Perhaps because you came back from the dead. I love my Riva dearly. But since you recommend it, I'll let her have her way.'

'You won't regret it.'

He peered at me as if convinced that I had come from another world. I left his shop. On my way back to the Bear Inn, I inadvertently stepped into some dog droppings. As I scraped my shoe clean on a metal grating, I laughed aloud at this totally convincing proof that I lacked the kind of supernatural powers with which I had been so absurdly credited.

NINE

When it was time for me to play my flute that evening, I persuaded Bertha to sit on Herr Müller's lap — Salka was away visiting her mother in a village some twenty miles distant. I told the audience that the music I was about to play described the antics of the Empress Catherine and her lover, Potempkin, as they tried to make love after taking purgatives prescribed by the court physician. Whenever I played F sharp on my flute Herr Müller would say: "I have to shit" and whenever I played E flat Bertha would say: "I have to piss!" The pantomime created unbounded mirth. Herr Müller laughed so much that he had a bout of coughing which almost brought about his demise. He congratulated me heartily, when the inn was finally cleared of customers.

Later, as I lay on my mattress I dreamed that a lion had savaged me because I had rebelled against scales he had set me to play on the keyboard. I had wanted to play a tone poem which described the cascading, fast running waters of a waterfall but I was obliged to perform the lion's will. How dull were those scales! How enchanting the waterfall! How ruthless the lion who demanded my submission!

The following morning, as I was working at my desk in Ben-Levi's house, I heard a clattering of hooves outside. A messenger from the castle knocked peremptorily on the front-door and handed me a written authorisation for Reb Chaim Ben-Levi to pay Gerschon for a year's supply of his loaves. Accompanying this message was a note commanding me to play at a ball celebrating the betrothal of Count Poceski's daughter, Marie Louise, to a subaltern in the Russian Imperial Guard.

I was delighted to be thus honoured.

Ben-Levi's mother brought me a mug of warm milk while I was working at the accounts. She is a tiny lady with a wizened, pinched face and a mass of brown hair, which I suspect may be a wig. After placing the mug on the desk beside me, she said in a thin, quavering voice: 'My son says you have seen the Other Side. What was it like?'

It took me a moment to grasp her meaning. I replied: 'Unfortunately, God rendered me unconscious while I was there, so that I am unable to describe the experience.'

Realising that she was seeking comfort for the day when she must make that same journey, I added: 'I suffered neither excessive warmth nor excessive cold while I was in God's care. I can truly report that he maintains a perfectly equable climate.'

She gave a little smile, murmured something inaudible and crept out of the study.

That afternoon, I handed Gerschon his money, for which he gave me a receipt. He informed me that Riva was already packing in preparation for her journey to Warsaw.

Later, I returned to the Inn, gave a performance and then composed a ballad for Leah containing saucy references to our love-making. I looked forward to reading it to her that evening. But as I approached Reb Shmul's house, I was disappointed to hear Shlotkin neighing in his stable, which indicated that Shmul had returned from his travels.

I knocked on the faded front-door, observing the tiny cylinder on the righthand doorpost, which Leah had once explained to me contained prayers written in Hebrew.

Welcoming me with a warm smile, she said: 'We are about to have our evening meal. I hope you will join us. My father has been asking about you.'

Reb Shmul was drying his hands on a towel as I entered the room. He exclaimed 'Ah! Johann Wunder himself. I hear you have put that flute to good use. Wasn't that a splendid exchange I made. Sit down. Sit down.'

I replied as I obeyed: 'I hope one day to pay you for it.'

'No need. You are the talk of the town.'

I told him of my invitation to play at the betrothal of Count Poceski's daughter.

'Make sure he pays you a fair reward. He treats the women around here as if their only purpose in being born is to satisfy his lust.'

He threw the towel over a rack and added: 'What is worse, he plots with the Russians to stop men from achieving their freedom. We shall give them all a bloody nose one of these days. So, on to more important things: have you remembered anything of your past yet?'

'Very little. I have remembered musical scores and some unimportant details connected with my childhood. Something is happening. One of these days I am sure everything will come back to me.'

Reb Shmul said a blessing in Hebrew, cut some pieces of bread, added some salt and handed them around. As Leah placed bowls before us, he announced delightedly that his journey had been very profitable. To celebrate his success, on his way back through the town he had bought a leg of mutton. Leah had turned it into an appetising stew, which provided a sumptuous meal.

A log fire was burning fiercely in the grate. As we awaited a pudding made of noodles and sultanas, Shmul went out to the storage room and returned with a bottle of vodka. He poured out a liberal portion for me, an even larger one for himself, muttered the word *L'chayim* and took an enormous swig. Soon afterwards, he began to reminisce about his past adventures, in each episode of which the hero turned out to be Shlotkin.

'You realise, Johann,' he said earnestly,' that if Shlotkin. hadn't stopped in his tracks to give his kind regards to a magpie, you would still be in St Mark's graveyard.'

I nodded agreement, gravely.

He went on: 'You may think that was a matter of pure chance. Not so.'

He replenished both our glasses and went on: 'I have learned during the twelve years I have owned that horse that he has a sagacity beyond that of a rabbi.'

He tapped his nose. 'Who can say that the one who came to see you when you were sick has a half of Shlotkin's good sense. The rabbi looks up in the clouds and sees us all floating to Jerusalem when the Messianic Age comes. Shlotkin looks down at his feet, his first concern being that they should not slip, which is much more sensible. If he followed the rabbi's example and broke his leg, I would be ruined. Rabbi Adler should spend more of his time considering the practical things of this life. But back to Shlotkin...'

I guessed from Leah's embarrassed look that she was accustomed to hearing her father's rambling discourses. It also occurred to me that Shmul deserved a sympathetic audience as a reward for the lonely life he led.

'Once in the town of Brno,' Shmul went on, 'I was offered a valuable picture painted by someone called Rubens — you have never seen such fat undressed ladies. The seller assured me the price was paltry compared with the value of the painting. Naturally, I enquired, "If it's so valuable why are you selling it?" He told me he needed the money urgently in connection with a law suit. "My misfortune " he went on, "happens to be your good luck. Look at the painting carefully — you can see quite clearly the signature Rubens." I looked and sure enough the signature was as clear as day.

'I consider myself shrewd. But even the cleverest businessman can have a bad day. The man then said: "Look, if you are still doubtful, why don't you come to the museum where you can see a very similar painting by the same artist." So I did and the one picture looked no better than the other. I agreed to buy it, although it was going to take all the money I possessed. My heart was pounding hard at the thought that I would be able to sell the picture at a profit and pay off all my debts.

'He carried the painting round to where Shlotkin was tethered. My money was hidden in a secret compartment in the wagon-- you know bandits can attack when you least expect it. By the time we arrived, the man was panting heavily. Believe me, that picture was in a very heavy frame. Shlotkin looked round, saw the painting and whinneyed loudly. Such a noise I had never heard from him before.

'I ignored him and went to collect the money from a secret recess in the floor of the wagon. Meanwhile, the man, tiring of his burden, placed the painting on the ground. A miracle then happened! Shlotkin neighed again, moved sideways and put his hoof right through the painting.

'Naturally, there was a violent quarrel. I had not yet put the money into the man's hand and pointed out that when the accident occurred the painting still belonged to him. He insisted that it was my horse which had damaged his painting and therefore I must pay for it. We came to blows. I was young then and gave him a drubbing. Then I jumped into the driving-seat, flourished the whip, Shlotkin let out a joyous neigh and away we galloped.

Reb Shmul smiled, reminiscently.

The candles were guttering and his face looked ruddy in the firelight. He said: 'Word came to me in the next town I visited that this man had machinery that was turning out Rubens's paintings faster than a printing press can turn out bank notes.'

I congratulated Shmul on his lucky escape.

Leah, who must have heard the story many times before, began to wash up in the sink.

'There was another occasion,' Shmul went on, 'when times were very hard. I had no money to buy goods and I was forced to barter an item I had taken from my home — Rachel, my wife, God rest her soul, was alive then. It was a fruit dish we had been given for a wedding present. We had no use for it because we couldn't afford fruit. There was a long street market held every Wednesday in the town of Brisdska. I stopped at the first stall and after a haggle exchanged the fruit dish for a cake-stand which took my fancy. At the next stall, I exchanged the cake-stand for a wood saw. At the next, I exchanged the saw for a dress which, if I couldn't sell it, might at least, fit Rachel. I exchanged the dress for a smoothing-iron.

That, in turn, was exchanged for a gold ring which I bit and it turned out to be brass. Nevertheless, I exchanged it for a pair of leather shoes and two groschen. By this time I was so hungry I went into a café with the two groschen and bought a glass of milk and a slice of brown bread. It was raining when I left the cafe and I soon discovered that the shoes let in water. So, at the last stall in the market, I exchanged the shoes for — that's right — you've guessed it — my wife's fruit dish. But I wasn't unhappy because I had made a decent profit — a glass of milk and a slice of bread.'

Leah and I exchanged glances. We were both thinking how very different the evening would have been if Shmul had not come home from his travels.

He went on tirelessly: 'A man cannot exist on such a slender diet as milk and a slice of bread. As usual Shlotkin turned out to be my saviour. We had gone onto the next village. I was tired and hungry and I stopped Shlotkin under the shade of a tree and drifted off to sleep. I dreamed that I was at a banquet being fed delicacies by beautiful maidens such as you read about in the Arabian Nights. When I awoke, we were in a strange place. Shlotkin had wandered off because I had forgotten to tether him!

'We were near a rubbish tip on the outskirts of the hamlet. And there, on top of the rubbish was a child's rocking-horse in beautiful condition. It required a mere lick of paint to make it suitable for a rich child. I stopped at a large mansion on my way home and a woman gave me enough money for it to feed my family for a week!'

'Amazing,' I murmured, and placed my palm over my glass to indicate that I had drunk enough vodka.

Standing up, I thanked my host and his daughter for the excellent meal and announced that I must go. It must have been at that moment that the ballad I had written for Leah fell out of my pocket.

TEN

While shaving the following morning, I looked at myself in the mirror and thought: 'Johann Wunder, who is this strange person who cannot remember his parents, his loved ones and his teachers? Is it not odd that he can play a musical instrument, and perform complicated clerical tasks? Someone taught you these skills. You must once have had parents who fed you, formed your habits and gave you a conscience. In the past you obviously took meals with other people, conversed, played music and made love. All the details must still be somewhere inside your brain.

I had heard one scurrilous rumour which suggested that Shmul had found me lying unconscious in a brothel. In that case my loss of memory might be due to a combination of debauchery and alcoholic poisoning. Another rumour maintained that I was an imp who had sprung into Shmul's britska from another world. This latter notion is easily refuted, because I have a belly-button, proving beyond doubt that I am man born of woman.

Salka was serving porridge when I went down to breakfast in the restaurant. I handed her my bowl and asked after her mother's health. She responded with a long list of deadly-sounding ailments, ending with the words: 'But she's all right, apart from that.'

I whispered: 'Thank you for your message.'

Salka hung her head over the jug of porridge, slowly filled my bowl and then whispered accusingly: 'Bertha told me you gave her a song to sing. Why didn't you wait for me to come back.'

'She said but four words during the performance, including one that was not very pretty. Some day, I'll compose a part specially for you.'

'Don't bother!' she replied sulkily and began to serve the next customer.

Amused by her childishness, I returned with the plate of porridge to my table and asked myself why she should display jealousy over such a trifling matter. I put it down to a desire to share in that small degree of fame my flute-playing had created.

While working in Ben-Levi's office that morning, I tried to recall the words of the ballad I had foolishly dropped in Shmul Perlman's house.

My flute and I dance attendance
On the sweetest of ladies called Leah.
My music she finds most enchanting
Its message will always be clear:
That my flute shall ne're be uprooted
from the site of that sacred grove
which Nature has granted my lady,
From which I swear ne're to rove.

Flesh of my flesh is my Leah
And flesh of myself is my flute.
It has captured the heart of my lady
And entered her up to its root.
We have kissed, we have danced,
We have coupled;
For Leah I have entered my suit.
My troth is plighted for ever
And so, indeed, is my flute!

I had imagined that I would give the little poem to Leah while we were in bed, convinced that in these circumstances she

57

would have appreciated its bawdy humour — the words had been composed while I was still tipsy from drinks thrust upon me while entertaining in the Bear tavern. I hoped against hope that her father had not found it.

*

I examined the invitation to play at the Count's ball. There was no mention of any payment. But I was in no position to decline.

Also in the safe was a bundle of documents which I thought concerned the Count's various mistresses. Examining them, however, I discovered correspondence between Ben-Levi and Prince Poniatowski, which made reference to the French Revolutionary Government's desire to restore Poland to its former glory. I had heard talk in The Bear tavern of how the revolutionaries in France proposed to usher in a new age of Enlightenment and Freedom. The suspicion now occurred to me that Ben-Levi's visit to Prague had a purpose that went beyond mere games of chess.

I hastily restored the bundle of letters to their original position in the safe and resumed my work.

I was due that evening to give another performance in the Inn. But before taking my evening meal in the restaurant, I set out to walk to my former place of residence, having made up my mind to inform Shmul Perlman of my intention to marry his daughter.

There was no reply when I knocked on the door. I could hear Shlotkin moving around in his stable. Yankel the hunchback was standing in the semi-darkness by the fence across the road. He called out to me but his words were borne away by the wind. I crossed the road and he repeated them.

'Leah has gone.'

'Gone where?' I asked in amazement.

'Her brother, Itzhak, has been badly wounded fighting with the French. She has gone to Holland to look after him.'

'By herself!'

'She is a strong, capable woman. I wished that she would have married me. But no one wants a hunchback.'

I was at a loss for words. Finally, I managed to stutter: 'But — but — why didn't she tell me?'

'When she came to say goodbye, she mentioned that she had left a message for you with her father.'

'Where is he?'

'In town. Ah, here he is ...'

I looked down the road and saw Shmul walking towards us, his body bent forward dejectedly, his hands sunk deep in his overcoat pockets. When he came within hailing distance, I said to him: 'Why didn't you tell me that Leah was going away?'

'There was no time. A friend of mine was driving a chaise to Vienna and she made haste to go with him. My son has had a leg amputated. He is very ill.'

'I could have gone to Vienna with her.'

'There was only one vacant seat. Anyway, I could barely afford Leah's fare.'

Reb Shmul Perlman then invited me into his house. He announced lugubriously when we got inside: 'This calamity has cost me a fortune. I had to borrow more money from Reb Abraham Koch to pay for Leah's journey. But at least he had the decency to say he would charge no interest.'

He then complained: 'Why did Itzhak have to go and fight for a foreign power? Of course, I know there is justice in their cause. But even if my son lives, which is by no means certain, he will be a helpless cripple for the rest of his life, always dependent upon charity. Do you know why he and his brother, Abe, decided to fight for the French? Because he thinks their revolution will improve the status of Jews. A vain hope. But young men will always go chasing ideals.'

I was about to ask why Leah had volunteered to go on such a long, hazardous journey. But there was no need to ask: her compassionate, stalwart heart would always go to the aid of the sick and oppressed. All I could hope was that her mission would be successful. It seemed unlikely that I would ever see her again.

'I have something for you,' Reb Shmul mumbled, tugging at something in his pocket. My heart sank, as I thought he was about to pull out my ballad. Instead, he handed me an envelope addressed to Johann Wonder in Leah's well-rounded handwriting.

I thanked Shmul and stuffed it into my pocket. But he said: 'Aren't you going to read it?'

Yes, of course.' I opened the envelope, The letter read:

To my Flautist from Heaven,

Dear Johann,

I have to go on a journey to rescue my brother, Itzhak, who is badly injured and lives in appalling circumstances in a village in Holland.

I shall be in Vienna for a few hours before resuming my journey. Knowing that you came from Vienna, I shall see reflections of you everywhere.

I am sure one day you will recover your memory and renew your position in Viennese society.

This is really to say that your ballad has raised me to the highest level of happiness, It will be in my heart forever. But I shall never marry you.

Your loving Leah.

'You are satisfied with what she has written?' Shmul Perlman enquired, frowning suspiciously.

I replied: 'I had grown very fond of her while I was in her care but she refuses to have me for a husband.'

He growled: 'You may have a wife in Vienna.'

'I have no recollection of being married. If Leah will marry me, I shall stay here in Korlishev.'

'Jews do not marry Gentiles.'

'I would make her a good husband — I may be poor now but, who knows, one day perhaps I shall be rich.'

'Jews only marry Jews,' he said in a voice that was slightly slurred. 'It is decreed by custom.'

'The world changes; customs must change, too. If you cannot be reconciled to your daughter marrying me, we will go and live somewhere else.'

Reb Shmul then became angry.

He shouted: 'Jews marry only Jews.'

'But why should there be such an absurd rule?'

'To preserve our message.'

'What is that message?'

He looked at me steadily for a few moments and then said: 'I need inspiration to answer that question.'

He went outside and returned with a bottle of vodka. I refused his offer to pour me out a cup. He sat at the table again, poured himself out a large measure and said: 'The message is that we must be ourselves and not become other people.'

'What is the matter with being other people?'

He replied drunkenly: 'They worship the Golden Calf.'

'So do some Jews.'

He gazed at me through blood-shot eyes for a full minute and said: 'If they do, they can no longer call themselves Jews.'

'All this nonsense doesn't explain why you forbid me to marry your daughter.'

'I don't forbid it. She forbids it herself.'

'We don't know if that is the case.'

'It may be years before she returns. By then you may be in possession of your estates in Vienna.'

'That will make no difference.'

He poured himself out another glass of vodka. Seeing my contemptuous expression, he said: 'Do you know why I am drinking? It is to forget my sad past. But at least I have a past, which is more than you can say.'

He stared at me for a while then added with a sad laugh: 'And that's another, even better reason why you can't marry my Leah.'

It seemed pointless to engage in further argument. I gave a helpless shrug, stood up and walked out of the house without saying a further word.

I regretted my ill-mannered behaviour on my way back to the Bear Inn. After all, I owed Shmul my life. He and his daughter were the only true friends I had in the world.

ELEVEN

People travel for miles from the surrounding villages to hear me play. They stuff coins into my pocket during and after the concert. I am saving to pay for my journey to Vienna, where I hope eventually to find out my true identity and establish my former place in society. Which reminds me that Shmul once joked that the last time he went to Vienna his only profit was a corpse, which to his astonishment came to life and afterwards proceeded to eat him out of house and home.

My memory shows little signs of improvement. My general health remains good, although I do suffer from occasional pains in my side. Music, like a bountiful stream of running water, runs through my head all the time. But I have no means of knowing whether it is newly composed, or is bubbling up from my unknown past.

Because I was experiencing difficulty in calculating the income from a large unevenly-shaped forest in Kamieneca, I was relieved when Ben-Levi returned from Prague. He looked cheerful enough and congratulated me when I told him of the solution I had found to the Riva Gerschon question. I asked about his games of chess but he put his finger to his lips, indicating that I should be cautious when mentioning the subject.

After a while, looking troubled, he drew a chair up to the desk, glanced briefly at my work and said in low tones: 'The truth of the matter is that I have been drawn against my will into dangerous waters. My sympathies, as you might guess, are with Prince Jozef Poniatowski, who has an ambition to free Poland. I did indeed play a series of chess games with him in Prague and won them all. But we spent much time discussing the military situation and assessing his chances of success in battle against the ruling powers. Because of my reputation as a chess player, he has a high opinion of my ability to assess risks. I warned him that while he and Thomas Kosciuszko might gain some initial success in a campaign to oust the Russians, in the long term the combined weight of the Prussian and Russian forces would crush him. He thanked me for my analysis but says he will go ahead with his plans — he is a gallant soul who believes that striking a blow for freedom is better than passive acceptance.

'Perhaps you are unaware of the history of this unhappy land. We Jews have suffered from periodic pogroms whenever there has been instability. In the last century Cossacks from the Ukraine devastated hundreds of Jewish settlements in these parts and slaughtered their inhabitants. Any relief we gain invariably turns out to be short-lived. Political unrest is being fomented all across Europe by the French Revolution. Poniatowski has been infected by its spirit and is intent on liberating Poland from the Russians and establishing a more liberal regime. I wish him luck. My only concern is to see that the Jews in the little town of Korlishev do not become the victims of his, or anybody else's, crusade. Jews suffer disproportionately whenever there is social disorder.'

I said politely: 'Forgive me, Reb Ben-Levi, but why are you telling me all this?'

He gazed at me for a while. Eventually, he broke his silence, saying: 'If it becomes necessary, I may have to say that it was your fault that I was not informed of Prince Poniatowski's presence in Prague when I went there to attend a chess tournament.'

I exclaimed: 'Why should I be held responsible?'

'I'll answer that question in a moment. In the meantime, did you get an invitation to play your flute at Count Poceski's ball?'

'Yes, I did. But he makes no mention of payment.'

'Don't worry. It was I who suggested that you should play at the ball. And I shall see that you get paid handsomely.'

'Thank you!' I then said in a sarcastic tone. 'That is hardly going to be adequate compensation for facing the Count's wrath in respect of the other matter you have alluded to.'

'It is unlikely ever to come to that,' Reb Ben-Levi said curtly. 'You are returning to Vienna shortly. Is not that correct?'

'That is my plan.'

'So, if the Count should ever suspect that my visit to Prague had something to do with Prince Poniatowski's presence there, I shall say that my former employee, Johann Wunder, present address unknown, destroyed a letter which might have warned me of his presence.'

'Why should I do that?'

'If the question should ever be asked, which is unlikely, I shall say that you were pressed to destroy it by a third party who has a grudge against me. Ironically, although I advised Poniatowski not to take military action, he clearly intends to ignore my advice. It is important, therefore, that the Count should not know that I had dealings with the Prince. He regards him as his worst enemy, because when he establishes a government of Poland, he plans to curb the power of the nobility. If the Count suspects that I went to Prague with the express intention of meeting Poniatowski, I could lose my trusted position, which would have very bad consequences for the Jews in Korlishev.'

'Then why did you go to Prague?'

'I was commanded to go there to play with some of Prague's best players. I couldn't refuse Poniatowski's invitation to meet him. The very nature of my position forced me to play a double game. When I offered you employment, I was not unmindful of the possibility that I might have occasion to use you in this way.'

I refused the mid-morning refreshment Reb Ben-Levi offered me and said testily: 'How do you know I won't inform the Count of what you have just told me?'

Ben-Levi stroked his beard.

'He wouldn't believe you — he believes me to be totally loyal. Which I am. It is only when my fellow Jews are in danger that I place his interests second. Let me explain, Johann. The risk to which I am subjecting you is extremely small. It is most unlikely that the Count will ever discover that I met the Prince. If, however, by some remote chance in the future I have to tell this harmless lie, by then you will be in a different province, lost in the anonymity of a big city.'

I said sullenly: 'It seems very unfair that I should be put at risk, however slight.'

'I have given you employment. Jobs are scarce enough here. And I have arranged for you to play in front of an eminent audience for which I shall see that you get payment. There is always a balance between good and evil whatever actions one takes. In the most unlikely event that I have to accuse you of destroying Poniatowski's letter, I shall take whatever steps are necessary to protect you. In any case, you will be leaving me soon. It is obvious that your future lies in music making.'

After a moment's thought, I replied: 'I see there is very little danger. But why did you bother to tell me?'

'It is forbidden to bear false witness. I have lessened the sin by telling you what I have done.'

I shrugged and said: 'Now I should like to question you about a problem of my own.'

'What is troubling you?'

'I believe I should seek professional medical advice to help me recover my memory.'

'All the geniuses of the past have failed in that particular area... All except one,' Ben-Levi said, struck by an afterthought.

'Who is he?' I asked, curiously.

'Just tell me more about your problem.'

I took a deep breath and said: 'Apart from being unable to remember my past, I keep getting reprises of music that I have never heard before. The score sheets come vividly into my mind. But I don't know whether they come from the life I led before I was discovered in a graveyard, or whether I am remembering the music of other musicians.'

Ben-Levi looked puzzled. He replied: 'Life is a complete mystery. I often wonder how storks remember from one generation to another how to travel vast distances and create nests among the chimneys of Korlishev. Some things God intend to be beyond our understanding — including also, apparently, how to assess an unevenly shaped forest.'

My shrewd employer had noticed on the desk my unsuccessful efforts at solving the problem of the forest in Kamieneca. He said: 'A combination of mensuration and inspired guesswork is the answer. Let me demonstrate.'

It was dark by the time we had finished our work.

I reminded him as I left for the Bear Inn that he had spoken of someone who might be able to help me regain my memory. He said: 'There is a certain Doctor Freulich in Brno who has achieved some remarkable results.'

He added: 'But he charges a great deal of money.'

*

It was a freezing night. I wrapped the threadbare coat that Shmul had given me around my body. The bitterly cold wind made my trousers flap against my legs. Nevertheless, I was cheered by the knowledge that there might be someone in the world capable of restoring my memory. I was also pleased at the prospect of obtaining a handsome sum for playing at the ball. I vowed that I would play with dazzling brilliance. Tuneful phrases rang in my ears as I ran and danced madly through the streets, trying to keep warm.

During my progress a harrowing vision of Leah came into my mind. I could hear the sounds of menacing explosions. Red bursts of artillery fire flashed in the dark landscape behind her cowering figure. This disturbing image stayed with me until I saw the familiar string of oil lamps and the hazy outline of the Bear on his pedestal.

TWELVE

Reb Ben-Levi and his mother were also invited to the celebration of the betrothal of Count Poceski's eldest daughter, Marie Louise, to Lieutenant Alexander Barnikov of the Russian Imperial Guard. To please his master, my employer was required to entertain the guests with a series of the dry anecdotes for which he was renowned. I found this close relationship between such contrasting personalities as the suave pleasure-seeking count and his chess-playing retainer difficult to understand. The Count single-mindedly desired to conserve the vast estates which enabled him to enjoy his hedonistic pursuits. Ben-Levi's main concern was to please him and thus ensure a peaceful life for the Jewish community of Korlishev. The only relief he enjoyed from his arduous duties was the occasional game of chess.

Because I lacked suitable clothing for the occasion, my employer kindly advanced money from my wages, which enabled me to purchase tan-coloured trousers and a dark blue tunic at a shop in town. I was extremely nervous at the prospect of playing before such a distinguished audience.

A carriage arrived to bring us to the castle. Reb Ben-Levi was dressed entirely in black with a large white cravat. His tiny mother was enveloped in a blue coat under which she wore a gown of tawny-orange colour that had lain in a trunk for many years. The grounds of the castle were full of splendid carriages, around which our driver skilfully manoeuvred until we arrived at the servants' entrance. We dismounted and walked through some candle-lit corridors, into a large kitchen where cooks were busy boiling and roasting an enormous quantity and variety of foodstuffs, including a huge boar which one of the chefs informed us the Count had killed himself the previous day.

The footman whom I had met on the previous occasion ushered us with his usual disdainful expression into a small room adjoining the kitchen, where a modest repast had been prepared. I could hear faint music. I wondered if the musicians who were playing might accompany me while I played my flute. However, I was confident from my experience in the Bear Inn that I could entertain the guests with or without their assistance.

Our meal, in deference to the Ben-Levis' Jewish dietary requirements, consisted solely of fish, potatoes, bread and butter and a bowl of fruit. While we were eating, we observed a procession of waiters carrying enormous platters of steaming food along the corridor.

There was little conversation during the meal. Ben-Levi's mother seemed in awe of everything around her. To make her feel at ease, I whispered: 'The Count believes that a few loaves of bread are sufficient to compensate Riva Gerschon for the loss of her marriage prospects. But for his own daughter he is willing to spend a vast fortune.'

'Marie Louise won't find it so easy when she goes to the Russian court,' she replied. 'They will treat her like a country bumpkin.'

I realised now from whom my employer had inherited his shrewdness.

Addressing me, Ben-Levi remarked: 'Today, I shall be the court jester, you will be the court musician. Let us hope we both perform well.'

It sounded as if even my redoubtable employer was also nervous.

Shortly after we had finished our meal, we were led along a corridor and then down one side of a large banqueting hall lit by numerous glittering chandeliers. Several hundred guests were sitting at trestle tables placed laterally across the room. Numerous officers from the Russian Imperial Guard were present, wearing splendid uniforms festooned with ribbons and medals. The women were clad in beautiful high-waisted gowns, their necks and bosoms shimmering with jewels.

The Count, his wife and family and the engaged couple were sitting below a raised platform from which came the strains of music. A young lady was playing the piano; two others were playing respectively a violin and a guitar.

A major domo, resplendent in a red uniform, instructed us to sit on chairs by the side of the stage. He mounted three steps onto the platform and waved peremptorily to the musicians. The music ceased. He then advanced to the front of the stage and addressed the guests, who were busy eating, drinking and talking: 'Les invités, dames et gentilhommes distingués, Monsieur Ben-Levi, le serviteur de Comte Poceski essaiera maintenant de vous divertir.'

He nodded at my employer, who then mounted the stage.

No one paid the slightest attention. The continuous buzz of conversations carried on as before.

Not in the least put out, Chaim Ben-Levi, turned his back on the audience and began ostentatiously praying to his Maker. He bowed this way and that, holding up his hands in supplication to the sky. Curiosity at this strange behaviour eventually produced a brief lull in the conversation. Reb Ben-Levi then turned round, held out both hands towards the audience, said: 'I was just praying for the roof to fall in. Pinned down, unable to move or talk, you would then be forced to listen to my jokes.'

Loud laughter.

He went on gravely: 'First of all, I must pay a tribute to my employer, a very generous man. If I broke my leg tomorrow, the noble Count would continue to pay my wages. If he learned, however, that I had wasted so much as a single groschen, he would break the other leg. But that's another story... My theme tonight is eggs.'

Addressing the Count, whose table was nearest the stage, he continued: 'Noble sir, for once in your life you have placed me above you. For this I am deeply grateful. But now I can tell you that the view from above is even more ridiculous than the view from below. I happen to know that you are as bald as an egg, as indeed are many of your distinguished guests. Only your wives and the wigmakers know who are the bald ones. Baldness is one of those quirks of nature which the good Lord uses — not very successfully in some cases — to deepen our sense of humility. It occurs to me that it is a pity the good Lord did not make us completely egg-shaped — because if you turn an egg upside down, it still looks the same. If we baldies had been formed in this manner, dear Count'— he removed his skull cap for a moment, exposing his own shining pate — 'we could stand upside down and no one would know the difference.'

Loud laughter.

'How many of you, I wonder, can boil an egg? For that matter, how many of you can slaughter a chicken? Valiant soldiers, it seems you are perfectly at ease slaughtering each other. But put you among chickens and you would all starve to death. Only the good sense of your ladies, who know how to wring a chicken's neck, would save you from starvation. On the other hand, you are entitled to credit for knowing how to pour artillery fire into a city, judging exactly the angles and velocity required to tear the limbs off its inhabitants.

'Do you know how I personally would lay siege to a town? I would bombard the population with — that beribboned gentleman with the purple sash over there. You sire, what should we use for ammunition? You can guess!... That's right, sire. Eggs, noble sire, eggs. I would put the fear of God into the population with eggs. No bones would be broken, no flesh seared, no limbs destroyed. But it would prove more effective than your customary strategy of hurling cannon balls. You, ma'am, that beautiful lady with the bosom I should love to cry on — what do you think my fierce bombardment would produce? An omelette! Exactly, a HUGE omelette! And the population of the besieged city, out of sheer gratitude for such a generous and unexpected distribution of food, would surrender immediately.

71

'There's a saying older than the hills that you can't make omelettes without breaking eggs. The metaphor is just as misleading as Zeno's paradox concerning the tortoise and the hare and it confuses us all into thinking that breaking heads is the same as breaking eggs. I can assure you from personal experience that there is a world of difference. So, noble gentlemen, I appeal to you, next time you are bombarding a city, which duty you will no doubt carry out with splendid accuracy and the highest and noblest of motives, consider seriously the rational alternative. Beat your swords into ploughshares, substitute eggs for cannon balls, and woo the natives with tasty omelettes. They will be more than happy to provide the salt and pepper themselves.'

Reb Chaim carried on in the same vein for fifty minutes, making fun of the military, the largest element in the audience. The army officers didn't mind. They were too drunk, apparently, to feel insulted. He even persuaded one elderly general to come up on the stage and pretend to be a constipated chicken laying an egg. The assembled company laughed until their corsets creaked and their cummerbunds snapped. I was laughing, too, quite taken with his performance.

Only when I remembered that I had to go up on the stage did I cease from laughing. Then my mouth went dry and my legs began to tremble.

When Reb Ben-Levi came down from the stage, breathing heavily from his exertions, he muttered to me: 'Get up there! Catch them while they are in a good humour.'

He sat down next to his mother.

I carried my flute up onto the stage and looked at the expectant faces in front of me. There were fierce-looking hussars with waxed moustaches, plump, burly colonels with mutton-chop whiskers, ladies with knowing, lecherous glances and inviting, pearl-encrusted bosoms. Directly in front of me the Count smiled up at me encouragingly, his dowdy wife was wiping something off her dark blue dress. The slim, vapid-looking subaltern, Alexander Barnikov, sitting beside her was holding the hand of his delicate, ingenuous bride-to-be. Her slender figure was clad in a becoming roseate satin gown. She looked up at me and smiled. That innocent smile established an instant bond between us. I smiled back at her, put the flute to my lips and blew a pretend fart.

A gale of laughter swept the hall.

I looked up at the elaborate ceiling and the ornate chandeliers and experienced an overwhelming sense of déja vu. If I had not been in this particular castle before, I knew for a certainty that I had been in many other, similar baroque establishments entertaining large audiences. In that instant I knew for the first time with absolute certainty that I had once been a professional musician.

'This is for the ladies,' I announced.

I played an impromptu piece called The Nightingale, which evoked the picture of a romantic evening in the countryside. I could have gone on playing variations on the theme indefinitely but stopped after a while, in deference to the mood of the audience. Scenting that they wanted comedy, I gave them the little item I had played in the Bear Inn. But instead of the Empress Catherine, out of tactful consideration for the Russian guests, I portrayed King George and Queen Charlotte of England jumping in and out of bed in the same fashion as I had depicted the Empress and Potemkin The joke went down as well as if I had been playing in the Bear Inn.

I went on to play Hungarian and Bohemian folk tunes to great effect. And then asked the audience if they had any requests. The Count's daughter asked in a clear voice if I would play Johann Sebastian Bach's Italian Concerto. The music started to run round and round my head with the speed of a gunpowder fuse. I was sure it would sound absurd on the flute. So I asked the lady sitting at the pianoforte if she would allow me to take her place. There was no rush of emotion as on the previous occasion I had looked at the keyboard. I played the piece with almost mechanical exactitude, my face twitching a little nervously.

A storm of applause greeted me.

I would have been happy to give them a reprise but the Count then stood up and instructed the major domo to prepare for dancing. I returned to the side of Ben-Levi. The female musicians played quiet background music, as the guests were led out of the banqueting hall into the ballroom.

A group of men and women, defying this general exodus, came over to congratulate me on my performance. The major domo instructed a waiter to bring drinks. I found myself being lavishly praised on all sides. The bewhiskered officer who had imitated the chicken insisted that I drink glass for glass of vodka with him, dashing each glass as he finished into an adjacent fireplace and urging me to do the same.

Ben-Levi watched with amusement as I modestly disclaimed the compliments being heaped on me. My perform- ance on the keyboard had come as much of a surprise to myself as anyone else. I could not believe that my mind or body which, I am not sure, had retained its knowledge of a composer whose name I could only faintly recall. But I was aware that I must once have revered him. His music seemed to have permeated every pore of my body how else could I have played it! I tried hard to recall a portrait of his face to no avail. In the meantime, I drank glass after glass of Russian vodka.

It was some time before I could escape the attention of my admirers. Eventually, the haughty footman appeared again and implored his guests to attend the ball. When they left, he instructed us with a severe mien to collect our coats and return to the servant's entrance, where our coach awaited us.

My success as a musician and the glasses of vodka had gone to my head. 'I — I was good,' I said, spluttering with excitement, as we climbed into the coach. You were good, Reb Chaim. We were both good. I had entirely forgotten that Johann Sebastian Bach shares my forename. I didn't know I could play the keyboard, but it seemed totally familiar when I sat down to play. Perhaps soon the rest of my memory will follow suit and I shall be able to claim my rightful place in Vienna. But you were magnificent, too, Reb Chaim. Wasn't he,' I added, turning towards his mother in the darkness. I then enquired of my employer: 'However, forgive me for asking, but why did you insult the Count, amongst other things drawing attention to the fact that he is bald. And why did you make fun of the officers in the Russian army. Might they not take it out of your fellow Jews?'

There was no sound but the clattering of hooves and the creaking of the elderly chaise in which we were travelling. Ben-Levi then answered, so quietly that I could scarcely hear him: 'Johann, try to imagine if the governing powers declared an open day for killing musicians. The hunters would injure some and murder others. But inevitably some of their prey would escape and continue to practise their art clandestinely. Next time the hunters required to be entertained, they would tolerate a limited number of insults, recognising that this was a prize they must pay for not running entirely out of musicians. That is the general principle which allows a humble Jew like myself to insult his superiors.'

Confused by the vodka, and not really understanding him, I muttered inconsequentially: 'I had no idea that Count Poceski was bald.'

I was still tipsy when I arrived back at the Inn. I climbed onto the pedestal in the courtyard and hugged the bear. The smell of his mangy fur reminded me of the pelts on the bed on which I had slept when I was living at Shmul Perlman's. I stepped down, staggered into the inn, lurched through the entrance hall, climbed up the three flights of stairs, clinging onto the balusters to preserve my balance and opened what I thought was my bedroom door.

A full moon was visible through a window opposite hanging motionless like a golden coin against a background of indigo sky.

'Who's that?'

It was Salka's voice.

I replied: 'Johann Sebastian Bach. No, I lie. It's Johann the flautist. He played tonight in front of the assembled nobility of Russia and Galicia.'

I tripped and fell onto the bed.

She said: 'Did you really play at the Count Poceski's ball?'

'Yes, and I was applauded to the moon and back. I shall be much in demand by high society in future.'

I lay beside her, her warm bosom nestling against my chest, and continued: 'Tonight, I played before the bald heads of Russia. Tomorrow, I shall play before the crowned heads of Europe. Of course, the crowned heads may be bald as well. Bald as eggs. I shall turn them into omelettes...'

'Johann, you're drunk.'

'And, Salka, you're beautiful.'

'You won't say that tomorrow when you're sober. When are you going to let me act a small part?'

'Soon. But meanwhile, treat me like I'm your loving sweetheart.'

'You are wicked, Johann. Stop doing that!'

'What?'

'What you are presently doing.'

'But you like it.'

'Who said I did?'

'I can tell. You are getting hotter and hotter and hotter.'

'What were they like?'

'Who?'

'The nobility. And their women. Were they beautiful? What does the Count's daughter look like? What colour dress was she wearing?'

'I can't remember. Oh, Salka, Salka, Salka... I am very drunk and I love you so. You are the quintessence of womanhood.'

'What does that mean?'

'I don't know. I know only that I love you, that I must have you.'

Salka was stroking my face.

'Silly boy. Oh! Oh! Oh!'

A moment later, she was hugging me to her with all her strength.

I became a wild Cossack. This way, Salka, my pony that way, Salka. Now, you're my brown bear clawing at me savagely and wantonly. Hold me Salka! Hold me!

We were savage Red Indians, giving vent to wild whoops. Arrows flew thick and fast, arrows of love, giving intense pleasure that set bells tingling and tinkling in my head. Salka! Oh. Salka! Oh, Salka!'

I recaptured the spirit of my youth in those ecstatic moments but not, alas, my memory.

My manhood ebbed and slowly died away and I dreamed that I was once again sleeping in St Marks churchyard.

THIRTEEN

How is it that I appear to have acquired a charm as irresistible as that of the famed Pied Piper? I am a pudgy little man with a mischievous face, so it cannot be my looks that make women swoon. But when I play my flute, or indeed any other instrument, they will do anything to prove their love and devotion. I consider sometimes they are simply paying a tribute to the heavenly music which flows through me.

I haven't forgotten, nor shall I ever forget, Leah, my nurse, my helpmeet, my heroine, who has travelled across war-torn Europe to give succour to her mutilated brother. It seems doubtful that we shall ever meet again. Perhaps it was to assuage my painful sense of loss that I slept with Salka.

It is not to my credit that I was very drunk at the time.

*

Count Poceski's ball proved a turning point in my fortunes. Two days after the event Reb Chaim Ben-Levi handed me a purse containing golden coins provided by the Count to show his appreciation of my performance at the banquet. The Count's daughter, Marie Louise, had added a quantity of silver thalers, with a note expressing her personal thanks and a request for some piano lessons. I also received an order from another member of the nobility to perform at a soirée to be given at his family seat some fifty miles from here. It stated that a coach would be provided.

When I had finished reading the letters, Reb Chaim looking very grave, informed me that I must leave his employment.

'Have I not given you satisfaction?' I demanded.

He replied: 'The quality of your work is admirable. But your gift for music vastly exceeds your talents as a clerk, which in themselves are not to be despised. You will earn considerably more money exercising your musical talents. It seems sensible that you should use that talent with which you have been so abundantly blessed.'

'But I prefer to continue in your service.'

He shook his head and replied: 'You have a remarkable gift. Make good use of it.'

He started pacing up and down, his hands behind his back and while he was doing so, I asked pointedly: 'Why do you want to get rid of me, Reb Chaim?'

He paused from his pacing and said: 'We are living in a dark, ignorant corner of the world. Radical new ideas that are sweeping the rest of Europe have passed us by. The peasants here consider that by tolerating the presence of Jews in their town they sstretch their capacity for goodness beyond its natural limits. They know that you rode into Korlyshev in the wagon of a Jewish pedlar. That, and your gift for flute-playing, marks you out as someone different from their normal, everyday experience. Some of these ignorant fools are saying that you are the devil incarnate.'

'That's utterly ridiculous!'

'Perhaps. But your capacity to play music of such unearthly beauty convinces them that you possess supernatural powers.'

'What can I do to disabuse them of these ridiculous notions?'

Reb Chaim stroked his yellow beard and then, as if addressing himself, said: 'The truth is their lives are short and brutish, their horizons narrow. When someone comes along with such an outstanding gift they think it must be against the natural scheme of things.'

I complained indignantly: 'But I'm just an ordinary person.'

Reb Chaim shook his head. 'Even the sophisticated Russian officers who have attended concerts in the court of St. Petersburg insist that you are extraordinary.'

'You, sir, made a remarkable address. They seemed to adore being insulted.'

'It's just as well they did not know about my encounter with Prince Poniatowski in Prague. If they knew, they would skewer me without compunction.'

He gave a little shiver and said, shaking his head: 'But other unpleasant things are afoot in Korlyshev. Notes have been pushed through my door accusing me of employing the Devil. I'm sorry but you must leave my employment at the end of the week.'

Soon afterwards he left to go on some mission for the Count. I found it difficult to concentrate on my work. The loss of my job worried me much more than the stupid rumours about my supernatural powers. It appeared that my musical gift was two-edged; on the one hand it made women fall in love with me, on the other it invited abuse and persecution.

Going home that night, as I approached the Bear Inn, I saw a tall, lean, swarthy man leaning against one of the iron pillars of a shed containing bales of hay. I recognised him as one of the ostlers. He released himself from the iron pillar as I approached the courtyard and stood before me. Spots of red stood out on his swarthy cheeks. His breath smelled of vodka.

He spoke at first in Polish and when I shook my head, changed to halting German. I thought he was praising my flute-playing, so I smiled and nodded. He then made a dramatic gesture of strangulation with both hands and I heard the word: 'Salka'. I assured him that I had no intention of stealing her from him.

He shook his fist, spat on the ground and then stood aside to let me pass. I went up to my cubby hole of a room, a little ashamed of the cowardice I had shown.

That night the collection of coins handed to me exceeded all my expectations. Word had spread of my sensational success at the Count's ball. More and more people wanted to hear me play. The knowledge that I could earn good money playing music relieved to some extent my disappointment at losing my clerical job.

I added the coins I had earned that night to the savings hidden under my mattress. There now seemed a real prospect of being able to afford the fees of the famous mind doctor that Reb Chaim Ben-Levi had recommended. With my memory and self-confidence fully restored, I would surely soon be able to regain the high position in Viennese society my instinct told me I had once enjoyed.

FOURTEEN

The following morning, Herr Müller intercepted me on my way down to breakfast. After congratulating me on my successful performance at the Castle, he said slyly: 'Now that you're a darling of the aristocracy, I suppose you'll think it beneath your dignity to play for the likes of us.'

While I continue to live here, I shall be happy to give performances for your customers.'

'And how much did your collection amount to last night?'

'It was satisfactory.'

'Was it now! In that case I suggest that you move from your present room to one that a travelling gentleman has just vacated. It will cost you double your present rent. But you'll be in surroundings more suitable for a fine musician such as yourself.'

I swallowed an impulse to decline the offer and said: 'All right. But you should remember, Herr Müller, that my music has brought prosperity to your inn. If you push me too hard, I shall go elsewhere.'

He muttered under his breath: 'You've been pushing Salka hard a little bird tells me.'

I ignored his remark.

I moved my few belongings into the new room that evening. It contained a fine bed and a cupboard for my clothes. From the window looking out over the courtyard I can see the stuffed bear from which the inn derives its name. Although I am prospering in this provincial backwater, I still yearn for the social position I feel I must once have enjoyed in the great city of Vienna. I can only guess what it must have been like, having no certain knowledge of that previous existence. All that remains are vague sensations and emotions. I can recall the bustling atmosphere but can form no firm images of its buildings or its inhabitants. Similarly with other towns the names of which struck a chord. Visions of buildings and spires in Salzburg, Mannheim, Leipzig occasionally enter my mind but they are shadowy and seems to have no association with people and events. I have a sense of once having owned a rich assembly of musical instruments and other worldly goods. But perhaps this is an illusion brought about by the fact that I am being feted as a musician.

A piece of music was running through my head the other day. As it changed key, the word 'Padre' came to me. But whoever was connected with the music was not, as the word implies, my father. Whenever I think of my true father, the word 'Lion' immediately leaps into my mind. I am unable to visualise his face, which is a great sadness to me.

I gave another performance tonight at the Inn. True to my promise, I gave Salka a little part to play in the singspiel I had devised. She played the part of a little filly in a paddock next to a stable in which were several stallions played by members of the audience, each one vying for her services. A little caprice made me call one of them Shlotkin. His common sense and wisdom finally prevailed over the other horses, allowing him the privilege of mating with her. I was pleasantly surprised to find that Salka could dance and cavort and kick her heels with great zest and style. I do believe that even the most unlikely people have talents which can be discovered when the right musical inspiration is provided. Music can unlock a wealth of human talent. Even Herr Müller, in spite of his great bulk, stood up on this occasion and pretended to paw the ground in front of the gaily-dancing Salka.

She came up to my room later that night, in a state of high excitement and asked me if she should become a professional dancer. I warned her that the training was arduous and the rewards niggardly.

'How do you know these things, Johann. What do you know of opera and the ballet?'

Opera!

The word evoked a host of vivid images. I sat down suddenly on my bed, an expression of frustrated longing on my face.

Salka said: 'What ails you, Johann?'

I shook my head slowly, without answering.

After a while, I said: 'I know something about ballet. It requires much training and discipline. Don't delude yourself, Salka. You will never be a dancer, although you have much natural grace and beauty. But now I think I should tell you that a tall, thin friend of yours has threatened to kill me, if I have anything more to do with you.'

'Oh, Fréderic. That ignorant oaf. Don't take any notice of him'

'He thinks you belong to him. Do you, Salka?'

'Of course not. He means nothing to me. You are my true love, Johann. Your way with music is truly fantastical! How do you do it?'

She sat on my lap and laid her head against my chest Then looking up at me, she said softly: 'But you must watch out.'

'You mean Fréderic?'

'No. not that fool,' Salka said contemptuously. 'But there are people in the town who say you are possessed of the Devil.'

'Why should they say that?'

'They ask how is it possible that a man who arrived in Korlyshev sick on a Jew's wagon can do such things as you can do. Nobody has ever risen so swiftly in the world. They say that either you are a murderer fleeing from justice, or else you're an imp in human form. Which are you, Johann Wonder?'

She stood up. I tried to grab her, but she evaded me and called out mockingly: 'Which of them are you, Johann? I want to know.'

'I am neither, silly girl. I am a musician who became very sick and lost his memory.'

'They say you died and came to life again.'

'They also say I was found unconscious in a brothel.'

'Which is true?'

'How do I know, if I was unconscious at the time? Come here, you silly girl.'

Salka came slowly towards me, a slightly fearful expression on her face. It was almost as though she believed these ridiculous stories.

I pulled her into my arms and kissed her. She murmured: 'I don't really care what you are, Johann. Your music is so beautiful. But you must be careful. There are some people in this town who would love to string you up. They say you are a crypto-Jew sent by the Prussians to spy on us.'

How ridiculous. Anyway, what's wrong with being a Jew? A Jew saved my life.'

'Jews are Christ-killers.'

'Jesus Christ would not condone the lynching of an innocent stranger. Anyway, who would benefit if they carried out their threat?'

Salka gave a cynical laugh.

'The citizens of Korlyshev would be getting just the kind of entertainment they like best. It is quite likely that they would make you play the flute before hanging you.'

Her statement made me feel sick. I tried to push her out of the room. She resisted at first, not realising how much she had upset me. She kept repeating as I struggled with her: 'Come and get me, Horsey. Get me if you can!' the words of the song she had performed the previous evening.

I finally managed to force her out and closed the door.

I sat down again on the bed, disturbed by her words and behaviour. I decided that I should start making plans for the future. If I continued to earn at my present rate, I should soon have enough money to visit the famous doctor who lived in Brno and stay with him until he succeeded in bringing back my memory. There was nothing left for me in this backward town, so full of hidden intrigue, malice and dark superstitions.

*

Apart from the entertainments I gave most nights at the Bear Inn, I have a further engagement three days hence with the Lord of Pugachov, who wishes to celebrate the completion of a building project at his family home. The invitation to give music lessons to Count Poceski's daughter was couched in vague terms. But I am determined to pursue the matter. I long to lay my hands again on a piano keyboard. Playing at the Count's ball has opened up a whole range of memories and possibilities. I am caught between two conflicting desires — should I write down compositions that are already in my head or produce new ones? The word Opera that Salka had mentioned struck a deep chord. I am convinced that at one time I was involved in such an enterprise. Unhappily, a heavy velvet curtain has fallen across my mind, shutting me off from my past. Even so, the word Opera evokes the memory of a glorious soprano voice, which I associate with an ineffable perfume. I vaguely recall arguments, tearful goodbyes and a conflict with the Lion.

The challenge of writing a new opera will help me through the difficult days ahead. I shall need a piano. The only one available belongs to Marie Louise, the Count's daughter.

FIFTEEN

Armies of workmen had toiled for years to refurbish and extend Lord Pugachov's baronial castle. They had added on an enormous ballroom, in which I played to a distinguished audience. Near the castle, scattered among forests of silver birches and fir trees, were tumble-down hovels housing the noble lord's wretched peasantry. It sickened me to hear the florid-faced, moustachioed Pugachov boasting in his speech of welcome of the useful employment he had given to the villagers by extending his castle. It had not occurred to him to improve their squalid conditions. However, I played my flute to the best of my ability, conquered the audience and received numerous enthusiastic ovations.

I had sent word to Count Poceski's daughter that I would be happy to comply with her request for keyboard lessons, adding that they might be curtailed, since I was planning to leave Korlyshev soon. Answering her invitation, which came quickly, I arrived at the Castle and was shown into the Count's library. Maria Louise was sitting at the piano, wearing a high-waisted muslin gown unbuttoned at her neck. She looked very young and innocent.

The footman ceremoniously bowed himself out. Marie Louise beckoned with her delicate-looking hand, saying: 'I am so glad you have come, Johann. I'm afraid that if I am asked to play the piano when I go to St. Petersburg I shall make a fool of myself. I had lessons when I was young but have forgotten much of what I learned.'

'Can you read music?'

'A little.'

There were music sheets on top of the piano. I found a simple piece by Haydn and placed it before her. From the moment her hands touched the keys I knew that I had taken on

87

a hopeless task. Her inability to play was not due to lack of practice or nervousness. I made due allowance for these frailties; it was simply that an undeclared state of war existed between the young lady and the Goddess of music. An artillery barrage would have been more pleasing to the ear than the sounds she was making.

I signalled her to stop.

She looked up at me enquiringly.

I said: 'My dear young lady, God has showered many gifts on you but not, alas, that of music. I suggest you write poetry, paint pictures or simply remain your most beautiful and enchanting self.'

Marie Louise closed the piano lid softly, apparently not too hurt by what I had just said. 'It is just as well I have found out in time. I feared that I might be called upon to play at the Russian court and would not meet their expectations. If I am asked, I shall decline. But now that you are here, will you grant me the great pleasure of listening to you play?'

I nodded assent.

She lifted the cover and yielded her place at the piano stool. I played the Haydn piece then launched into a movement of a piano concerto, the theme of which had been haunting my imagination all the morning. Orchestral instruments thundered in my head as I played, blending with the main theme which ran into numerous fanciful tributaries before returning to reach a splendid climax. I recognised the concerto as something I had composed during that forgotten portion of my life before coming to Korlyshev. When I had finished, I gave a despairing sigh and hung my head.

'What ails you, Johann?' the Count's daughter enquired, softly.

I replied wearily: 'Somewhere there is a catalogue of music which sporadically enters my memory. Occasionally, it releases accompanying pictures of musical scores. But more often than not it is surrounded by emptiness.'

'You played with such passion it made my heart beat faster. I would give up everything to be able to play like that.'

'Would you give up your forthcoming marriage?'

'Yes.'

'I would not advise it. Music is a hard taskmaster. I think its heavy pressures have crushed me into the ground. I'm totally confused. I cannot always tell whether the music I play is my own, or whether I have stolen it from other composers. It makes me feel as if I am sleep-walking.'

'You poor man.'

Marie Louise came and stood behind me and draped her arms around my neck as I sat at the piano stool. I impulsively kissed her hand and then stood up, turned round and apologised, adding that I was deeply moved by her sympathy.

'No need to apologise. Tell me, Johann, how did you come to work for Ben-Levi?'

I explained how Leah had obtained the position for me.

'He's a wonderfully clever man, Ben-Levi. I believe he beats the best chess players in Europe. Come and sit on the sofa.'

She led me towards an elegant settee covered in turquoise and gold silk and said after we had sat down:: 'My father plays chess but has never managed to win a game against Ben-Levi. I believe, though, he did once achieve a stalemate. Have you ever played chess with Ben-Levi?'

I shook my head.

Marie Louise was gazing me intensely, her moist red lips slightly open. Wondering for a moment if my music affected her as it had other women, I quickly reminded myself that Lieutenant Barnikov would chop my head off with his sabre, or at the very least challenge me to a duel, if he suspected me of stealing the affections of his fiancée.

'Does it require a special cast of mind, do you think?'

'What?'

'Chess — is it like music, requiring a very special talent?'

She tilted her head charmingly, as I struggled to collect my thoughts, wondering why she was so interested in my employer.

I answered: 'Probably.'

'So you think it does require a special talent that most of us lack. I was born without any musical talent, alas. Obviously, it was implanted in you to the maximum degree possible. So, answer me, is Ben-Levi just a natural genius at chess? Does he study a great deal?'

Why is she so interested in chess, I asked myself — a subject which interests very few women. I studied her innocent face on which sat a youthful bloom and wondered whether she was as innocent as she appeared.

'I do believe my employer has a natural gift for playing chess. He has a vast literature about the subject on his bookshelves. It is impossible to succeed at the game unless you are thoroughly acquainted with all the classic opening gambits. I have never actually seen him studying chess. He spends most of his time on your father's business. Incidentally, do you play?'

'My father once taught me the basic moves. The knight jumps, if I remember correctly.'

'That is correct.'

'So tell me, Marie Louise went on earnestly, 'Does the game require a high degree of cunning?'

'It requires memory and intelligence. Both are equally important. I suppose that applies to any game.'

'Does it apply to the game of love?' Marie Louise enquired, smiling.

'Certainly. But love is more of a battle than a game.'

Marie Louise made a sudden move with her shoulders, which outlined the shape of her breasts against the flimsy material of her gown. She then said wistfully: 'In a battle there is always a winner. In a true love-match both parties are victorious.'

'Of course!' I gave her statement my hearty assent. 'You seem most fortunate in the match you have chosen.'

Marie Louise looked down at the floor and said softly: 'He is a military man and will be away a good deal while I am stuck in St. Petersburg.'

'A splendid city.'

'I shall be very lonely there. Do you think you might be persuaded to come there and play?'

'I am only a humble flautist.'

'Johann, you have great powers on the keyboard as well. There is a tremendous future ahead of you, I am sure of it. You will play in all the great capitals of Europe. It seems incredible that you emerged from a graveyard with your capacity for making music unimpaired. I think I would almost be prepared to suffer that dreadful experience if it would enable me to play the piano.'

'Why bother when you do so many other things to perfection?'

'Such as what?'

'Such as looking ravishingly beautiful and making charming conversation.'

'Did you realise that I had another purpose in inviting you to give me piano lessons?'

'It was very cruel of me to give such a harsh verdict on your playing.'

'I am satisfied that your estimate is correct. Would you like a cup of chocolate?'

'No, thank you.'

'The other purpose to which I refer concerns our friendship, Johann. Will you write to me when you leave Korlyshev?'

'Certainly.'

'And will you keep me informed about your musical career. You must compose more music.'

'I should like nothing better. I am thinking of writing an opera.'

'Would you include me in the cast of characters?'

'Of course. How would you see yourself?'

Marie Louise thought for a moment, glancing up at the ornate ceiling. Then she replied: 'As the loving admirer of a great composer, who would do almost anything to advance his career.'

'You flatter me. But you shall become part of the plot. Everything is possible in the world of operatic make-believe.'

I gave a small, self-conscious laugh.

Marie Louise said earnestly: 'I shall make it my business to advance your interests whenever possible. The Empress of Russia adores music I am told. I shall try to obtain an invitation for you to play at her Court.'

'Thank you. I am deeply touched. But it looks as though I shall have to remain a flautist, because I don't own a piano.'

'You may use this one whenever you feel like it.'

'Thank you, dear lady.'

I took her hand and kissed it.

She responded by lightly touching my cheek, remarking: 'Does your employer have sympathy for those who protest against Russian overlordship of Polish territory?'

Not wishing to answer this dangerous question, I went down on one knee in an exaggerated gesture and exclaimed: 'Why waste time on such matters! I have loved you sincerely ever since I saw you looking up at me during my performance at your betrothal ball.'

Marie Louise seemed not too displeased at this declaration. She rebuked me half-heartedly, saying a little breathlessly: 'Johann Wunder, you know full well that my husband-to-be would run you through if he even half-suspected that you had designs on me.'

She paused and then continued, wistfully: 'But we shall remain good friends. I shall leave word with the servants that you may call at the castle whenever it takes your fancy to practise at the keyboard.'

'Thank you a thousand times.'

I stood up, thinking the time had come for me to leave. But she restrained me, placing her hand on my arm and saying: You haven't answered my question.'

'What question was that?'

'I asked if your employer was sympathetic to the Polish Freedom movement.'

'He has never discussed it with me.'

'My father is concerned that when he went to Prague recently Ben-Levi may have been in contact with Prince Josef Poniatowski, who is believed to be plotting an uprising.'

'I doubt it. My master's sole concern is in winning at chess.'

Marie Louise took both my hands in hers and with a worried expression, said: 'You do understand that it was my father who asked me to put these questions to you. He is very concerned about certain political developments. And now, since you have been truthful with me about my musical ability, I shall do as you suggest and try something else that suits my temperament.'

I replied: 'You will outshine everyone else at court with your youthful beauty.

She said fervently, as I departed: 'Come again soon to play the piano, Johann.'

It was a warm day. I strolled back to Korlyshev feeling puzzled. The Count obviously entertained suspicions about Reb Ben-Levi's Prague visit. His daughter seemed keen for me to return to the castle. But too close a relationship with her might be dangerous. I had no wish to be forced by Lieutenant Barnikov into choosing between swords or pistols. Music from an opera expressing turbulent emotions over sexual jealousy rang faintly in my ears as this unpleasant thought came to me. And this, in turn, induced in me a strong desire to return to that wonderful piano in the castle.

I breathed in deeply of the scent-laden air as I walked and watched the white puffy clouds moving slowly overhead.

Beautiful melodies came unbidden into my mind and I resolved to save them for my opera.

Nearing the outskirts of Korlyshev, the name of the librettist of an opera called Don Giovanni poised itself momentarily in my mind. I could see a bridge over a river and then the elusive image evaporated. The experience was so frustrating that I began to run at full pelt. The idea came to me, as my legs swiftly carried me over a path worn smooth by hundreds of servants and supplicants, that I should make the loss of memory, which I personally found so irksome, the theme of my new opera.

SIXTEEN

Ben-Levi's prediction that I would earn more money with a flute than my pen proved correct. Money began to pour in from concerts I gave at cafés, inns and private dwellings in Korlyshev and the surrounding villages. I continued to live as frugally as before, aware that it was going to take a long time to save enough money for the expensive course of medical treatment available from Dr Freulich. It was vital for me to undergo this cure because I could not possibly re-establish myself in Vienna while still suffering from memory loss. As soon as the memory of my past life was fully restored I intended to sue those who had consigned me prematurely to the grave and make legal claims for the recovery of my estate. I felt encouraged by a slight improvement in my memory, especially where music was concerned.

There was a splendid collection of musical manuscripts in Count Poceski's library and I was overjoyed to find that I could do full justice to them on the piano. One piece, however, caused a cold shiver to run down my spine. When I held this particular musical score in my hand, the image of a raging lion appeared in front of my eyes. To avoid a repetition of this uncomfortable experience, I placed Mozart's composition at the bottom of the piano stool and tried to forget its existence.

I called one day at Shmul Perlman's house to enquire if he had news of Leah. His face was flushed; he looked older than when I had last seen him. His speech was slightly slurred. He had been drinking heavily. There had been no word from her. He told me he feared his daughter had been abducted during her long journey across Europe.

A week later, when I called at the house again, there was no answer. I crossed the road to enquire from Yankel if Shmul Perlman was away on his travels. Chickens were flapping around Yankel's feet as he showered grain from a round wooden container. He told me that Shmul Perlman had undergone a nervous collapse and was undergoing treatment.in the Jewish poorhouse. He had been asked to look after Shlotkin while his master was away.

Deeply disturbed by the news, I remarked that it was time for me to repay Shmul Perlman for all the expenses I had caused him. Yankel said: 'Wait until he is fit again and then lend him money to help him stock up his wagon. This isn't the first time he has over-indulged and it won't be the last. He is only really happy when he is on the road.'
He added: 'Have you noticed he talks to that horse as though it's a human being.'

'Travelling all alone in the forests and mountains, he obviously needs someone to talk to.'

'The big question is: does Shlotkin understand what he's saying?'

'I think he probably understands more than we give him credit for.'

'If I started talking to my chickens,' Yankel remarked with a laugh, 'I wouldn't have the heart to hand them over to the slaughterer.'

As I was about to leave, Yankel placed his hand on my arm and said hesitantly: 'I should like to ask you a question.'

'Go ahead.'

'I'm asking you because you are a remarkable person. You came back from the dead and you have the power to charm the Devil himself with that flute of yours.'

'I'm just someone who has had the misfortune to lose his memory.'

'It's said all over town that you are very popular with the ladies. Alas, because of my appearance, no woman will sleep with me. If I went to a house of ill repute, would I be more wicked than a normal man who goes into his wife?'

'What does your rabbi say?'

'He refuses to say yeah or nay. He says it must be my own decision.'

'Perhaps he is concerned that you might catch a disease.'

'I am prepared to take my chance.'

'Then, as he advised, it must be your own decison.'

Yankel shifted from one foot to another, grinned sheepishly and said: 'Is it true that when you play your flute women fall to the ground and beg you to make love to them?'

'It's not quite like that. But they certainly appreciate music.'

'It must be Heaven.'

'There's a price to pay for everything.'

'What price do you pay?'

'I have paid the price of not knowing who I am.'

Yankel nodded and said with superstitious awe: 'Perhaps God is punishing you for having too many women.'

'Perhaps,' I replied.

I smiled at his naive expression and set off for the town. It was late summer and flocks of birds in the blue sky above were flying south. I had by now saved almost enough money to pay for my course of treatment with Dr Freulich. He had agreed in his response to my letter to accept me as a patient, warning me that I might have to stay at his establishment for several months. Meanwhile, I was upset by the lack of news of Leah.

I consoled myself as I walked by reflecting on the progress I had made since I had started to use the Count's piano. My new opera was progressing apace. The theme concerns a young mayor living on the island of Cyprus who suffers a loss of memory and courts a second wife because he lacks recollection of his first. The Greek Goddess, Mnemosyne, has playfully placed a bewitched boundary stone on the border between two villages. Whenever the mayor passes this stone he is able to remember the wife in the village towards which he is travelling, but not the one he had just left behind. The plot becomes complicated when the women become similarly affected.

I had already completed the libretto and the music of the first Act; the characters and plot were firmly fixed in my mind. I was acutely aware that my script lacked the polish of a professional librettist but I was confident that the music would make up for this. I was only too aware that no one would stage the outpourings of an unknown flute-player, scratching a bare living in a remote Galician village. I had no patron, no influence, no true friends other that Shmul Perlman and his daughter, neither of whom was now available to give advice. Nor could I any longer rely on Reb Chaim Ben-Levi's assistance. I could only hope that when I returned to Vienna someone would recognise the opera's merits.

Meanwhile, a coolness has entered into my relationship with Reb Chaim-Levi. I believe he suspects that I have become too close to Count Poceski as a result of my frequent visits to the Castle. In fact, I rarely see the count during these visits.

My friendship with Marie Louise, however, continues to develop. I very much enjoy her company and she, in turn, is very appreciative of my music. Although not gifted musically, she has an excellent insight into musical and dramatic principles and frequently makes useful suggestions. Sometimes she leaves me alone so that I can work; at other times I play and sing to her the arias I am composing for Cypriana. Her fiance, Lieutenant Barnikov, is away in Georgia on some campaign of pacification, to use the Empress's euphemistic term for mass slaughter. It reminds me of Reb Ben-Levi's sarcastic remarks when he addressed the military commanders at the ball. I think he was a little imprudent on that occasion.

A few days before my conversation with Yankel, I had called on Reb Ben-Levi to ask him to keep some of my earnings in his safe, I learned that relations between the Christian and the Jewish communities in Korlyshev had deteriorated. His mother opened the front door and regarded me suspiciously. After a pause, she muttered: 'Yes, do come in. But he is not himself today. Something is worrying him.'

She opened the door of the office. Although it was nearly midday, Reb Ben-Levi was still in his nightgown. He was seated at the desk with a faraway expression on his face. But when he recognised me, he addressed me cordially and offered me a glass of wine, which I declined.

'Well, Johann Wunder, your fame I hear has spread far beyond the confines of Korlyshev. What can I do for you?'

'I was wondering...'

Before I could finish my sentence, Ben-Levi interjected: 'Do you see Count Poceski very often?'

'No. I sometimes see his daughter, Marie Louise, when I practise on the piano in the Castle library.'

'A problem has arisen concerning Riva Gershon. Unfortunately the settlement you so capably negotiated has come unstuck.'

'What happened?'

'Riva's aunt in Warsaw wrote to her father, Eli, to say that the Count had made his daughter pregnant. Yesterday, Eli foolishly went up to the Castle, threatening to kill him. He was arrested on the Count's orders and brought back into custody in the jail house. I interceded for him unsuccessfully. He will either be shot or sent to Siberia for sedition. Poceski was in a particularly angry mood. He threatens to sack me if I pursue the matter any further. '

'That's terrible.'

I thought for a moment and than said: 'Could you perhaps put pressure on the Count by threatening to tell his wife of the affair?'

Ben-Levi gave a cynical laugh.

'The Countess knows all about his affairs. So do all his servants. So for that matter does the whole world. I have been racking my brains to think of a solution. Recently, the Count questioned me about my visit to Prague. He has learned that Josef Poniatowski had clandestinely visited the town and enquired if I had met him. I explained that I had made arrangement months before to play in a local tournament and that the Prince, on his arrival in Prague, had insisted on playing against me in the tournament. I went over each individual move in the match to throw the Count off the scent. But I think he still suspects me of sympathising with the Free Poland movement.'

'Did you tell him that I had destroyed a letter informing you of his intended visit?'

'For the moment he seems satisfied that my meeting with the Prince was purely fortuitous. I am keeping that ruse you mention in reserve, in case at some time in the future, he accuses me of collusion with Poniatowski. When he mentioned the Free Poland movement. I assured him, as I have done countless times before, that the loyalty of Jews towards the reigning monarch need never be questioned. But he was in one of his awkward moods and accused me of insolence when I addressed the Russian officers at his betrothal ball. He has threatened to make the whole Jewish population of Korlyshev pay for Eli Gershon's effrontery. There is no limit to his arrogance. He even had the audacity to declare that Gershon should be proud that his daughter was bearing his bastard!

'I have worked for Poceski for many years and know his every mood. Although he is a dreadful tyrant, it is sometimes possible to coax him into making a generous gesture. On this occasion he was in such a frenzy I could see no way of bringing him round. However, after another angry outburst concerning Eli Gerschon, I said to him calmly: "Sire, do you remember when one of your women ran stark naked through the Castle grounds because she claimed you had neglected her and how I calmed her down, wrapped her in a blanket and took her back to her home?"

'The Count gave a great guffaw at this reference to one of his conquests. I took advantage of this sudden change of mood to remind him again about the game of chess I had played against the Prince. I described the Prince as amateurish, knowing this was what he wanted to hear; in fact Prince Poniatowski is a fine player, if somewhat impetuous. I then played my last desperate card. I said to him: "Do you suppose you could beat me at chess, if I was blindfolded?"

'He looked astonished and said: "Why do you ask?"'

I replied: "I am throwing down a challenge. If I win, I shall expect you to release the baker, Eli Gerschon, without further charge. If I lose, his punishment can stand."

'The Count agreed to my terms but insisted on playing the best of three games, which of course tilts the odds in his favour.'

'How can you remember all those moves when you are blindfolded?'

'In much the same way as you remember the notes you play on your flute.'

'When is this epic match going to take place?'

'Whenever it suits Poceski. It will be the biggest challenge I have ever faced in my life.'

'Why do it? You don't owe Eli Gerschon anything.'

'I am doing it for the sake of justice and for the cause of peace in this town. Eli Gerschon is a fool but he doesn't deserve such a punishment.'

At that point I asked if I could leave my money in his safe. But Ben Levi turned down my request, on the grounds that if the house burnt down he would be unable to repay the debt.

His words had an uncanny prescience.

*

As I re-entered the town, after my conversation with Yankel, the faint acrid smell of smoke came to my nostrils. I assumed somebody was burning rubbish. But I was too busy with my thoughts to pay much attention.

Salka was standing in the entrance to the Bear Inn, wearing bright clothes: a red bonnet, a white embroidered blouse and a blue flared skirt. I guessed she had just returned from visiting her mother. She said to me excitedly, when she saw me: 'Have you heard there was to be a fete tomorrow with music and fireworks to celebrate Count Poceski's famous victory at chess over the Jew Ben-Levi.'

101

So Ben-Levi had lost the unequal contest. I felt sorry for him.

Salka went on, pouting sulkily: 'But the celebration has been cancelled.'

'Why?'

'Because the Jews said they did not want it to take place. One of their number died in a fire. People are saying that the real reason is that they are ashamed their champion lost.'

I said urgently: 'Tell me what happened.'

Salka explained that the Count was so delighted at beating Ben-Levi at chess that he ordered a celebration. As a generous afterthought he ordered Eli Gershon to be released from prison. It seemed that Gerschon, on being freed, then went back to the bakery, set it on fire and died in the flames.

I went up to my room in a sombre frame of mind. Reb Ben-Levi had made it his life's work to maintain good relations between the two communities. But it was beyond even his powers to counter the overwhelming sense of injustice brought about by this mad act of self-immolation. Bakeries of course, are notorious for catching fire. But even if it was an accident, the Count was still guilty of cruelty towards Eli Gerschon and his daughter. I could see why the Jews were unwilling to attend the fete. But it prompted the thought: why couldn't the two communities continue to live together in harmony? The answer was that the forces of fear and superstition were too strong.

Salka came into my room a few minutes later. She sat on the bed and said with a sly grin: 'Some say it wasn't the Count that put Riva in the family way. They say it was your flute that did it.'

'It didn't make you pregnant,' I replied, rudely.

That's because I wasn't born yesterday,' she replied. 'Would you like to play on your flute again?' She roguishly pulled up her skirts above her knees.

'Which flute are you referring to?'

'The one in your trousers, what else.'

'Frédéric wouldn't be very happy if I did.'

'Are you frightened of him?'

'No. But I'd rather play you a tune on my musical instrument.'

'I suppose I'm not good enough for you now that you're seeing the Count's daughter.'

'She is betrothed to someone else.'

'And I am betrothed to Frédéric. That didn't stop you from having your will with me when you barged into my room.'

'I'm sorry. I was drunk.'

'So I'm only good enough for you when you're sozzled.'

'Nonsense, Salka. And there's nothing between Marie Louise and me. She just likes to listen while I play on her piano.'

'Don't give me that. I bet she drops her drawers for you. I should have known that it's true what they say about you.'

'What is that, pray?'

'That you're a sorcerer, a creature of the night. What the Jews call a dybbuk.'

'What's that for God's sake?'

'Someone who has sinned in a past life and has come to life again to frighten other people.'

Infuriated by her words, I shook her violently and shouted: 'Don't say that you wicked girl. I'm neither an imp nor a dybbuck. I'm just a man who has suffered gross misfortune.'

I let her go and sat on the bed, nearly sobbing with desperation.

Salka hissed at me as she departed: 'You belong with the Jews and the rich aristocrats. You're not one of us and never could be.'

SEVENTEEN

Areputation once acquired in this small town becomes as permanent as a birthmark. Because of the unusual manner of my arrival here, local peasants are convinced that I possess supernatural powers. Even Yankel believes I cast a spell over women. The truth is that Leah gave herself to me because of something inexpressibly beautiful which happened between us. In Salka's case, I stumbled into her bed by accident. I am certainly no Casanova. Strangely, reference to that name conjures up an image of a haughty, bewigged man with an imperious but charming manner. Perhaps he is someone I met in my previous life. On reflection, though, it is much more likely that his image came from a book or magazine.

I discussed the loss of my memory with Marie Louise when I called at the Castle the following morning to practise at the piano. I had played a piece by Franz Joseph Haydn and commented afterwards that I could almost feel his physical presence in the room.

Marie said — I was on intimate terms of address with her by now: 'Do you think you knew him before you became ill?'

'It is possible. But what difference does it make now? There is little or nothing left of the person I once was.'

'Don't talk like that, Johann. When you see this famous doctor he will help you to recover your memory and you will find out exactly who you are.'

I played an arpeggio on the piano keys that expressed flashes of lightning and said bitterly: 'God composes such a brief life for us. Perhaps during it, we hear faint echoes of a previous lifetime.'

'What do you mean?' Marie arched her fine eyebrows in puzzlement.

'I have a feeling that each time we are granted new life we play exactly the same music but on a different orchestral instrument.'

'Do you believe in reincarnation?'

'The illusion of having once played music with Joseph Haydn is so strong in my mind that it has almost persuaded me that it is true. But it is my body that seems to remember rather than my mind. Perhaps I am a dybbuk, as some of the people in the town are saying.'

Full of anger and frustration, I banged angrily on the piano keys with my hands.

Marie Louise then remarked with an expression of sadness: 'Johann, you were born to entertain and delight other human beings who live sad and ugly lives. I wish you would stay here for ever instead of going away.'

I stood up and enquired: 'What is the matter? Have I upset you?'

She shook her head, and then to my surprise, burst into tears.

I put my hands around her shoulders and immediately withdrew them, thinking that I heard the soft pad of the footman's slippers. Marie Louise, understanding my concern, shook her head and said disdainfully: 'It's all right. There's nobody there.'

'I didn't want — '

'You don't have to worry. The servants are trained not to see or say anything.'

'Might they not tittle-tattle?'

'Their lives would not be worth a wooden groschen if they did. My father sees to that.'

'But everyone knows about his affairs.'

'Only because he wants everyone to know what a heroic seducer of women he is. If he heard any rumours concerning the chastity of my mother or my sisters, he would remorselessly track down the originator of the rumour and have him killed.'

'Might not the servants tell your father, if you committed an indiscretion?'

'There is no chance of that. My mother pays them money to keep their mouths shut.'

'That being so, I shall embrace you again.'

Holding her tightly, I said: 'What is it that is bothering you, dear Marie? I can't bear to see you unhappy.'

Marie Louise gave a deep sigh and said: 'I don't love my fiancé. In fact I hate him.'

'Then why did you agree to marry him?'

'Because his family occupy an important position in Russian society and my father gains prestige by the marriage.'

'Could you not resist the match?'

'I have tried. But my mother joins in with my father and I cannot withstand their combined pressure.'

'Why don't you simply refuse to go through with it?'

'My father would throw me out without mercy. I have no way of earning a living. I would starve.'

'Alexander seems a perfectly nice chap.'

'He's good at nothing but cutting people's heads off.'

'That's his job as a soldier.'

'Oh, Johann,' Marie said piteously, 'If only he was cultivated and understanding like you. He knows nothing of music, art and literature and even less of the ideas of freedom and equality that are sweeping across Europe.'

'He is young and can learn about these things.'

'He laughs in my face whenever I mention them.' She looked up at me and pleaded: ' Johann, when you go away, may I go with you?'

I bent down, kissed her upturned face and said: 'Marie, I should love to take you with me. But I simply cannot. Your father would send soldiers after us and have me killed if I took you away. I have enough problems, as it is, through not knowing who I am. Incidentally, The family with whom I lodged when I came to Korlyshev gave me the name Johann Theophilius Wunder. Theophilius means the same as Amadeus.

He — Amadeus Mozart — by all accounts, was thrown into a common grave in exactly the same way as I was.'

A remarkable thing then happened. Weary and doom-laden music sounded in my head — a   Requiem carrying such profound and deeply sad associations that I fainted.

When I came to, I was lying on a sofa in an ante-room just off the main entrance hall whither the servants had carried me. Marie was sitting by my feet, an absorbed expression on her face.

She said to me: 'Are you all right, Johann?'

I shook my head and enquired: 'What happened?'

'You fainted after saying that you shared the same fate as Mozart.'

'Did I? It's not surprising. He must have stolen some of my music and passed it off as his own.'

'How do you know?'

'There's a piece among the music in the library which was familiar to me. I am sure I wrote it before this terrible thing happened to me.'

'Musicians don't steal other people's work.'

'Sometimes they plagiarise without realising they are doing so. But it is particularly hurtful when an eminent musician such as Mozart succumbs to the temptation.'

'Are you sure you did not steal it from Mozart?'

'I am not sure of anything any more.'

I lay motionless on the sofa for a while, trying to recall when I had composed that particular piece of music. But the effort was too much for me.

I gave a great sigh.

Marie then came and lay down on the sofa beside me and kissed my face. I responded warmly. Soon, I found that I had ignited a passionate flame of whose existence I had been unaware.

'Wait, my little porcelain doll,' I said hurriedly and went over to the door and locked it.

By the time I had got back to the sofa, Marie had loosened her outer garments. We were too engrossed in what we were doing to take much notice of a distant commotion going on outside. Soon, however, hearing the sounds of angry shouting, I stood up on the sofa and looked through a small window set high in the wall. Smoke was billowing forth from some houses in Korlyshev. Red flames burst fitfully through the smoke.

I said: 'The town is on fire. Come and look.'

Marie stood up on tiptoe and we both looked at the destruction that was going on in Korlyshev.

'What do you think is happening?'

I shrugged,

'God knows. But there is nothing we can do to help.'

'Let us finish what we began.'

There was a flurry of white undergarments as Marie, almost swooning with desire, swiftly undressed. I followed suit and went into her with determination to appease a truly aristocratic lust. I felt conscience-stricken because of what was happening outside.

'I am Nero who fiddles while Rome burns,' I gasped.

'Oh, Johann keep playing. It is delightful!. More! More! More!'

Marie twisted and turned like an eel, screaming and hugging me to her, with a look of demented bliss on her face.

*

By the time I left the Castle, the noise and hubbub in Korlyshev had subsided . A banner of black smoke still hung over the town. Walking through the Jewish quarter on my way to the Bear Inn, I saw that a number of dwellings had been burnt down. Vaporous fumes pervaded the scene. The foundations of the houses that had been burnt down were strewn with blackened rushes and charred toys and pillows. Remnants of clothing were scattered on the ground. The streets were deserted.

I saw nobody until I reached the courtyard of the Bear Inn. Salka's boyfriend, Fréderic, was standing outside the stables.

'What started the fire?' I asked.

'You did,' he said with a nasty leer.

'Don't be stupid. I was at the Castle.'

'Licking the Count's arse, was you?'

As I started to walk towards the entrance of the Inn, he followed me, grabbed my shoulder and said with an insolent expression: 'There was supposed to be a celebration today because the Count beat Ben-Levi at chess. What happens? The baker is released from the jail house. And then the lousy yid sets his own shop on fire.'

'That was yesterday.'

'The Count promised us free booze and food galore. What do the Jews do? Out of sheer spite they asked the Count to cancel the party. So a few of us went up there today and started our own bonfire.'

'You mean you burnt down Jewish houses?'

'Serves them bloody well right for spoiling our fun. It's not every day the stingy Count gives a party. It might be years before it happens again.'

'So what was the point in burning down people's homes?'

'We was promised a bonfire,' Fréderic said with a sly smile. 'And by God we got one. The only pity is that we didn't burn you as well.'

'Why do you say that?'

'Because you seduce our women, you shit-faced sorcerer.'

He raised his right arm in a signal. Three ruffians appeared from behind the shed and began to pummel and kick me with all their might. I tried to fight back but was rapidly knocked to the ground. Kicks and blows flew at me from all directions. Luckily for me, as I lay trying to protect my head with my hands, Bertha came into the courtyard and let out a piercing scream. My assailants ran off , leaving me lying motionless on the cobbles.

Bertha helped me stand up. I managed to stagger into the

entrance hall. I expressed my gratitude and limped up to my room. Thanks to Bertha's timely intervention, my injuries were not serious.

I lay on my bed for a while, nursing my wounds. It struck me that the time had now come to leave Korlyshev. The superstitious peasantry not only harboured strange ideas about my origins but could not forgive me because their womenfolk worshipped my music.

I got up, washed the blood off my face in a bowl of water and brushed my clothes, I was about to leave when Salka burst into the room. She flung herself against me, shouting hysterically: 'I'll kill that bastard Fréderic.'

'Did you ask him to beat me up?'

'No, course not. Are you all right?'

'It's just a few bruises.'

At that moment I noticed that my right hand was extremely painful — one of my attackers had stamped on it during the fracas. I flexed my fingers, wondering if I would ever be able to play my flute again.

I said: 'Salka, you might as well be the first to know. I am going away shortly to undergo a cure for my loss of memory.'

'How long will you be gone?'

'I don't know if I shall ever come back. I don't seem to be very popular here in Korlyshev.'

'You are immensely popular, Johann. The town has never heard music like yours and never will again, if you don't return.'

'I won't be able to play for a while — the villains have crushed my fingers. Keep well, Salka. I am going now to take leave of some of my friends.'

I gave her a peck on the cheek. She said plaintively: 'Don't go, Johann. It'll be horrible after you've gone.'

I gave her another kiss, this time on the lips.

Slowly and painfully I descended the stairs and hobbled towards the Jewish quarter.

EIGHTEEN

I asked a passer-by to direct me to the Jewish poorhouse. He peered at me suspiciously and asked my business, thinking perhaps that I was a hooligan intent on making further mischief. I told him that I was Johann Wunder and wished to see Shmul Perlman. He exclaimed: 'So you are the flautist! I didn't recognise you with that swollen face and black eye!'

He directed me to a squat wooden building with a tiled roof in a small field surrounded by silver birch trees.. As I walked towards it, he shouted out: 'Ask them to attend to your face while you're there,'

A small stream ran through the grounds. A flower bed near the front door was planted out with flowers in the form of intersecting triangles. A plump, fair-haired women wearing a white apron over her frock emerged from the entrance and asked my business. I told her I should like to speak to Reb Shmul Perlman. She informed me that he was out walking and directed me to a chair which stood just inside a room containing about twenty beds. The occupants were mainly old men but among them were two young boys with bandaged hands and arms — victims of the fire that had consumed their homes.

I sat down, pleased that Shmul was out walking, which suggested that he was making a good recovery. The old men I could see appeared frail and haggard; one looked as though he had not long to live. My eyes then alighted on the yellow beard of Reb Chaim Ben-Levi. His left leg, bandaged down to his foot, stuck out awkwardly from under the bedclothes. I approached him, holding out my left hand — the one free from injury — and said cheerfully: 'What happened to you, Sir?'

'Do you think I fell out of my bed?' he enquired, petulantly.

I shook my head.

He peered at my bruised face and enquired: 'Were you involved in the strife as well?'

'Some young men accused me of being a sorcerer and beat me up. They were very angry because the fete was cancelled. They boasted that they had burned down some Jewish houses. What exactly happened?'

Ben-Levi tugged at his beard and replied: 'We Jews do not celebrate while we are still mourning the death of a member of our community. I asked for the fete to be postponed. The trouble started when Eli Gerschon, God rest his soul, burnt down his bakery. Some of the sparks were caught by the wind and set fire to the thatched roofs of neighbouring Christian houses. The owners assumed that the Jews were settling scores in retaliation for what had happened to Gerschon's daughter. So they came down yesterday carrying pickaxes, cudgels and spades to wreak vengeance on us. Some of the Count's soldiers tried to arrest them. Scuffles and fighting broke out. I tried to make peace and got this for my pains.'

He winced and indicated his broken leg.

He went on: 'The Talmud says that when you commit one small sin you are opening the way to committing an even worse one. So it was with the Count's seduction of Eli Gerschon's daughter. In committing that sin he opened the way to the destruction of Korlyshev.'

'It hasn't been destroyed, sir,' I admonished him gently. 'A dozen houses have been burnt down. They will be rebuilt and in time the wounds of this dreadful occurrence will heal.'

He gave a resigned gesture and muttered: 'I hope so. I hope so. I have been working for most of my life to avoid this kind of catastrophe. But still, when it happens, it comes as a shock.'

'Will it affect your relationship with the Count?'

'I think not. He has been here to visit me. He left me those apples and a bottle of fine wine. We have been through too many storms for this to ruin our relationship. He is a mass of inconsistencies. Utterly ruthless in the defence of his privileges, he appreciates virtue in others. He insists I am a good man. But the truth is that I have one terrible weakness.' He grinned weakly and went on: 'And that is that I would play chess with the Devil himself, if I thought he could give me a decent game.'

I whispered: 'Did the Count really beat you at chess whilst you were hooded?'

Ben-Levi gave a rueful smile and whispered: 'Between you and me I now realise that it would have been much better if I had beaten him — which was well within my capability. In that case, Gerschon would probably have been sentenced to ten years in Siberia. But at least he would have survived and I would not have sustained this broken leg.'

'It seems that God punishes the innocent and lets the wicked flourish?'

He shot a sceptical glance at me and said: 'Let those who still have their health ponder those mighty questions. I am not well enough to think about them.'

I then asked: 'But why did you let him beat you, knowing that this would let Eli Gershon's punishment stand?'

'Because I know the Count better than he knows himself. If I had beaten him, he would have perversely refused to keep his side of the bargain. But if he could boast that he had beaten the champion, he would find it easy to show mercy. I therefore won the first game and let him win the next two.'

I said admiringly: 'Now I know why your fellow Jews have such faith in your judgment.'

'My judgment failed me dismally on this occasion.'

Shmul Perlman came into the room at that moment. He looked much fitter than when I had last seen him. His face was ruddy and he carried himself jauntily. I took leave of Ben-Levi, walked over to Shmul Perlman and enquired: 'How are you, sir?'

'Cured. But you look as if you have been in the wars.'

'It's nothing compared with what some of these people have suffered. I'm very glad to hear that you are better.'

'Yes, they have drained the alcohol out of my system. No more drinking except perhaps for an occasional glass of schnapps. It is safer than vodka, which rots the liver and gives no warning of the damage it is doing. Schnapps, on the other hand, gives you a well-deserved headache next morning, to remind you of your previous night's folly. If my daughter Leah was back with me I would have no difficulty in stopping drinking. All I want now is to get on the road again. Come outside.'

As we stood in the garden in the pale evening sunshine, he said: 'You are still hoping to get your memory back?'

'Of course. I hate being Johann Wunder, when I know all the time I am someone else.'

He said pensively: 'I should like to be Mayer Rothschild. But I have learned to accept that I am just Shmul Perlman, a poor pedlar who drinks excessively.'

'That is not a true parallel,' I replied, aloofly. 'I was somebody else and I am entitled to recover my true identity.'

'You may not even like the person that you once were. You probably belonged to that selfish elite of Viennese society who are continually vying with each other for more money than they can possibly spend. Now you have learned to make an honest living with that flute, why not settle down here in Korlyshev and make a good life for yourself.'

'Is it so wonderful here, when Jewish houses are burnt down and I get a thrashing because I can make music?'

'In a few weeks it will all be forgotten, you'll see. We like having you in this town. You provide badly-needed entertainment. I have attended several of your concerts in the Bear Inn and other places. I was amazed. I couldn't believe you were the little fellow I rescued. So why not stay here? I have learned during my years of travelling that we carry our own burdens with us wherever we go. Going away won't help you. Stay here and be happy.'

I shook my head and said: 'I am determined to find out who I am. When are you going on your next journey?'

'Tomorrow I am going via Ostrava to Zilena and then on to Brno, where some of my best customers live.'

'Would you take me with you? I have made arrangements to see a well known doctor who lives in Brno. I am hoping he will cure me of my loss of memory.'

'Of course!' Shmul said heartily. 'Be at my house tomorrow morning at cockcrow.'

On my way back to the Bear Inn, I experienced a painful doubt. Shmul had referred to having rescued me. This time he had not actually mentioned St. Marks graveyard. Was it possible that the scurrilous rumours concerning my origins were correct and that he had, in fact, found me lying unconscious in a place of ill repute? His own daughter had said that he would think nothing of going into a brothel to make a sale. However, be that as it may, I still had a duty to set out on a journey to find my true self.

On my return to the Inn, I saw the bulky figure of Herr Müller in his accustomed chair by the bar. I ordered a glass of schnapps. Bertha served me. As I stood there, Herr Müller said:

'Have you seen Salka during the course of your travels.'

'Not since midday.'

'She was supposed to be serving behind the bar this evening.'

I threw back my glass of schnapps. My resolve strengthened by the fiery liquid, I went upstairs to my room and began to pack, in order to be ready for an early departure the following morning. By now I had acquired sufficient clothes to fill the leather bag I had bought recently in the local market. Having completed my packing, I searched under the mattress for the money I had saved for my journey. I could feel nothing. I moved my hand further and further along, then in desperation, turned the mattress upside down. My money had gone. Once again I was a pauper.

NINETEEN

Perhaps Frèderic had told Salka to rob me. Neither he nor Salka ever returned to the Bear Inn. I was obliged to cancel my journey and begin the long, painful process of saving for my treatment all over again.

During the next few years I entertained thousands of people in taverns, restaurants and fine houses — sometimes in towns, sometimes in villas perched in high places in the mountains or in farm houses standing in vast areas of lush meadows. My enthusiastic audiences stuffed money in my pockets, or threw coins on the ground in front of me. Occasionally I hired a hall and gave subscription concerts. Many of the people in this region had never heard music of this quality before. I played on harpsichords or pianos when they were available. But for the most part I played my flute. The audiences loved the bawdy jokes I told during the intervals.

I wrote to Dr Freulich informing him that my journey to see him had been delayed through unforeseen circumstances. In the meantime, an uprising occurred and Prince Poniatowski, as Ben-Levi had predicted, was defeated by the Russian army. Two years later, Riva Gerschon was killed during the massacre that occurred when the Russians captured Warsaw. I formed the impression that Count Poceski had unquestioningly accepted Reb Ben-Levi's account of how he had come into contact with Prince Poniatowski while in Prague, because he showed no signs of animosity towards me. In fact, after Marie Louise married her Russian subaltern, he continued to allow me to practise on the piano at the Castle.

Eventually, having saved enough money for my course of treatment, I settled on a date to travel with Shmul Perlman to Brno, where I hoped Dr Freulich would cure me of my amnesia.

A rooster standing on top of the sagging straw roof of Yankel's tumble-down dwelling announced sunrise, as I approached Shmul Perlman's house. Shlotkin, anxious to start his journey, kept moving impatiently a few yards backwards and forwards along the road, as he waited for Shmul to load the wagon. It seemed only yesterday that I had arrived here at this very spot sick in mind and body. Now, with my physical health fully restored, I was about to embark on a journey that I hoped would lead to the restoration of my memory and reveal my true identity.

Dr Freulich was a disciple of the famous Dr Anton Mesmer. I had heard of the latter's amazing performances, during which he occasionally persuaded patients to talk about the most intimate details of their lives. I was perfectly willing to submit to this process, however painful and embarrassing, if it would restore me to that eminent position in society I was more than ever convinced I had once enjoyed.

TWENTY

Shlotkin's ears quivered as we began to move forward. I remarked that he seemed very keen to start on our journey, to which Shmul responded: 'Horses, like human beings, are happiest when working.'

The streets of Korlyshev were empty and silent at this early hour. The Jewish houses burnt down during the riot had long since been rebuilt. We passed their synagogue. Poceski's castle loomed on our left. I wondered how Marie Louise was getting on in St. Petersburg. Then we took the right fork and began our ascent into the mountains.

Shlotkin plodded at an even pace, his harness jingling. Larks flew above us into the clear blue sky. It was a warm, sunny day but Shmul had warned me that the journey would be long and arduous and we might even encounter snow before reaching the town of Brno. We would be making many detours in search of customers for his merchandise. I had with me all my worldly possessions, including the flute with which I had earned my living during the past few years. I was indebted for this, and indeed for life itself, to the strange, red-faced, gray-bearded old man sitting by my side.

Shmul had received two letters from Leah, who was now nursing Itzhak, her wounded brother, somewhere in the Low Countries. She worked as a seamstress and a waitress, in order to provide food and shelter for them both. She had written that she hoped one day to save enough money for them to come home. I remembered with affection her kindness and tender love-making.

'You can lay the responsibility for the ruination of your family on the French Revolution,' I remarked. 'So much for their promise to bring deliverance to mankind.'

'My sons were fighting for a great and good cause,' Shmul said sternly.

I refrained from replying, not wishing to become involved in a futile argument with the old man.

We climbed slowly, the britska creaking and rumbling as we passed over stony ground on our way to a pass through the Carpathian mountains. A cold wind was blowing. Shmul reached behind me and took out a couple of rugs. As we covered ourselves, I saw an eagle ascend from the top of a nearby pine tree and dive soundlessly on a small bird winging its way through the valley. The eagle soared high with the pathetic furry bundle trapped in its beak.

'Poor bird!' I exclaimed, sorry to see its life ended so suddenly.

'An eagle must do what his nature commands,' Shmul commented. 'But when a man kills one of God's creatures, he has a duty to offer a prayer of thanks to the Almighty for providing him with sustenance.'

I enquired mischievously: 'Would you eat Shlotkin, if you had to?'

'Without Shlotkin, I would soon starve.'

'You could easily buy another horse.'

'He wouldn't be Shlotkin. When he dies, I shall die, too.'

The statement suggested to me that Shmul's spirit had been weakened by his misfortunes. His former ebullience had gone. But his sententiousness continued to try my patience. I fretted in case this journey on which I had staked so much would end in disappointment, leaving me still without a memory of my previous life and leading a life as lonely as Shmul's. Bored by the ceaseless rumbling of the wheels beneath us, I asked him: 'Were you ever tempted by loose women when you were away from home?' Listening to one of Shmul's interminable stories seemed preferable to the monotony I was experiencing.

'Not by harlots. Their brazen ways put me off. It was a respectable woman who tempted me.'

'What happened?'

Some fifteen years before, the young wife of a shopkeeper in the town of Zilena had tried to seduce him.. But at the crucial moment Shlotkin had blundered into the shop doorway and, as he put it, "interrupted the business."

'So you see,' Shmul said with a wide grin, 'Shlotkin saved me from the sin of adultery.'

We stopped by a mountain stream for lunch. Shmul hung Shlotkin's nosebag round his neck. We sat on a fallen tree trunk by the side of the stream, dined off the bread and cheese Shmul had prepared for us and drank copious, refreshing draughts of beer held in a cask at the back of the wagon. I could see fish darting through the stream in front of us. Its diamond-pure waters tumbled down towards the distant valley, leaving a frothy wake behind rocky boulders. Magnificent mauve and black peaks rose before us, their pine-clad tops shimmering in the sunshine.

Having eaten, we resumed our journey. Shmul remarked that we must reach the town where we were to spend out first night before darkness fell.

As we travelled, a confusing thought entered my mind. I had lost my memory. But even though I couldn't recall my previous life, logic demanded that my memory must still be somewhere. If another person had acquired it, had he become me? And supposing he, in turn, lost his memory and it was somehow acquired by someone else, would that person also become me? The notion was so disturbing I vowed never to consider it again.

Our route took us through dark pine forests. On our left I could see the edge of a canyon which fell precipitously down towards the winding ribbon of a river thousands of feet below. To combat boredom, I took up my flute and played a merry tune. A smile appeared on Shmul's face. He commented: 'That sounds familiar.'

'I have only just composed it.'

'Are you sure you didn't remember it from your former life. You were certainly a musician.'

'Yes, I suppose so. Incidentally, I have yet to pay you for this flute.'

'No need. It cost but little and has provided much pleasure.'

We drove on for several more hours. On one occasion I saw a wild boar snuffling through the undergrowth. Some time later, I caught a glimpse of a bear and pointed it out to Shmul. He immediately launched into an account of how, some years before, while he was making a call of nature, Shlotkin had warned him of the presence of a large bear by neighing loudly. The warning, he said, had saved his life.

I was getting tired of listening to the praise Shmul lavished on his horse at every opportunity. An animal's intelligence is, after all, much inferior to that of a human being. Shmul had persuaded himself that his horse was his guardian angel. The native North American Indians believe that eating wild animals enables them to absorb their qualities of courage and endurance. With Shmul it was the other way around; he had acquired the notion that because he talked to his horse he had acquired human understanding. Since Shlotkin was his only company during his long journeys away from home, I forgave him his weakness.

My flute impromptu helped to pass the time. Johann, I told myself, as the horse seemed to adjust his stride to the music, now you are falling victim to the same delusion as you ascribe to Shmul.

I glanced at Shmul. His craggy features seemed as ageless and indestructible as the mountains through which we were passing. But I guessed that behind his impassive countenance he was torn with worry about his daughter and crippled son and the need to earn enough money to feed himself and his horse

The sun was beginning to sink, leaving a fiery white glow behind the mountain peaks. Shmul announced that it was time to stop again for refreshments. He brought Shlotkin to a halt, lowered his bulky form from the driving seat and began searching for twigs with which to make a fire. He brought out an iron pot from the rear of the wagon containing a broth he had prepared. The horse meanwhile found a patch of grass a few yards away on which to graze,

I wandered off as Shmul heated up the soup and admired the breathtaking view. The mountains on the other side of the river glowed with an unearthly radiance, throwing the valley into purple shadow. There was an almost palpable silence and the phrase The Master of the Universe came into my mind. I experienced an indescribable feeling of awe in the face of Creation and tried to remember a prayer I had been taught as a child. But the exact words escaped me.

Frustrated at my inability to remember, I wandered to the edge of the ravine and stood on some black rocks, looking down a cliff face that dropped abruptly to the winding thin blue river far below. How insignificant I seemed in relation to this magnificent scene. What did it matter in the whole scheme of things, if my memory was defective?

Suddenly my feet began to move involuntarily, as I slid and slithered helplessly down a slanting granite outcrop worn smooth by aeons of erosion. In a frantic effort to save myself, I threw myself sideways. But in a second I had tumbled helplessly into empty space, succumbing to gravity like a lamb led to the slaughter.

Rocky outcrops of the cliff face passed before my eyes. I resigned myself to being dashed to pieces on the rocks thousands of feet below. Leah's face flashed through my mind and helped to reconcile me to my fate.

I tried to grab tufts of vegetation that were passing rapidly in front of me and managed briefly to slow down my fall by clutching momentarily at the branch of a small tree projecting from the cliff face. But I continued to crash through a succession of the leaves and branches until, miraculously, another larger tree blocked my descent. I lay with the breath knocked out of my body across a tree trunk, precariously poised above a sheer drop to the rock-strewn river that lay thousands of feet below.

When I had recovered my breath, I shouted out feebly for help.

There was no answer.

I shouted again.

Shlotkin's head appeared, peering out between some bushes a hundred or more feet above me. I thought I heard a faint neighing sound. Soon, Shmul's bearded face appeared where Shlotkin's head had been before.

He called: 'Don't move.'

I fumed at this redundant piece of advice, painfully aware that the slightest movement on my part would bring about a fatal fall into the abyss below. I remained perfectly still, clutching the bark of the tree as a child clings to its mother, praying that I would somehow be rescued.

Some time later, a rope descended towards me.

After several unsuccessful attempts, I managed to grasp the end and tied the rope firmly around my shoulders and waist. The rope tightened and I heard the voice of Shmul urging Shlotkin to further effort. I was gradually dragged upwards through branches and leaves towards the lip of the cliff. For several minutes I dangled horrifyingly over sheer emptiness. Then I felt Shmul's arms comfortingly around me as he dragged me across the granite outcrop, the initial cause of my downfall. He continued to hold me as the horse pulled me to a point of safety. Shmul then shouted out to Shlotkin and I came to an abrupt halt.

'Any bones broken?' he enquired gruffly, as he untied the rope.

'I think I am in one piece.'

I groaned, as I moved my aching arms and shoulders.

'Once again you have saved my life, Shmul. How can I thank you?'

'It was Shlotkin who saved you,' he replied gravely.

Soon afterwards he made me drink a cup of vodka but declined to drink himself.

We then partook of the nourishing broth Shmul had heated up. When it was time to recommence our journey, I climbed up on the driving seat of the wagon, feeling ashamed of myself for having doubted Shlotkin's sterling qualities. After we had travelled a mile or two, however, common sense returned and I realised that the horse had been made curious by an unaccustomed noise and had simply looked over the ledge out of curiosity.

My narrow escape had taught me that life was precious. I said to Shmul: 'One day I may ask your daughter to marry me?'

There was silence for a while, as Shmul digested my words. Then he muttered: 'It is customary for Jews to marry Jews.'

'Supposing I were to become a Jew.'

He gave a cynical laugh and then said: 'Yankel, the hunchback, is fond of telling the story about a man who told him: 'I have decided to give up being a Jew. He answered: 'And I have decided to give up being a hunchback. It illustrates the point that being a Jew is something you inherit. Anyway, the priest in Korlyshev concluded that you are a Christian.'

'I have no recollection of my religion, so I might just as well become a Jew.'

'A musician's music is his only true religion.'

'Then do I have your permission to ask your daughter to marry me?'

'Time enough to consider such a question when we have found out who you are. You may be married already.'

His words sharply reminded me that my loss of memory deprived me of any right to marry. But Shmul was correct in one respect. Music was, and always would be, my true religion.

TWENTY-ONE

My ribs ached abominably for the next few days. But I was grateful to be alive. To please Shmul, I gave full credit to his sagacious horse for my lucky escape. Certainly, it seemed that God had ordained that I should create more music and perform more useful deeds before taking leave of this earth.

We called on many small towns and villages on our meandering route through the mountains. Time and time again Shmul surprised me by his skill in handling his customers. He seemed able to divine their weaknesses and play on their secret desires. His shrewdness and guile, however, did not always achieve the desired result. One innkeeper demanded too much for a night's lodging and all Shmul's bargaining pleas proved in vain. Neither party would budge and we were obliged to sleep huddled under blankets in the britska, under the stars.

One night in late October, we camped by the side of a narrow river. I collected sticks for a fire. Shmul cooked a savoury meal from beans and potatoes. He had shown considerable flair that day in bartering and selling goods. When I complimented him on his skill, he replied: 'A good pedlar plays on his customers as skilfully as a musician plays on his fiddle. Not everyone has that ability. It's not a bad way of life. It has dangers but also its compensations.'

'Such as?'

'One sees the whole range of human nature. I have known Jew-haters who threatened to kill me because they said I was cheating; and others who thought that I should die because I had shamed them by being too honest. I have met harlots who were saints in disguise and rich aristocratic ladies who were no different than harlots. But all in their time have shown some consideration for old Shmul the pedlarman. I have yet to meet someone really evil.'

'What about the leaders of the Revolution in France, whose activities have killed one of your sons and mutilated the other?'

'The French have declared they wish to bring us Jews into the mainstream of civilised life. For that reason I forgive them.'

'Why do people make such distinctions? One doesn't ask whether Shlotkin is a Jew or a Christian.'

'Exactly. But don't fool yourself. Horses dispute among themselves as well as human beings. I have seen them fight as viciously as the soldiers fighting the battle of Lodi. Shlotkin, however, is undoubtedly a Jewish horse.'

'Why do you say that?'

'Because he is totally loyal to his Master.'

Shmul smiled as he poured another portion of beans and potatoes onto my wooden platter from the steaming bowl.

I lay awake for a long time, thinking about the medical treatment I would shortly receive from Dr Freulich. I had heard talk of magnets which had strange effects on the human mind. An innkeeper in one of the towns we had passed through had said Dr Freulich's method was barbaric and against nature. Shmul told me not to worry about such stories. People would not pay the doctor good money, if he did not cure his patients.

Reassured, I fell asleep and dreamed that I was wearing a crimson-lined cloak that grew longer by the hour. Elegantly-dressed women, handsome men and beautiful children flocked around me. The air was full of a sweet fragrance as voices cried out: 'All Hail Theophilius Wunder, Creator of sublime music.'

TWENTY-TWO

Shlotkin's shoulder muscles bulged, as they took the weight of the wagon during our steep descent into the town of Brno. On our right stood the forbidding bulk of the Spilberk fortress, where Shmul informed me, numerous malefactors and enemies of the Emperor Francis were imprisoned. Apprehensive about the unusual medical treatment I would shortly receive, I asked Shmul if, instead of going straight to the doctor's residence, I could spend the day accompanying him during his round of bargaining, a routine to which I was by now accustomed. But he shook his head vigorously and replied: 'No, Johann. let us go to Dr Freulich, so that he can start as soon as possible the task of restoring your memory.'

I replied: 'When the doctor has cured me, I intend to go and claim my inheritance. But I should be obliged while you are in Vienna, if you would make enquiries about the waistcoat I was wearing when you found me.'

'Certainly, and I shall let you know if I find out anything useful. But if things do not turn out as you would like, do not despair. The good Lord may have other plans for you.'

'Will you let me know if you have any news of Leah?'

After a prolonged pause, he answered: 'Yes.'

We entered through the town gates. At this hour there was little traffic. Shmul navigated unerringly through the narrow streets of the town and drew up beside a small house with a gable standing opposite a church. Outside, was a brass plaque inscribed with the words: Dr Freulich's Mental Institute. I collected my belongings from the wagon, bade Shmul goodbye and patted Shlotkin on his flank.

I rapped on an ornamental knocker covered with a patina of verdigris. For some reason the lion-shaped knocker sent a shiver of fear through me.

A porter wearing dark green livery opened the door.

Beyond the passage-way in which he stood, I could see a narrow road leading through extensive, wooded grounds to an imposing stone-built three-storey mansion. I informed the porter that I was a new patient of Dr Freulich. He directed me towards the house. Encumbered by my heavy bag and my flute, I walked through fallen leaves and shrubberies, passing as I went, two other smaller structures on each side of the grounds. From one of them there came bloodcurdling sounds. It came as quite a shock to realise that Dr Freulich numbered madmen among his patients. I calmed my fears by assuring myself that my own illness did place me in that desperate category.

A cheerful, apple-faced maid opened the weathered oak front-door of the main house when I arrived and led me into a hall panelled with dark wood.

'Are you the Wunderman?' she enquired.

Amused by this play on my name, I nodded assent. She said: 'Dr Freulich is expecting you. But first his daughter Fraulein Bella wishes to speak to you.'

She directed me to a small ante-chamber, where I sat for some time on an uncomfortable, high-backed, well-worn armchair, twiddling my thumbs and wondering whether my decision to come here had been wise. It seemed that my fame as a musician had preceded me. This opinion was confirmed when a comely, titian-haired young woman entered the room, introduced herself as Bella, Dr Freulich's daughter and assistant, and announced briskly: 'Herr Wunder, we are pleased and proud to welcome someone of your remarkable musical accomplishments. There are certain conditions attached to your receiving treatment. My father, as you know, is a follower of Dr Anton Mesmer, whose unorthodox methods have been

129

condemned by the medical establishment. In order for you to be eligible for this treatment, it will be necessary for you to sign a document swearing that you have received only conventional methods such as leeching and medicaments. Are you prepared to sign to this effect?'

'Certainly,' I replied. 'But are there any risks associated with the treatment?'

'None whatsoever. My father has treated hundreds of patients. Most have shown signs of improvement. None has suffered any harm.'

I said hesitantly: 'I shall not consent to live with the poor, deranged creatures who inhabit one of the buildings I have just passed.'

'The Citadel, as we call it, is used exclusively for disturbed patients who might be a danger to themselves or others. You will be accommodated in a room on the top floor of this house. I shall show it to you shortly.'

'When am I due to meet your father?'

'You will dine with us tonight and tomorrow he will commence your treatment. Before I show you to your room, would you care to pay one month's advance payment of the amount you agreed with Dr Freulich?'

I opened my bag and counted out the money. She locked it in an iron safe then led me up a narrow flight of stairs. Arriving on a landing, she directed me to a small room containing a single bed covered with a white woollen counterpane. It was plainly furnished with a wooden press and a narrow chest-of-drawers. A pitcher of water and an earthenware bowl stood on the latter. I placed my flute inside the press.

Bella said: 'My father and I hope you will honour us by playing our pianoforte while you are here. We have had it specially tuned.'

'I am flattered to learn that you have heard of me.'

'Several people have told us of the Wunderman who is such a remarkable musician. My father guessed it was you when you first wrote to him. It must be terrible to lose one's memory.'

'It would have been intolerable, if I had not retained my ability to make music.'

'You said in your letters that you were found unconscious in Vienna. Have you been back there since?'

'No, I am nervous of going there while still in a state of forgetfulness.'

Bella frowned and a little of her former prim officiousness returned. She said: 'I hope my father will be able to help you. You must entirely submit to his will, if the treatment is to be efficacious. Your neighbour across the landing is a lady undergoing a similar cure for another ailment.'

'What does she suffer from?'

'Compulsive snuff-taking, an addiction to which she succumbed when her husband died.'

Bella Freulich informed me that if I was hungry at any time the cook would supply bread, milk and cheese. Breakfast, midday and evening meals would be served in the dining-room on the first-floor. She added with a charming smile before leaving that I would be free to play on the piano in the living-room whenever the fancy took me.

I lay on the soft bed and thought how lucky I was compared with Reb Shmul Perlman, now pursuing his weary round throughout the town. I remembered him saying that he had once been so faint with hunger he had exchanged a sack of Shlotkin's droppings for a slice of bread.

I was lucky to be alive and thrice blessed to possess a gift for music that enabled me to earn my living. I hoped the ministrations of Doctor Freulich would cause the shadows of forgetfulness to fall away. All the evidence supported the thesis that I had once been a highly successful musician. Soon my true self would be restored and I would be in a position to renew the splendours of my former life.

TWENTY-THREE

D r. Freulich was a slightly-built man of about fifty. His nose was a little too large for his pale, narrow face. He wore the powdered wig, long black frockcoat, cravat and waistcoat typical of his profession.

At our first encounter I was struck by his composed manner. But I discovered later that he was capable of becoming angry, especially when reminded of the unjust treatment meted out to his mentor, Dr Anton Mesmer. He told me he felt obliged for the sake of humanity to continue using his controversial treatment, even though it was frowned on by the authorities. Oddly, as soon as he mentioned the name Mesmer a familiar tune ran in my ears. I formed a mental picture of the orchestral arrangement but could remember nothing else about it.

My preliminary session with Dr Freulich took place later that morning. I told him that the name Mesmer had evoked musical memories. As I spoke a vision leapt into my mind of an even-featured, elderly man with a mild-mannered, solicitous expression. I described him to Dr Freulich and he said that I had given him a fairly accurate impression of his former mentor. I then mentioned that a work by the late Wolfgang Mozart had once caused me to faint. He lost his temper and snapped at me: 'I have enough Genghis Khans, Vlad the Impalers, and Charlemagnes in there,' pointing towards the building opposite where his severely mentally-impaired patients were incarcerated. He added cynically: 'Don't therefore try to pull the wool over my eyes by pretending that you are the late Wolfgang Mozart.'

'You don't see any significance in these experiences?'

He replied, in a softer tone: 'No, my dear fellow. The reason you have experienced sensations of what the French call 'déjà vu' is obvious. You are above all else a musician. Music profoundly affects your emotions. My daughter, incidentally, is looking forward to hearing you play the piano. What we are going to try to do is to establish the primary cause of these delusions and your accompanying loss of memory. High fever and delirium can sometimes be responsible. The length of time you have suffered from this condition, however, suggests that the lobes of your brain have been impaired. Is it possible that you suffered a blow on the head?'

'As I told you in my letters, I was thought to be dead and thrown into a pauper's grave, It is possible that when this happened my head struck a rock or some other hard object.'

As I spoke, I was smouldering with resentment at the implication that I had some kind of childish wish to be mistaken for Mozart. Nevertheless, on the whole I was impressed by Dr Freulich's scholarly bearing as well as his kindness towards his patients and the general atmosphere of cheerfulness that prevailed throughout his establishment.

I dined with him and his daughter, Bella, that night in a room resplendent with crystal chandeliers, velvet curtains and gold-encrusted furniture. A fine piano stood in one corner. I couldn't refrain from commenting on the contrast of these domestic comforts with the experiences of poverty I had recently endured.

Bella wrinkled her nose and said: 'It must have been very trying when you were living in the home of that impoverished pedlar.'

'Fortunes's wheel can cast a man down one minute and lift him up the next. It was a good lesson for me. I even became familiar with Yiddish, the Jewish language. It has a lot in common with German.'

Bella responded, as a maidservant poured potato soup into our bowls: 'What is amazing is that you enjoyed living with someone so far below your social level.'

I replied, sarcastically: 'When someone saves your life, you do not then scrutinise his pedigree.'

133

Dr Freulich intervened: 'Don't misunderstand my daughter. She has a scientific interest in the question of social mixing. It was this which prompted her question. Is not that so, Bella?'

Bella nodded, gravely.

He went on: 'Your experience, must be unique, Herr Wunder. And you have no recollection of who you were before this dreadful thing happened to you?'

'Practically none. But I must tell you an odd thing — whenever the word lion is mentioned a roaring takes place in my head. Even the lion-shaped knocker on the front-door of your gate-lodge disturbed my peace of mind. In my dreams I see towns and places I cannot remember ever having visited. Apart from these sparse images there is absolutely nothing I can recall of my past life.'

'You have the manners of a gentleman. Did you consider going back to Vienna, in the hope of finding someone who might recognise you?'

'Whatever possession and estates I owned will have long since been appropriated by others. I need to be in full possession of my faculties, with a strong and accurate memory of my past life, before I can establish a legal challenge to have them returned to me.'

Dr Freulich nodded, sagely.

'I understand your dilemma, Herr Wunder, and I hope my treatment will help you. My daughter tells me you have signed the document which swears you to secrecy regarding my method of treatment. I cannot promise you miracles. I have never had a case before of complete loss of memory. We shall have to work slowly and patiently. It will be painful at times, especially when you eventually come to remember the dearest members of your family.'

'Thank you, doctor. I have every confidence in your skill and wisdom. I am a little puzzled, though, as to why it was necessary to swear me to secrecy.'

Dr Freulich's face reddened and his voice trembled slightly as he replied: 'The reason is that my mentor, Dr Mesmer, the founder of this type of medicine, has been scorned and derided by the authorities in both Vienna and Paris. They have made his method of treatment unlawful. But I feel intensely that it would be wrong to deny its huge benefits to my patients, especially since it has proved extremely useful in my own field of mental illness.'

After the meal, Bella asked me if I would play some music. I walked over to the piano, stood facing them and mischievously improvised a simple little piece with my right hand, assuming an expression of utter amazement at my feat of musicianship.

They both laughed at my clowning.

Before I returned to the table, I bent down and examined the pedal mechanism. There was something missing. But I could not remember what it was. I sat down, shook my head to clear away some confused thoughts and then enquired about the other patient who was resident in the house.

Dr Freulich replied: 'She is Madame Estelle Toussaint, the opera singer. She prefers to dine alone in her room. Occasionally, she practises singing. I hope she doesn't disturb you.'

'Don't worry on that account.'

'She has an extensive knowledge of music and musicians. She told me she once dined with Padre Martini, the great music teacher in Bologna, who taught Mozart, Salieri and other great musicians.'

Soon afterwards, feeling tired after my long journey, I excused myself and bade them goodnight. A maid handed me a candle and I made my way upstairs to my room. I felt quite confident that Dr Freulich would soon be able to break the impasse in my mind that prevented me from reaching back into my past.

The following morning, when I came down to breakfast Bella was already seated at the table. We were served boiled chicken and bread. She told me her father had already started his rounds of the Institute. I asked out of curiosity if he was widowed. She informed me that her mother had succumbed to an illness brought about by nursing the mentally ill and was now herself a patient living in a private room in the building known as The Haven.

I replied: 'It is sad to think that those who treat mentally sick people can succumb to the very illness they are trying to cure.'

'Exactly.' She added with a smile: 'Fortunately, no one has ever suggested that loss of memory is a contagion that may spread.'

The maid asked if I should like wine or beer. I chose the latter. While we were eating, I looked up and saw a tall lady with a mahogany complexion and a mass of curly gray hair studying us through the half-open door. She closed it rapidly when she saw me staring at her.

'I presume that is the "snuff lady",' I remarked to Bella.

'Yes, she keeps herself to herself. She is from Martinique, where, incidentally, Napoleon's mistress, Josephine de Beauharnais, was born. I presume you have heard of Napoleon he is an up and coming general in France.'

'You are well acquainted with the latest news,' I remarked.

'It was the coincidence that interested me. I am making a study of coincidences. I sense in them a clue to some of the rules that govern nature.'

'You have a scientific bent of mind like your father.'

'Yes. I hope one day to follow in his footsteps, although it is very difficult for a woman to enter the medical profession.'

'Do the strictures of the establishment on Dr Mesmer's method worry you?'

'No. I am sure that in the end those who are against it will change their minds. No other method has provided such an effective treatment for mental sickness. Someone once said that the human mind is as unexplored as darkest Africa. Magnetism, which has enabled sailors to navigate the globe by means of a magnetic compass, may well prove equally useful in exploring the mysteries of the mind.'

'I hope it will cure me,' I said, giving a nervous shrug. 'Is it painful in any way?'

'Not in the least. A great peace will overcome you and it will release many noxious elements that are causing your present forgetfulness.'

I examined Bella Freulich a little more closely. Her nose a smaller version of her father's perfectly suited a delicate face framed in bountiful titian curls. Her somewhat brusque manner had repelled me the previous night. But I was impressed by the enthusiasm she showed for scientific knowledge. It was evident in her glowing amber eyes and excited tones. I warmed towards her because her love of science seemed to mirror my own love of music.

TWENTY-FOUR

D r. Freulich's office was situated in the smaller of the two wooden buildings; it was called the Haven. My treatment began there the following morning. Portraits of Dr Freulich and his wife hung on one wall of his office, along with testimonials to his medical skills. The front of the doctor's desk was engraved with scenes from the Holy Bible. A cartographer's globe stood on one side of it; on the other a colourful stuffed parrot. Behind his desk was an extensive bookcase containing numerous leather-bound volumes. A skeleton in one corner of the room looked as though it has just stepped out of the ancient suit of armour which stood beside it, complete with sword and scabbard. The polished wooden floor was strewn with oriental rugs.

Dr Freulich drew thick brocade curtains to shut out the pale autumn sunshine and instructed me to drink a mug of liquid, which he told me contained some kind of iron solution. He assured me that it would do me no harm. While I was drinking the liquid, which had a taste not unlike that of the China tea I had been offered during some of my concerts, he explained the basis of the cure I was about to undergo. 'Our bodies are full of fluids. They are no more immune to the pull of gravity than the oceans which rise and fall with the moon, giving rise to tides. This pull also has a powerful effect on human emotions and is the cause of a number of ailments. By affixing magnets to various parts of the anatomy, it is possible to alter the flow of "animal magnetism" within the human body, providing beneficial results which are as yet unexplained.

Dr Freulich then declared that while an enormous amount of work remained to be done to analyse and refine the healing process, he felt the system had already proved itself a thousand times over; it had enabled him to discharge many patients deemed incurable by other physicians. He corresponded regularly, he informed me, with the Marquis de Puységur, a layman with a profound interest in the subject, who had discovered how magnetic healing could be used to induce a somnambulistic sleep state in which disturbances of the mind could be resolved. This particular procedure, Dr Freulich explained, would hold the key to my cure.

He then asked: 'Herr Wunder, why do you wish to recover your memory?'

'Because I desire to become a full and whole person once again.'

'Of course,' Dr Freulich replied approvingly. 'We are but the sum of our memories. But I must warn you that bringing back your memory will be a long and arduous process. Too rapid a cure might prove dangerous. The dam holding back your memories must be allowed to crumble away slowly under its own weight, so that you gradually become aware of your true identity. Do you understand Herr Wunder?'

'I do.'

Dr Freulich then attached magnetised bars on two leather straps around my abdomen and my chest. I felt nothing at first but when he suggested that the magnets were taking effect, I felt a soft warmth spreading gently around my whole body. I remember thinking perhaps the reason the authorities were against the treatment was because they believed that it was too good for the common man and wished to keep it exclusively for themselves.

'Herr Wunder, you say you don't know who you are. How did you come by your name?'

'I was given the name of Johann Theophilius Wunder by the daughter of the old pedlar who rescued me. I had not realised

139

that I was known as 'The Wonderman' until I came here. I suppose it is a tribute to my music-making abilities.'

'You say you were found in a Viennese graveyard — do you recall the Imperial Summer Palace, the Schonbrunn?'

'No.'

'Saint Stephen's Cathedral?'

'No but ...'

'But what?'

'I associate it with a celebration of some kind of wedding.'

'Did you ever go to the Theater an der Wein?'

'I don't remember.'

'Did you ever walk in the Weinerwald?'

'I don't remember.'

'Nothing comes back to you of your past life.'

'Nothing ... except?'

'Except what?'

'It doesn't matter. It's not important.'

'You must tell me. Even the most insignificant trifle may be important.'

'I had a pain in my heart when I played the violin.'

'You can remember playing the violin?'

'I think so.'

'Who taught you to play it?'

'A lion.'

'How can a lion teach music?'

'I don't know. But that is all I see — a lion that growls and attacks me if I make a mistake.'

'Were you a musician?'

'I believe so. My head is always full of music. I often hear instruments in the orchestra crying and answering each other as though they are human beings in excited conversation.'

'Why do you think you were also affected by the lion-shaped knocker?'

'Something to do with the name Leo.'

'Are you by any chance referring to Leopold Mozart, the father of the late Wolgang Mozart?'

I detected hostility in Dr Freulich's voice and hesitated to answer. I sensed that he was uneasy about my reference to Mozart. But feeling bound to tell the truth, I repeated what I had already told him; namely that I had once fainted on picking up one of his works.

Dr Freulich said harshly: 'You must not persist in trying to exploit any connections you may have had with the late, lamented Wolfgang Amadeus Mozart. You resemble him to the same extent that a coarse earthenware mug resembles Meissen porcelain. I have attended several of his concerts. He was a splendid fellow. I met him at the opening night of the Marriage of Figaro he was wearing a crimson pellisse and a gold-laced cocked hat...'

Dr Freulich paused for a moment, relishing the memory. He then continued: 'So don't keep referring to Mozart. Try to remember the names of some other musicians you may have encountered during your life in Vienna. Did you perhaps meet Joseph Haydn, Salieri, Gluck, JC Bach?'

As he mentioned each musician, I was able to recall the char-acteristics of their compositions. Haydn's music, especially, came roaring in full flood into my ears. But I simply could not remember any other details relating to these individuals.

I replied: 'I can remember the music but not the musicians.'

Dr Freulich then asked me if I had ever done anything in Vienna of which I might be ashamed.

I thought for a while and then replied: 'The only thing I am ashamed of is of having been cast like a dead animal into an unmarked grave.'

'Is it possible that the old pedlar hit you on the head and then tried to rob you?'

'No! No! No!' I cried out.

'We don't know for certain what happened. But we must try to elicit information relating to your life before that episode. Try to remember other incidents.'

I protested: 'But, Dr Freulich... if I could remember, I would not need your assistance.'

'Very well, Johann Wunder. We are at an early stage in your cure. Soon, I shall put you into a trance and we shall see what that reveals.'

'What year were you born, Herr Wunder?'

'Seventeen ninety-one.'

'That's impossible. It would make you six years old! You are a middle-aged man. You must have had a childhood and a young adulthood. Who were you?'

'I don't know.'

'Can you remember the name of your birthday saint?'

'No.'

'Would you please count backwards from one hundred in steps of seven. I will give you the first answer ninety-three. Please carry on from there.'

'Eighty-six, seventy-nine, seventy-two ... '

'That is good. Your arithmetical memory is unaffected and your musical memory and linguistic ability are, as far as I can judge, unimpaired. Everything from your earliest infancy must still be there in your mind prior to the year when you became Johann Wunder. I am now going to pass a magnet in front of your eyes in a series of rhythmic movements and you will find yourself going into a deep sleep. You will be able to talk to me in exactly the same way as you are talking to me now. I will question you about certain events in your life. Is that perfectly clear?'

'Yes, Doctor Freulich.'

At that moment, the stuffed parrot, red, blue with a yellow breast, became alive and flew through the luxuriant leaves of a jungle in perfect harmony with its surroundings. Trying to translate its gliding motion into music, I hummed a tune under my breath. Dr Freulich was examining me intently as he contin-ued waving his hands.

'Per..per...Papagei, 'I said, 'You poor creature.'

Dr Freulich shook his head impatiently.

'Don't fidget and stop humming. You are relaxing into a sleep-like condition that will allow you to continue hearing my voice.

I muttered. 'Papagei, papagei, papagei. You remind me of per —per—Papageno. He, too, wears feathers. He's a funny fellow like a parrot — he plays simple tunes on his chimes: Papa — Papa —Papageno —Papageno.'

Delightful music sounded in my ears. I laughed out loud.

Shortly afterwards, or so it seemed, Dr Freulich snapped his fingers and brought me back to my senses.

TWENTY-FIVE

The vision of a man dressed in feathers like the stuffed parrot kept recurring when I returned to my room. The image obstinately refused to go away. I washed my face in cold water, attempting to banish this unwelcome avian visitor from my mind. While I was thus engaged, I heard a delightful aria coming from the room opposite. The name of its composer, Cristoph Willibald Gluck, suddenly flashed through my mind and encouraged me to believe that Dr Freulich's treatment had started to work.

I hastily dried my face and knocked on the door of the room from whence the sound was coming. Madame Toussaint appeared, wearing an olive-green house-robe. Yellow traces under her nostrils indicated that so far Dr Freulich's treatment had failed to cure her addiction. She peered at me suspiciously.

'I said: 'Pardon me, Madame, I have called to let you know that I am familiar with that beautiful piece of music.'

'And are you not also familiar with the voice of the famous soprano, Estelle Toussaint?'

She tilted her head in a self-mocking manner.

'Alas, my memory has been wiped out by an unfortunate accident. But your voice is powerfully affecting and I immediately recognised the name of the composer.'

'The aria, is, of course, Divinités du Styx from Gluck's Alceste, in which I played the leading role. My own memory is, alas, not what it was. I am addicted to tobacco in its most noxious form. It has affected my voice as well as my memory. But I hope one day to regain my former powers. Mozart, the incomparable Mozart, once said that my voice was like that of a nightingale in love.'

'You were praised by Mozart!' I exclaimed. 'Someone once said that I bore a faint resemblance to him.'

'I don't think so. No — not in the least.'

She then muttered with a sad expression: 'Poor Mozart! Died so young. He lost several of his children, but he always remained cheerful and engaging. There will never be another Mozart.'

My hopes of basking in reflected glory having thus been rudely dashed, I asked Madame Toussaint if she would honour me by singing some arias from an opera I had composed. She replied haughtily: 'I would not stoop so low as to sing inferior music composed by a dilettante.'

Then noting my disappointed expression, she relented and added graciously, 'Catch me in a good mood one day and I might change my mind.'

I returned to my room.

That night I dined alone with Bella. Dr Freulich was attending his sick wife in the Haven. When I told Bella about my conversation with Madame Toussaint, she said it was just as well she had refused my request to sing my compositions, because her voice was well past its prime. She begged me to play the piano. I promised to do so after we had dined.

During the meal I told her about the strange effect the stuffed parrot had had on me. Even as I was speaking, the title of an opera, 'Die Zauberflöte' sprang into my mind. I ran to the piano, played some passages and shouted jubilantly to Bella that the parrot had triggered important musical memories.

I sat for a while, gazing at the keyboard, regretting that I did not own a piano. My flute could not compare to a piano when it came to composing. I even regretted the naughty ballad extolling the flute I had composed for Leah. I would not have given it to her if I had known that she was about embark on a long and dangerous journey. But I told myself not to despise the ancient wind instrument which had enabled me to earn a living and discover that in my former life I had been a musician.

A rush of sombre images brought on by Die Zauberflöte then came into my mind: men in magnificent uniforms, Egyptian gods and goddesses, strange hieroglyphics and statues of animals. I had no time to reflect on these grotesque visions, because I had to return to the dinner-table. Bella then insisted on talking about the parrot in her father's study. She told me that her great-grandfather had requested it should be preserved when it came to its natural end. He declared in his will that he had confided so much to it during his lifetime that he considered it a valuable repository of information about the family.

I remarked: 'It might have served your great-grandfather's purpose better if he had written his memoirs.'

'My father would agree with you but he often says he is glad he kept the parrot, because it seems to encourage his patients to talk. Incidentally, I have no recollection at all of my great-grandfather but fragments of his personality seem to exist in Ziggy.'

'Ziggy?'

'That was the parrot's name.'

A delightful aroma arose as the maidservant served a pot roast.

I enquired: What exactly do you mean by "fragments of his personality?"'

Bella replied. 'Our personalities consist of many separate elements, as proven by the fact that we react differently to every person we meet.'

'But there is a unifying element in us which constitutes our personality.'

'It may be just an illusion. There is no conclusive evidence for its existence. Take Mozart, for instance. He seemed to possess many sides to his nature. He was a scamp and an angel, a wonderful musician, a profound philosopher and a lover of wine and women.'

'I enquired with a smile. 'Which among those elements do you see in me?'

She studied my face and said, with mock gravity: 'I suspect that you may be a womaniser.'

'Not a philosopher or an angel?'

'I would guess that your strong desire for the female of the species frequently overrides other considerations.'

'May I take that as a compliment?'

'Take it how you will.'

'But going back to Mozart, there was surely a unifying element in his nature, as there is in all of us.'

'I think he spent so much time consumed by music that for much of his life he had little consciousness of himself as an individual.'

Bella gave me an enigmatic smile and then addressed herself to the potroast.

I was still puzzled by her analysis of 'selfhood,' the vital part of every human being that motivates our every action.'

I said: 'Do we then all see the parrot differently?'

'Yes, and even our individual perceptions of the parrot vary from day to day. One day you might remember Ziggy for his redness; his blueness, his yellowness and so on. Another day you might be struck by his capacity for talking, on yet another by his flying ability. This shows that your perceptions and, by implication, your personality, is changing all the time. Incidentally, if my great-grandfather's object in bequeathing the parrot was to be remembered, he succeeded very well, because whenever the parrot is mentioned my great-grandfather comes into the conversation.'

'They say we are alive as long as people remember us.'

'That is a rather superficial view. Genghis Khan is remembered for his massacres. But is he more alive than my great-grandfather, who by all accounts, was a dear, kind man?'

'Well, let us agree that Ziggy is still alive, in the sense that his stuffed remains continue to help people recover from their illnesses. Incidentally, do you believe in life after death?'

'I do not take the conventional view that God issues entrance tickets to Heaven according to how we have behaved. I share the belief of the Red Indians of North America who say that every object has its 'shade,' that is to say its corresponding reality in another world. And that each shade has yet another shade in yet another world, and so on ad infinitem.'

Her unorthodox opinion amazed me, even though I did not completely understand it. The word Papageno rushed into my mind at that moment, along with a melange of images, including that of a feathered human being, a mysterious woman known as the Queen of Darkness and the words: Wisdom, Nature and Reason. I walked over to the piano and played several more pieces of music evoked by these bizarre images. Bella remained seated and watched me with an expression of amazement.

The title of an opera, Die Zauberflöte, again came into my mind but this time there were no accompanying images. My memory had failed me once again. The Magic Flute had lost its magic. I put my head in my hands and sobbed. Tears coursed down my face.

Bella came over, put her arms around me consolingly and said: 'Don't cry, dear Johann Wunderman. It must be a great trial having all that music inside you bursting to get out. Soon, your memory will come back and you will be your true self once again.'

TWENTY-SIX

During the next session of my treatment I described to Dr Freulich the vivid and disturbing images the parrot had produced in my mind. He had a copy of: Die Zauberflöte in his library and was amazed by my familiarity with the music and the text. I even managed to describe the costumes to him in considerable detail. 'You must have been a fanatical admirer and devotee of Mozart,' was his response and added with a derisory smile: 'It would almost seem that you are Mozart.'

'You scorned the idea yesterday.'

'I scorn it today as well,' he replied, making it clear from his expression that he did not consider it remotely possible. 'Who would believe that a man of wealth, talent and renown such as Wolfgang Mozart would suffer the indignity of being thrown like some ignorant, poverty-stricken peasant into an unmarked grave! Even taking into account the recent reaction against over-elaborate funerals, there would have been a huge public outcry if he had been buried in this disgraceful manner. The likeliest explanation for your familiarity with Mozart's works is that you were one of his pupils. We shall find out more in due course when I put you into a magnetised trance.'

'You suggested yesterday that you saw a faint resemblance between myself and Mozart.'

Someone once said I resemble Michael Kelly, the opera singer, but that doesn't mean that I can sing. I was merely trying to tease out from you why you have this obsession with Mozart. I could find a hundred men in the streets of Brno this morning who look more like him than you do. Why do you so relish the idea of being Mozart? Answer me honestly.'

'I don't really relish it to tell the truth it frightens me. The pedlar who rescued me from the grave once said that a Jew can no more escape from being a Jew than a hunchback can escape from being a hunchback. None of us, including the Emperor Francis himself, can escape his destiny. The only reason for my obsession with Mozart is that his music haunts me all the time.'

I looked questioningly at Dr Freulich. He was standing over me, holding a brace of magnets in hands which seemed quite large for such a slight man. A sympathetic look appeared on his face and he mumbled something inaudible.

He then said: 'His music haunts a lot of people besides you, Herr Wunder. It is a common enough fantasy to dream of becoming rich, talented, handsome and powerful. But even if you succeeded in remembering the most intimate details of Mozart's life from the time he took his mother's milk to the time of his death, I could still not accept that you were he...' He paused and added, smiling: 'Because that, as I am sure you appreciate, would violate the laws of nature.'

He went on, lowering his voice: 'Let me also say this: that if it became known outside this Institute that by some form of alchemy I had transformed you into Wolfgang Amadeus Mozart, I would be prosecuted for practising witchcraft! As it is I incur enough opprobrium by using Dr Mesmer's methods.'

He added sarcastically: 'So should we not keep secret these astonishing recollections, Herr Wunder?'

I muttered: 'Of course,' as he began to tie the magnets round my person.'

The familiar flow of warmth began to enter my body. He waved another iron magnet gently in front of my eyes and said: 'You are feeling relaxed as though floating on a cushion of air. You are now falling very gently into a somnambulistic slumber. Soon, you will be asleep but you will still be able to hear me and talk to me. I flourish the magnet so and you are asleep...'

It seemed that only seconds had passed when I saw Dr Freulich frantically snapping his fingers at me. He was shouting: 'Wake up, Herr Wunder. Wake up. You are now out of your trance. You are in Dr Freulich's study. Wake up! Wake up!'

A host of colourful scenes that had been passing in front of my eyes vanished from view, leaving behind Dr Freulich's frowning visage.

I shook my head violently.

'Strange,' he muttered. 'Very strange.'

'What is strange? I enquired,. in a state of confusion.

'I almost came to the bizarre conclusion again while you were under the influence of the magnets that you were, indeed, Wolfgang Amadeus.'

'Remarkable,' I replied, sarcastically. 'I, who above all should know the truth, deny that I am Mozart. And you now say that I am he. What makes you so sure?'

'While you were in a trance-like state I asked you if you once had a music teacher called Padre Martini and you answered: Yes. I then asked you what subject he taught and you replied counterpoint. I also asked for a musical item you had composed in 1791 the year you supposedly died and you declared that you had composed a piece of music for your Masonic lodge, a cantata called — ' Dr Freulich looked at his notes — 'Kleine Feimaurer. Do you remember that composition?'

I shook my head.

Dr Freulich regarded me suspiciously.

But there are also certain inconsistencies in your responses. You insisted that you married Aloysia Weber, who is, in fact, the sister of Constanze, Amadeus Mozart's wife. So on the one hand we have compelling evidence that you are Mozart and on the other equally compelling evidence that you are not.'

'I said wearily: 'Does it matter?'

'It obviously matters a great deal. You stated that you wished to find out who you were so that you could claim your estates and possessions in Vienna.'

'That is my ambition. But more important is my desire to become a whole person with a complete memory of his past like everyone else.'

'Well, we are making progress. You made certain statements while you were in a magnetic trance that suggests you are a

151

Freemason. I am a Freemason myself and when I tested you, you made the correct responses. That, plus the fact that you are aware of a cantata composed for a Masonic occasion, suggests to me that, if you are not Mozart and of course, we have effectively ruled that out, you almost certainly knew him intimately. The likeliest possibility is that you were a member of his Masonic lodge. This would explain how you came to be familiar with the cantata specially composed for the consecration of his lodge temple.'

I mumbled: 'I have no knowledge of Masonic ritual and cannot remember being a member of a lodge.'

'Your Masonic memory may be faulty,' Dr Freulich said with a smile. 'But not your musical memory. My daughter remarked when she heard you playing the piano that it comes as naturally to you as breathing.'

I frowned heavily and said: 'Things keep coming back to me. Your excellent piano possesses an unusual pedal mechanism. I seem to recall that it was his invention.'

'More confirmation that you were indeed well acquainted with Mozart. Herr Wunder, we are getting somewhere. The search is narrowing. Incidentally, while you were under the influence of the magnets you muttered something about Leipzig and documents bearing the signature of Johann Sebastian Bach. I hope you won't claim to be the great contrapuntist just because you also happen to be familiar with his works.' He gave an excited laugh and added: 'For the very good reason that Bach was in his grave long before you were born!'

TWENTY-SEVEN

At dinner time that evening, as we waited for our steaming hot bowls of broth to cool, Dr Freulich reminisced about some of the Mozart concerts and operas he had attended. Turning towards me, he remarked: 'You have a faint Salzburg inflection not dissimilar to that of Mozart, so you may well have known him during your boyhood. The fact that you recalled the name of his music teacher confirms my theory that you were intimately acquainted with him.'

He glanced across at his daughter and said: 'Do you not agree with me, Bella?'

Bella said: 'I looked at your case notes, father, and I am a little doubtful about the method by which you reached such a conclusion.'

'My dear girl, it is obvious. This man remembers Father Martini. Estelle Toussaint has affirmed that Mozart was one of his pupils. The likelihood, then, is that Herr Wunder was a fellow student of Mozart under Father Martini in Bologna. The fact that he has shown familiarity with certain Masonic signs and rituals is also highly significant.'

'Father, leaving aside the latter, it was you who mentioned Father Martini to Herr Wunder'

'When?'

'On the evening when he arrived at the Institute. So if he now remembers the name, it is because you had already made him familiar with it.'

'Yes, but during his magnetic trance he remembered another important detail, namely that Padre Martini had taught him counterpoint.'

'What else would he have taught him? A well qualified musician only needs to add refinements to his skills, the foremost of which is counterpoint. It was you who put the suggestion into his mind in the first place. When subsequently during a magnetic trance, he remembered it, you triumphantly proclaim that he knew Father Martini! That's precisely the kind of mistake you warned me against making when I am allowed to practise magnetic healing.'

'Hmph. Yes. I see your point.'

Dr Freulich peevishly turned his attention to his bowl of soup.

Bella then added pointedly: 'Which so far you have not allowed me to do.'

'You are too young to listen to some of the shameless admissions I have to listen to when my patients are in a trance-like state.'

'Father, I know the facts of life. If I am ever to practise medicine I must know all about human weaknesses, too.'

'Yes. Well... Herr Wunder, would you object if Fraulein Bella attended our sessions?'

I toyed with my spoon and answered: 'Are you not concerned that I might become unwilling to talk in the presence of a member of the opposite sex?'

'An interesting point,' Dr Freulich remarked, looking stead-fastly at his daughter.

'It could be valuable from a purely scientific point of view to see if that is true. It would help us to determine whether patients can consciously withhold information when they are in a magnetic trance.'

A further exchange then took place between Dr Freulich and his daughter about confessions made under the influence of the magnets, during which my presence was totally ignored. It seems that when professional passions are aroused, good manners go out of the window. However, it gave me the opportunity of observing that Bella Freulich's arguments, even though she had no formal academic training, often seemed to prevail over her father's. It was a genuine case of the pupil transcending the master.

At the end of the meal, Dr Freulich left to visit his sick wife in the Haven.

Bella then reminded me of my promise to play for her. I played a passage from a piano concerto in D major which evoked uneasy memories of a king being crowned. I became so absorbed in the music that nothing else seemed to exist. I was aroused from my trance-like state by the sound of furious applause. Bella was clapping her hands, enthusiastically. Her face had gone quite pink.

She came over to the piano.

I remarked: 'You are obviously a true lover of music.'

'You possess the divine touch of the master.'

Extending my lower lip lugubriously, I said: 'Age has cramped my style and coarsened my musical sensibilities. But I am truly glad that you enjoyed it. To show my appreciation I shall compose a little piece that will sum up your delightful personality.'

I drew out some trills and fol-de-rols from the keyboard then remarked, shaking my head: 'Perhaps that is a little too frivolous. You are really quite a serious person.'

'Yes. But I am also a vulnerable woman.'

'Vulnerable in what manner?'

I should hate to suffer my mother's fate.'

'What happened to her?'

'She was nursing a young woman who had suffered rape at the hands of soldiers after the battle of Arcola. She then began to feel as though she had herself suffered the full horror of the experience. My father calls it 'vicarious injury.' He is giving her magnetic healing and hopes in a few weeks that she will be fully cured.'

Bella's right hand rested lightly on my shoulder. The look of adoration in her eyes strongly suggested that my piano-playing possessed powers surpassing those of Dr Freulich's magnets.

Was I an arch seducer of women, like the infamous Don who descended into Hell? A mental picture of Don Giovanni suddenly came to mind and with it a frightening surge of music.

155

Bella's cool cheek was touching my own as she whispered: 'Johann Wunder, I must tell you that my father is quite baffled about who you really are. But I am determined to unravel the mystery. I hope, when I join him in the healing process, that you will trust me with your deepest secrets.'

'What does it matter?', I replied dejectedly. 'I am nothing but a wandering musician, with no past and no future.'

'No, you are a great musician. I love you with all my heart,' Bella announced softly. She suddenly kissed me.

All my worries and fears magically disappeared as our lips met. But seconds later, just as we were about to embrace, a wild-eyed bearded man wearing a stained nightshirt burst into the room, brandishing a sword. 'Where is the accursed doctor?' he screamed.

Bella interposed herself between me and the frightening appa-rition. I remained seated at the piano. He advanced menacingly, repeating hoarsely: 'Where is the doctor?'

Bella said in a conciliatory tone: 'The doctor is not here, Louis. He has remained in France. When you are fully recovered, you may go and seek him there.'

The man then shouted in deafening tones: 'He should have his head cut off as he cut off mine.' He pointed to a livid scar on his throat.

'Louis, I swear he is not here.'

Pointing his sword at me, he demanded: 'Who is he?'

'He is just another inmate. He will do you no harm.'

'He is not the doctor?'

'No, just a patient like yourself.'

The man's face twisted into a scowl. He slashed furiously with his sword again, making a whistling sound and growled: 'Doctors who kill other people must be tortured as I was. Are you sure he is not a doctor?'

'Absolutely sure. Tell him, Johann.'

In a trembling voice, I said: 'Assuredly, I am not a doctor. I am Johann Wunder, a humble musician.'

'You look like a doctor.'

'I assure you, sire, I am not.'

Hoping to deflect him from his murderous intentions, I played a brief passage on the piano. The creature lowered the sword and stared at me open-mouthed. After a moment or two, he said: 'I am bound to find Dr Guillotine and kill him.'

'He is not here, Louis. I have told you he is still in France.'

'Then I must kill someone. I'll kill him instead.' He nodded at me.

'Please don't, Louis,' Bella pleaded. 'The Dauphin doesn't like bloodshed.'

'The Dauphin is dead!'

Angry tears rose into the man's eyes. He wiped them away with the sleeve of his nightshirt and then raised his sword, preparing to carry out his threat.'

Bella whispered urgently to me: 'Play, Johann! Play as you've never played before!'

I plunged both hands onto the keyboard and launched first into a stirring march and then, as I stole a glance out of the corner of my eye, a gentle lullaby. A puzzled-looking Louis slowly lowered his sword. His expression softened and he rocked his head gently from side to side in time to the music.

The door sprang open. Two uniformed attendants rushed forward, knocked the sword from his hand and pinioned his arms to his side.

As they dragged him out of the room, one of them said to him good-humouredly: 'It's all right, votre Majesté. The Revolution is over. You'll soon be back on your throne.'

I looked up at Bella, gave a deep breath and remarked: 'My God, that was a lucky escape. He could have killed us both.'

'Poor man, he was wounded fighting against the Revolutionary Forces of France. Ever since then he has fancied that he is Louis Sixteenth and seeks revenge on Doctor Guillotine, who invented the dreadful machine that goes by his name. How he managed to escape from the Citadel, I can't imagine. He must have stolen the sword from my father's office.'

We were about to resume our tender embrace when Madame Toussaint appeared in the dining-room, demanding to know the cause of the commotion. Bella explained. Madam Toussaint nodded briskly and then turning to me, said: 'It is most fortunate for you that I have been diverted from my nightly reading of the Bible. If you would now like to show me the arias you told me about, I will endeavour to sing them for you. Do kindly remember, however, that my voice temporarily lacks its former purity of tone.'

'I am highly honoured, dear lady,' I assured her. 'I shall go upstairs and bring down the music.'

While I was engaged on this errand, I could hear her practising her scales. Her voice was hopelessly cracked in the lower register and somewhat wobbly in the higher. However, I was eager to hear parts of my opera sung by a professional opera singer and learn her opinion of its merits.

Estelle Toussaint selected three arias. She gave a sympathetic rendition of the first two, laughing at their humorous content. The third, sung in the finale when husband and wife are reunited in love, she found so powerfully affecting that she mopped tears from her eyes with a handkerchief.

I thanked her profusely. She assured me that if my opera was ever staged she would be proud to play a leading role. Before leaving, she whispered to Bella that she had not taken snuff since early that morning and hoped to go through the night without any.

Bella reminded her of the acclamation which might yet await her in the opera houses of Europe, if she managed to shake off her dreadful habit.

After the opera singer had left, I asked Bella what she thought of the arias from Cypriana.

'Absolutely splendid.'

'Did you appreciate the jokes?' I enquired eagerly. 'Our young mayor suffers a complete change of personality when he arrives at the magic boundary stone. All the action stems from his loss of memory.'

Bella then asked: 'Do you have any recollection of being married?'

'No. But the name Aloysia frequently comes into my mind.'

'I believe that in your case,' Bella said thoughtfully, 'it is music that evokes memories rather than the faces of human beings. Did the name Johann Sebastian Bach mean anything to you when my father mentioned it?'

'Yes.' I shut my eyes for a moment and said: 'He wrote rich, complex music. I can recall some now.'

'Go and sit again at the piano.'

I obeyed Bella's command.

'Play some of his music.'

The keyboard drew my hands towards it. I began to play a piece by Bach. Its majestic quality touched my heart.

'Beautiful,' I pronounced when I had finished. 'Beautiful!'

'What is it called?'

'Toccata and Fugue in F Major.'

'What is a fugue?'

'A flight of fancy. It consists of a theme repeated a fifth above or a fourth below an original statement. Listen —' I played the music again. 'And then it runs away from the original theme and returns to it again. The theme is woven contrapuntally into many variations before returning to the original. Here's another example.' I played a brief excerpt from another fugue which had just entered my mind. 'Do you like it?'

'Yes, yes, delightful. You play beautifully. You were right to liken it to a flight. The word Fugue derives from fuga, meaning flight. It suggests to me another way in which you could have lost your memory.'

'What way is that?'

'I cannot say just yet. I must discuss the theory with my father.'

At that moment Dr Freulich appeared. It had been raining heavily and water was streaming from his astrakhan hat and his cloak.

He looked extremely worried, held out both hands towards us and said: 'I must apologise for what has happened. This is the first time an inmate has ever escaped from the Citadel. We shall have to change the way we manage such patients. Thank God you have come to no harm.'

TWENTY-EIGHT

A heated argument was going on between Bella and Dr Freulich concerning my treatment when I came down to breakfast. They both agreed that my recollections of Mozart's *Die Zauberflöte* and Johann Sebastian Bach's Toccata and Fugue were highly significant. They disagreed strongly, however, about my future treatment. Dr Freulich wished to try to continue trying to evoke memories of my personal and social life. Bella believed that the key to my recovery lay in prompting further musical memories.

Oddly, a vivid memory of childhood episodes had come to me the previous night as I lay in bed. I held a violin closely to my chest, to ease a constricting sensation around my heart. When the one I knew as the "Lion" reprimanded me and forcibly replaced the violin on my shoulder, I cursed him, saying: "Shit in your pants," I remembered also pulling down my sister's drawers because she played two wrong notes while we were playing a duet on the pianoforte. And I remembered spying on a fraulein in the house opposite when she was taking off her clothes.

I saw no point in mentioning these embarrassing memories to Dr Freulich. But I did consider telling him of an idea that the cartographer's globe on his desk had suggested to me: namely that my life having passed from the heat of the Equator, was now descending rapidly towards the Antarctic ice cap of old age. It seemed appropriate, therefore, that I should seize as many pleasures as might still be available.

During breakfast a maid came in and handed me a letter from Shmul, which had been transcribed by a friend in Vienna into German script. He expressed the hope that I would soon be cured. His enquiries about the brocade waistcoat had not yielded any useful information. Leah and her brother had left the Low Countries and were on their way to Leipzig, where they intended to stay for a while.

After reading the letter, I remarked to Bella: 'You take a scientific interest in coincidences. Here is one for you. I had some recollection last night of Leipzig. It now appears that Shmul's daughter intends to stay there for a while before returning to her father's home in Galicia.'

'Yes, that is an interesting coincidence. Perhaps it suggests some kind of telepathic communication between you both. Is she attractive?'

'A wonderful girl with a heart of gold,' I affirmed enthusiastically and described how Leah had bravely travelled across Europe to give succour to her mutilated brother. Bella briefly acknowledged what I had said and then made haste to tell me about the plan she and her father had devised for my future treatment. They were now both firmly of the opinion that I had moved in the same musical circles as Mozart. My familiarity with his works strongly suggested that I had been his pupil. Bella said she would like to question me further about his music.

'Perhaps I am Mozart's 'shade,' I suggested to her in jest.

'Science has yet to prove that we can carry our personality into another lifetime.'

Her father declared impatiently that he despised such talk, which could take the world back to the dark age of superstition. He left the breakfast table to visit his patients. As soon as he was gone, I whispered urgently to Bella: 'When and where can we be alone?'

'Do you want me to mesmerise you without my father being present!' she replied, deliberately misunderstanding me.

I exclaimed, fervently: 'You have already mesmerised me! Incidentally, how did that madman manage to escape from the Citadel?'

'The building was not expressly designed for its present purpose. We really need a new house to suit our special needs.'

"New house!" The equivalent Italian translation leapt into my mind — *Casanova.* It brought to mind the image of a haughty-looking gentleman with a fine profile, whose amorous exploits were well known. And this in turn reminded me of another famous philanderer: Don Giovanni. I told her this and she exclaimed excitedly: 'Our plan is beginning to work! We can build further on that scaffold of musical memories in your mind. Does Don Giovanni remind you of anything else?'

'A man with the name of a bridge. He has a large nose. That is all.'

I tried to embrace her. But she easily evaded my clutches and ran to the door. On reaching it, she turned round and declared that if I behaved well during my treatment that day she would consent to walk with me in the grounds that evening before dinner.

I went to my room, enormously excited by the prospect ahead of me. I was in a jovial mood when I walked into Dr Freulich's office for another session of magnetic treatment. I assented readily to his proposal that Bella should attend that morning as part of her medical training. He quickly got down to business, placed the magnets around my person and made a fluent gesture with his hands which put me into a deep somnambulistic sleep.

Later, he showed me the transcript of what took place while I was in that strange state, adding: 'Herr Wunder, thanks to your willing cooperation, we have made what I believe to be some important discoveries about your past life. Some of them may possibly be false memories induced by suggestions I inadvertently made. But by comparing recollections of events which we know have occurred with those that have not, we shall move closer to the truth. Gradually we are building up a picture in which everything about your past life is falling into place. It will soon enable us to establish your true identity.'

*

'You are going back in time and are now thirty-one years old. Who sits on the throne?'
'Joseph the Second.'

'My daughter tells me that you remember a man called Casanova. Can you tell me something about him.'

'He boasts of having seduced over a thousand women.'

'Was anybody else present when he made that boast?'

'A converted Jew called Lorenzo da Ponte. He suggested to Mozart that they should compose an opera called Don Giovanni based on Giacomo Casanova's life.'

'Where were you at the time?'

'In a Viennese tavern.'

'How did you come to overhear that conversation?'

'I don't remember.'

'Who are you?'

'Johann Wunder.'

'And who were you then?'

'The same, I suppose.'

'Not Amadeus Mozart?'

'No, he spoke coarsely of women. I would not have dared. The Lion would not let me.'

'How did the conversation go?'

'Da Ponte suggests we order a bottle of wine. Why not a flagon says Mozart — when inspiration is flagging we need either a flagon or a flogging. Let's have the former it is less painful. Giacomo Casanova, did you not experience sometimes a little difficulty in rousing yourself for your next conquest after a hard week's debauchery.

The answer came: No more than you, Wolfgang, have difficulty in starting a new string quintet when you have just finished a quartet. My kind of music consists of a lady's cries of delight when I pleasure her. I play on women as you play on a guitar, a piano or a flute. Especially the latter — emboucher — if you get my meaning.

Mozart then asks: Are you never in danger from jealous lovers or husbands.

Yes, indeed, replies Casanova. It adds piquancy to seduction. When all is said and done, it is the chase rather than the kill which gives the hunter the supreme pleasure. So with

164

*the game of love. The harder the chase, the more pleasurable
the consummation.*

*Da Ponte then chimes in: You might think that we have in
Giacomo's lurid confessions the very stuff of our proposed
operatic drama. But repetitious couplings might offend the
Emperor, the Archbishop and some strait-laced members of the
nobility.*

*Mozart giggled and said Shit on the Archbishop! And added
seriously: Do you recall that when we collaborated on the
Marriage of Figaro, the Emperor got hot under the collar But
it was Figaro's over-familiarity with the Count which upset him
— not the bedroom scenes, which hardly disturbed him at all.
We can get away with an account of Giacomo's debaucheries,
if we dress it up in a moral framework. Mozart then added
sorrowfully: Incidentally, the few sopranos I have tucked into
my drawers hardly count alongside Giacomo's numerous
seductions...Or should I say I tucked myself into their drawers!
He laughed unrestrainedly and then turning to Casanova, said:
Giacomo, my own wife is always urging me to be faithful and
yet there is nobody she admires more than a thorough-going
rake such as yourself.*

Life is full of such paradoxes, Giacomo responded.

*Mozart replied merrily: It is more full of doxies than
paradoxes. Those mutually opposite objectives: chastity and
lust strive for supremacy in human beings like cats fighting in a
bag. They will never come to terms. Do you have no fear of
punishment for your misdeeds, Giacomo?*

*He answered; You might as well blame the tiger for being
carnivorous as blame me for being amorous. Women, who are
supreme realists above all else, respect this law of nature,
which is why they never reprimand me for my so-called
misdeeds.*

*Mozart then commented: Not so their husbands, Giacomo.
And that would explain your itinerant life — you are always
being chased by cuckolded husbands.*

165

Turning to da Ponte, he said: Our dear, lecherous friend always manages to escape without penalty. Can we not ease the qualms of the Emperor and the Archbishop by causing our amorous character in the opera to suffer a condign punishment?

Da Ponte replied enthusiastically: Splendid idea. Let's send him to Hell. That will solve the problem Let's get to work on it straight away.

*

'I am now going to snap my fingers. This will bring you back to the present.'

Snapping sound.

'Are you Wolfgang Amadeus Mozart?'

'No.'

'How did you come to be acquainted with that conversation?'

'I overheard it.'

'You were eavesdropping?'

'Perhaps I was a waiter.'

'A waiter would only hear snatches of the conversation..'

'Perhaps I made it up.'

'Why should you do that?'

'It is one of the things I like doing.. I have written libretti, you know. I have written one recently called Cypriana.'

'What is it about?'

'A man who forgets he has a wife whenever he passes a magic milestone.'

At that moment Bella, who was sitting quietly in a chair in a darkened corner, said quietly: 'When you were talking under the influence of the magnets, you referred to Mozart's wife. Are you sure you yourself have not passed a 'magic milestone,' which caused you to forget that you had a wife?'

'I sometimes remember a girl called Aloysia Weber. But I have no recollection of marrying her.'

'Do you think Mozart's music might bring that period in your life back to you?'

'Perhaps. I am entirely in your hands.'

Dr Freulich became a little impatient at that moment. He said: 'I now propose to put you back again into a magnetic sleep. You may listen, Bella, and learn from the experience.'

*

He waved the magnet, snapped his fingers and put me again into that waking sleep.

'*Who is Leo the lion?*'

'*Mozart's father.*'

'*Not your father?*'

'*I have no father.*'

'*Everyone has a father.*'

'*I had a progenitor, not a father.*'

'*Mozart's mother's name began with the letter A. Do you recall her full name?*'

'*Aloysia?*'

'*No. You must remember your own mother. Every man remembers his mother.*'

'*Perhaps she died when I was born.*'

'*Bella intervened and enquired: 'Do you recall Mozart's Paris symphony in D Major?*'

'*Yes.*' I hummed the first movement.

Bella: 'Do you remember Mozart's Concerto for flute, harp and orchestra?'

'*Yes, indeed. Mozart confessed to me that the flute seemed too dominant at first. He told me he wrote it while his mother was sick in Paris. But he was too sick with love for Aloysia to notice how ill his mother was. He said it grieved him tremendously when she died.*'

'*When did Mozart tell you this?*'

'*I can't remember. Why do you keep tormenting me with Mozart this and Mozart that!*'

Dr Freulich then intervened: 'Are you Wolfgang Amadeus Mozart, Anna Maria's son?'

'I am Johann Wunder.'

Bella: 'But you remember Aloysia?'

'Yes, she sang like a love-sick nightingale.'

Bella: 'But she was not your wife?'

'She was the love of my life.'

At this point, Dr Freulich took over the questioning again. 'Herr Wunder, did you marry a girl known as Constanze?'

Pause.

Dr Freulich repeated; 'Did you marry Constanze Weber?'

'I am not a bigamist. She was Wolfgang Mozart's wife.'

I declined to answer any more questions. Dr Freulich snapped his fingers and I returned to my normal waking state. He stared at me for a while with a puzzled expression and then said: 'Wolfgang Mozart married Constanze Weber. If you are Mozart, then Constanze was your wife.'

That ended the session.

TWENTY-NINE

Waiting impatiently for the hour of my appointment with Bella, I sought to pass the time by composing a flute concerto in honour of Shlotkin. I imagined him trotting through forest glades with jingling harnesses and lightly clopping hooves. But the image changed after a while and I seemed to be transported into a horse-drawn coach rolling through the verdant hills of Tuscany.

I lay down my flute. Dr Freulich's magnets seemed to be mysteriously working in the aftermath of our last session, casting aside veils in my mind that separated me from my past. Memories came flooding back, including haunting passages from *Die Zauberflöte*. Vivid images appeared of Pamina, Sarastro, Tamino, Papageno and Papagena — all in colourful costumes.

But the images faded as suddenly as they had appeared. Were they real I asked myself. Had I composed the work, or were they simply recollections of visits I had made to the opera? I had no means of knowing which was true.

I picked up my flute again and consoled myself by playing the overture from Cypriana. That, at least, I could be sure was my own composition. The forgetfulness visited on the young mayor, Alexander, when he passes the magic milestone mirrored my own affliction. I now began to ask myself whether the doomed love affair with a young woman called Aloysia I had mentioned to Dr Freulich had actually happened to me or to someone called Wolfgang Mozart, whose music kept haunting me. It seemed impossible that I should be Mozart. For one thing he was reputed to be an impulsive creature as full of frolicsome pranks as a schoolboy. That was someone utterly unlike me! Unless, that is — and this was a possibility I could not ignore — we were the same person, the difference being that my former lighthearted self had now been lost under the spreading flesh of middle-age.

The excruciating confusion brought about by this notion left me in a state of near panic. Only the knowledge that I would shortly be meeting Bella enabled me to avoid crying out in a mixture of rage and sorrow.

Once again I sought refuge in the Shlotkin flute concerto. Soon, however, my work was interrupted by a loud knock on the door. I called 'Enter' and the tall, gaunt figure of Estelle Toussaint drifted in. She slowly cast her melancholy eyes round the room and then informed me that I played the flute like the God Pan himself. She added as an afterthought, shaking her head ruefully, that as much as she admired my music, she could never bring herself to make love to a man the top of whose head only came up to her bosom. I replied that I would be happy to wear stilts and she laughed delightedly. I judged, though, from her nostrils that she was still not yet fully cured of her affliction.

After glancing briefly at the musical score I had scribbled, Madame Toussaint declared it charming, and swept out of the room.

It was now time to meet Bella.

I put on a coat and walked to the gate-lodge. Clouds were racing across a dark sky. Glancing back to the main house, I saw above it, piercing the gloom, a fiery trace from the dying sun. Bella emerged from the rear door, holding a key in her hand. Looking up at the sky, she said she thought it might rain. I took her hand and we strolled slowly among the shrubberies. The mad creatures in the Citadel were quiet. A seductive perfume clung to Bella's face and hair, arousing my senses. As we walked towards the Citadel, I asked how Louis the Sixteenth was faring. Bella assured me that a combination of magnetic treatment and medicine was slowly restoring his sanity.

I slipped my arm around her. She gave a little start and exclaimed: 'I heard you playing your flute this afternoon; it was superb. What were you playing?'

'I was composing a concerto in praise of a horse who once saved my life.'

'How do you remember the different orchestral parts for all those instruments?'

'As a horse is formed to pull a cart, so my head is formed to compose music.'

'And yet how strange that you cannot remember your own past.'

'Some vivid episodes came back to me today. The treatment is beginning to work. I seem to be two different people.'

She squeezed my hand and said, smiling: 'Both of you are remarkable.'

I swung her round towards me, planted two kisses upon her lips and said, breathlessly: 'The first kiss was from me, the second from my döppelganger.'

A shower of rain soaked us in a few seconds. Bella said: 'Come, we had better take shelter.'

She led me back through the shrubberies towards the Haven, urging me to tread very softly, and opened the main door. We passed Dr Freulich's study, tip-toe-ed through a gloomy corridor and climbed a staircase at the end. Bella drew me into an empty room. In the dim light I could make out a bed, a chair and a small bedside cabinet, on which stood a small, iron candleholder. Bella struggled with a flint-box and lit the candle. She then sat on the bed, took my hand, pulled me towards her and kissed me with an abandon that inflamed my senses.

Soon, when I met with an obstacle to my urgent desire, Bella beat madly with her hands against the pillow and begged me to persevere. When I at last succeeded, she gave a whoop and then a gushing sigh of relief. A rapturous concordance of clarinets, triumphant trumpets and silvery-sounding cymbals sounded in my ears, followed by a blissful silence.

We both slept.

171

Bella was still fast asleep when I awoke. I drew the coverlet over her and whispered: 'Why, did you do that, my beloved girl.'

Bella sat up, wiped herself and declared: 'I swore that I would only yield my maidenhead to a genius. I am satisfied that it is now accomplished. Tomorrow would have been too late.'

'What do you mean?'

'Johann, I have to tell you that you are in extreme danger.'

'What have I done?'

'The Emperor's secret police are after you. They intend to imprison you in the Spilberk fortress.'

'Why should they do that?'

'Two men called on my father this afternoon.. I was asked to leave the room. But I eavesdropped. Are you acquainted with someone called Count Poceski?'

'I met him when I was living in Korlyshev.'

'And did you know a man called Ben-Levi?'

'Yes, he employed me as a bookkeeper for a while.'

'The men told my father that Ben-Levi has been arrested on suspicion of being involved with the Kosciuszko attempts to free Poland. They charged Ben-Levi with meeting Prince Poniatowski, Kosciuszko's accomplice, in Prague on the pretext of playing chess with him. Ben-Levi told Poceski you had confessed to destroying an invitation from the Prince which would have provided foreknowledge of his presence in that city. They don't believe his story and want to question you, in order to obtain further proof against him. They also say that you lived with a Jew whose sons fought on the side of the French Revolution and believe that you may be the composer of *Die Zauberflöte*, a seditious opera about Freemasonry, which preaches that all men are equal. They suspect you of having feigned your own death in order to escape punishment for that crime.'

Her story destroyed my blissful state. The thought of undergoing interrogation by the Emperor Francis's secret police in the dreaded Spilberk fortress filled me with foreboding.

I told her: 'If I was a Freemason in my former life, I have forgotten everything about it. Did your father tell them he suspected that I might be Mozart?'

'He said he wasn't sure but to gain time said he would try to squeeze information out of you during the next session of treatment. That was as much as he could do on your behalf. Because his method of healing is suspect, he cannot afford to provoke the civil authorities. Nevertheless, he has succeeded in delaying your arrest by one day.'

'Bella, my love, before I make any decision, tell me who I am and what I am suffering from?'

She replied: 'What does a fugue suggest to you Johann?'

'A composition in counterpoint. Different themes take flight —'

She interrupted me. 'that is it — your mind has taken flight. In other words, you cannot bear to remember your past life and your true self.'

'Why should I not want to remember?'

'Some events in your previous life have proved so wounding that you cannot bear to contemplate them.'

'Then do you truly believe that I am Mozart?'

Bella took my hands, pressed them firmly against her soft breasts and said: 'Part of me says you are Johann Wunder, the other part says you are Wolfgang Amadeus Mozart. But whoever you are, you are indeed beloved of God and act as a channel through which he sends messages of surpassing beauty.'

I replied irritably: 'Thank you for your kind compliment. But I came here to discover who I am, not to be told I am a musician, which I know already. You say I am in danger of being imprisoned. What shall I do?'

'The secret servicemen will come to arrest you tomorrow. One of our servants is driving into Vienna early tomorrow morning to collect medicines from an apothecary. I have told him to take you with him. He sets out at dawn. Will you make yourself ready?'

'It seems I have no alternative.'

'When you get to Vienna, hide under another name and make discreet enquiries. If you can succeed in convincing people you are Wolfgang Amadeus Mozart, you will regain his estates and you can then use your wealth to defend yourself against these scurrilous accusations. You will proclaim that *Die Zauberflöte* simply preaches belief in Nature, Wisdom and Reason. The Emperor won't dare to imprison a powerful figure who wins applause from the multitude. You will then be able to resume your rightful position in Viennese society.'

'But how shall I prove that I am Mozart?'

'The sights and sounds of that great city will revive your memories. You will go to shops and banks and theatres where you were known. Finally, you will make yourself known to Constanze, who was Mozart's wife. That meeting, if you are indeed Mozart, will provide the ultimate proof of your identity.'

I kissed her fervently and said: 'How can I thank you, dear Bella, for what you have done?'

'The knowledge that you will be free from further persecution is sufficient reward. I am bent on following a medical career. But I shall always cherish the knowledge that I have loved a genius.'

I kissed her again.

We dressed and made our way stealthily out of the building.

THIRTY

Carrying my flute and a leather bag containing all my worldly possessions, I walked very quietly down the winding path towards the gate-lodge, worried in case the Emperor's police agents were lying in wait for me. The first pale streaks of dawn were visible above the church spire. I increased my pace, convinced that unseen eyes were observing me. However, I arrived safely at the gate-lodge, where Josef, the attendant who had greeted me when I first arrived at the Institute, was waiting with a horse and cart.

I handed up my luggage and joined him on the driving-seat. His mother tongue was Bohemian, a language discouraged by the authorities. But he seemed to understand German passably well.

Little was said until we had left the town well behind us. He then became quite talkative and confided to me that there was a great deal of sympathy in Brno for Dr Freulich. The townsfolk spoke in awed whispers of his magnetic healing. He personally owed the doctor a debt of gratitude, because he had helped him to forget the dreadful bloodshed and carnage he had witnessed while serving in the Austrian army. He pulled up his leather jerkin and showed me a puckered livid scar where a French musket shot had passed through his side without hitting any vital organs.

He enquired whether Dr Freulich had succeeded in curing me.

'Not completely. I am still suffering from gaps in my memory.'

Josef, pointing to the horse, said: 'That old nag is lucky — he remembers nothing but his nosebag.'

'My memory has failed me to the extent that only God knows who I really am.'

'If God knows who you are, that is all that matters,' Josef assured me.

175

We rattled along at a fast pace.

Soon, the clouds thinned out. A pale sunshine illuminated the surrounding hills. Looking back at the massive fortress dominating a hill top, I repressed a shudder. Josef reached down into a bag by his side, took out two rosy apples and offered me one. I was not inclined to eat at first. But as our distance from the fortress increased, I regained my appetite and munched the apple.

Josef confessed that having on several occasion heard me playing the piano, he had told his local priest that the sound had made his very soul flutter with joy. The priest had told him that God gave music to man as a foretaste of Heaven.

I appreciated his remark so much that when we arrived in Vienna late the following night, I gave him a large tip.

I stayed at an inn that Josef recommended. Wrapped about my person in various parts of my clothing was the balance of the money I had reserved for my stay at the Institute. I had enough left to keep me for several weeks.

*

During the next few days I wandered around the great city. The long-hoped for flood of memories did not come to me. But I was comforted by recalling Josef's remark that my Maker knew who I was. I told myself that it was really of no great consequence whether I was a friend of Wolfgang Mozart or Wolfgang himself. Equally irrelevant was whether I had been found in a graveyard or a brothel. The important truth was that I was someone in his own right who could enthral a crowd by playing on a musical instrument and was able to create sublime music out of my own head. My gift also turned women into adoring slaves. What more could any man wish for?

The answer was a wife and a family.

I had told Dr Freulich while under the influence of the magnets that a girl called Aloysia was the love of my life. But it seemed she could not have been my wife. Dr Freulich had told

176

me that Wolfgang Mozart had married her sister, Constanze. The defining moment would come when I asked her if she recognised me as her husband.

The keeper of the inn where I was staying recommended that I should entrust an attorney of his acquaintance with the task of finding Constanze's whereabouts. Sounding her out would be a delicate task and must be done tactfully; it would come as too much of a shock if she were confronted by me without warning. He directed me to the lawyer's office, situated in a narrow house in the centre of town. I waited several hours in a basement room. Eventually, after being summoned to appear before the attorney, I threaded my way through filing cabinets and dusty bundles of documents tied with pink tape. Lawyer Schuster, a corpulent man with numerous chins, was sitting behind an elaborately-carved, leather-topped desk, his carelessly-placed wig partly exposing his own sparse, graying hairs. He stared at me through half-closed eyes that resembled glittering blackcurrants.

I addressed him: 'Sire, I am Johann Wunder and have been absent from Vienna these past seven years. Have you heard of a man called Wolfgang Amadeus Mozart?'

'He was a musician. He died some years ago.'

'Did he leave a widow?'

'Yes. How is it that the news of his death did not reach you?'

'I have been living in a small town in Galicia.'

'What did you do there?'

'I earned my living as a bookkeeper and later as a musician.'

'What is it you require of me?'

Unwilling to claim that I was Mozart at this early stage, I temporised by saying: 'I am owed a debt by the deceased. Would it be possible to recover it from his estate?'

Lawyer Schuster gave a cynical laugh.

'Mozart was heavily in debt when he died — the Emperor had recently turned down his request to employ him as a Cappelmeister. He sponged off a friend of mine, Michael Puchberg, and died owing him a great deal of money. His wife was left penniless. But I believe the present Emperor has since granted her a small pension.'

I gave a sigh and said: 'My mission then appears to have been in vain. Do you happen to know where his widow lives?'

She's no longer a widow. It was reported in the newspapers recently that Constanze Mozart has remarried. I believe her new husband is a Danish diplomat.'

I fainted.

When I came to, a woman was fussing over me fanning my face with a large sheet of paper and saying repeatedly: 'You poor man, you poor man.' Lawyer Schuster was gazing at us both with an amused expression.

When I had sufficiently recovered, he showed me a cutting from a newspaper. It spoke of the recent marriage of Frau Constanze Mozart, widow of the late Wolfgang Amadeus Mozart, to a Danish diplomat, Georg von Nissen. The passage referred to her first husband as 'the late lamented and celebrated composer of The Marriage of Figaro.'

I blurted out thanks and took my leave.

Outside it was raining heavily. A wild wind was bombarding the pedestrians and horse-drawn carriages with leaves from the linden trees. Tears running down my face, mingled with moisture from the rain. My last chance of finding out my true identity now seemed irretrievably lost.

I took refuge from the storm in the depths of a tavern and ordered a glass of schnapps. A young, beguiling, red-cheeked prostitute with a half-exposed bosom came and sat beside me. I brusquely waved her away.

Shortly afterwards, I tried hard to recall the woman to whom I was supposed to have been married, According to the newspaper cutting, Constanze had born me six children, of whom only Karl Thomas and the baby Xavier Wolfgang had survived. She had been ill after Xavier's birth and had recuperated by taking the waters in Baden. It seemed that we had been much apart.

178

A determined effort on my part to remember her features brought a picture of a woman sitting in a chair suckling a baby. But even this did not convince me that it was a genuine recollection. It could just as easily have been a phantom memory evoked by the newspaper cutting. As Bella had demonstrated, memory can be inserted into one's mind as easily as a new instrument can be added to a musical score.

I ordered a schnapps and then another and another and another. Trying to rack my brain for a recollection of Constanze, there came to mind a faint image of a wedding ceremony in St. Stephen's cathedral. I shook my head, trying to bring the memory into focus. As I did so, the faces of the drinkers in the crowded tavern in the smoky atmosphere became as distorted as the faces in a fairground mirror. Nevertheless I succeeded in clarifying my thoughts. There was no point, now that Constanze had remarried, in burdening her with my presence. My reappearance, when she thought me dead, could only unbalance her mind, estrange her from her present husband and bring about great unhappiness for everyone concerned.

The harsh truth was that Wolfgang Amadeus Mozart had been bankrupt at the time of his supposed death. If I managed to establish a claim to his estate, I would simply encumber myself with debts.

So what should I do now?

Vienna, the city which had ruined my health and my finances, had nothing more to offer me. I did not relish the thought of returning to the poverty-stricken, backward town of Korlyshev. Secret servicemen were seeking me in Brno and possibly elsewhere. Leah, the only person in the world who cared a jot for me, was living in Leipzig, a city renowned for its musicians. The composer of that magnificent unfinished work The Art of The Fugue, Johann Sebastian Bach, had lived there. I would search the city for the girl who had nursed me back to health. When I had found her I would love her for as long as we both lived.

179

I shivered in the darkness that night in my bed at the inn. Nevertheless, I felt content with my decision. Giving up the quest for my dubious past would enable me to become a new person living under a new name. I need no longer carry the heavy load of an earlier life with its heavy overtones of sadness. Bella had said that she believed that under extreme strain our minds can cause us to fly from painful recollections. If this was what had happened to me, I would become someone else and celebrate the achievement by composing my own masterly fugue.

As I drifted off to sleep, I remembered that famous poem by the English playwright, William Shakespeare: The Seven Ages of Man. In my dream state it seemed to convey a message that the person 'full of wise saws and modern instances' can scarcely remember himself as the 'infant mewling and puking in the nurse's arms.' As we grow older and develop new personalities, we fly from our earlier selves. It seemed a suitable theme for my new fugue.

This exciting idea for a musical composition offered some compensation for my recent tribulations. The following morning, I gave up the greater part of my savings in payment for a seat in a coach bound for Leipzig. The cadences of my new fugue, The Seven Ages of Man, sounded gloriously in my head as I boarded the coach.

THIRTY-ONE

One of my companions in the coach, a lean, spry fellow called Alfred Schneider, was carrying a violin. I guessed he was on his way to join an orchestra. He, in turn, noticed my flute. As our coach bumped along the rutted highways we got to know each other well. During our overnight stays in various inns and hostels, we delighted our fellow passengers and guests by playing duets. Sometimes we swapped instruments, Schneider proving as adept on the flute as I was on the violin. We improvised pieces of music and had enormous fun. Unfortunately, my tendency to act the buffoon led to a regrettable disagreement.

On our third overnight stay, I played the flute concerto dedicated to Shlotkin I had composed in Brno. Alfred wove a quiet, unobtrusive accompaniment on his violin in the background. Enormous applause followed. By this time I had drunk several steins of beer. When the applause died down, an impulse came over me to repeat the comic routine that had pleased audiences in Korlyshev. The effect was astounding. The crowd appreciated my bawdy humour even more than my flute-playing. Drinks appeared from all directions. A collection was organised by an attractive young lady, who gave me a slobbery kiss after handing me a bag of coins. By this time I was very drunk.

I hadn't noticed that Schneider had disappeared.

The following morning, when I boarded the coach, he was already sitting in his usual place in the corner. I said jocularly: 'We gave a great performance last night, did we not?'

There was no reply.

I tried to press on him half the money which the enthusiastic young lady had collected for me. He refused.

181

'Why not?' I demanded 'You contributed as much to the entertainment as I did.'

He shook his head and said in a low voice: 'No. And that is why I am in honour bound to refuse.'

'But you gave a very good performance.'

He shook his head again and stared mournfully out of the window.

It was midday before he confided to me his reason for not accepting his rightful share of the money. He said I played both the flute and the violin, his own instrument, with a prodigious talent that put his own playing to shame. He talked of giving up music.

I spent the next two days trying to restore his confidence. I told him of my experience of being found with no money and scarcely a decent garment to my name. When I described to him how I had been taken up, literally from the grave, and had been succoured by an old Jewish pedlar, his expression changed. He listened intently as I went on: 'You are a professional musician. You have played in well-respected orchestras. More important, you have shown that you can keep body and soul together by these means. You must continue to develop your talent and your career.'

I had earlier told Alfred the reason for my journey to Leipzig, mentioning that it might prove difficult to find Leah. Later that evening, when we arrived at our next stop, which happened to be Alfred's destination, he took me into a dark corner of the inn and whispered: 'There is something I must tell you. I am a Jew. I hide the fact, in order to be able to get a position in an orchestra.'

'Why are you telling me this?'

'To help in your search for the daughter of your benefactor. Your best plan is to enquire in a synagogue in Leipzig. She will have gone there to seek succour.'

'Alfred, that is sound advice. You are a good friend. I shall never forget our journey. I hope we'll play together some other time.'

*

I took Alfred's advice. Within two days of arriving in Leipzig, I had ascertained the address where Leah lived with her brother. I set out for her lodging house and discovered it in a crowded part of the city. I walked up three flights of rickety stairs, taking care not to touch the balustrades, which were covered with drying laundry. I knocked on the door and experienced three shocks in rapid succession as it opened.

The first came from the unearthly shriek that Leah gave when she saw me. The second was from noticing how pinched and haggard she had become. The third and greatest, was from the recognition of my own features in the face of a small boy sitting on the lap of a younger, clean-shaven, one-legged version of Reb Shmul Perlman.

Leah had stayed away from Korlyshev all these years to save her father the shame and humiliation of knowing that she had a child born out of wedlock. I hugged her and swore we would never part. We now live under a new name, one which I adopted having seen it inscribed over several shops and businesses in the area. I play my flute — and occasionally the fool! — in taverns and coaching houses. I hope soon to get my music published by one of the publishing houses that abound in this historic town.

Part two

THIRTY-TWO

Gwen Bateson had already started looking for premises for her new business, having convinced herself that the Mozart manuscripts were about to make her very rich. She had a passion for Art Nouveau furniture and harboured a dream in which she travelled the world in style, searching for the works of master craftsmen such as Henry Van der Velde and Louis Majorelle. She imagined dealers and collectors, in awe of her extensive knowledge and refined taste, flocking to buy the rare and exquisite pieces displayed in her West End showroom. She attributed Professor Beinmender's hesitation about authenticating the manuscripts to a natural caution and was convinced that secretly he was as excited about them as she was herself.

A dealer telephoned the showroom with an offer to buy a Victorian secretaire which Tom had bought some time before. She promised to ring back. As she searched through the stock records, it occurred to her to offer Beinmender a percentage share in the manuscripts as an inducement to him to speed up the task of gaining recognition. Aware that he had been a little drunk when he had made that ridiculous proposition, she told herself it must mean that he found her attractive. An affair with a good-looking man seemed an appropriate response to her belief that her husband was playing around.

Tom had volunteered to take the walnut secretaire off the hands of a golfing friend, unaware that it had been clumsily repaired — she guessed they had both been drinking in the golf club bar at the time. She decided to accept the dealer's offer, even though it meant accepting a small loss.

When Tom came in at midday he was in jubilant mood, having bought several pieces of furniture at a bargain price. She told him that Beinmender had come to dinner the previous night and mentioned his doubts about the authenticity of the documents she had found.

'I wouldn't waste any more time on them.'

'He showed me a translated portion of the journal. That alone could turn out to be of tremendous historic interest.'

'You'll be telling me next that Elvis Presley is still alive.'

'A lot of people believe he is.'

Tom guffawed and asked if she had sold anything that morning. Annoyed with herself for her foolish remark, she told him about the secretaire and castigated him for buying it.

'Everyone gets caught out once in a while.'

'There's no excuse for someone with your experience.'

'I bought it sight unseen. I wasn't to know he'd messed about with it.'

He gave a resigned shrug and asked: 'What does Carla think about Beinmender turning his thumbs down on your find?'

'He hasn't exactly done that. She doesn't know yet. She stayed overnight with Nathalie.'

'She spends far too much time away from home.'

'She can't practise in this flat. We should have stayed in our own house.'

'Blame the bank manager for that. Incidentally, you should have waited for me to get back before inviting Beinmender to dinner.'

'I was desperate to know whether the music sheets are valuable. We don't know anyone else with his kind of specialist knowledge.'

'And now he says it's a lemon.'

'Not exactly. He is of the opinion that the rest of the journal will produce valuable information.'

Tom looked tired — there were bags under his eyes. Gwen wondered if he had a mistress in Birmingham, where he went frequently on business.

She said sharply: 'I hate this shop. Half the time people come in just to get out of the rain. And they make such inane remarks.'

'So what would you do instead?'

'I should like to spend more time buying.'

'We'd be broke inside of a year.'

'I have a knack for spotting good pieces.'

'But you're absolutely hopeless when it comes to haggling. Would you like a cup of coffee?'

Typical of him to dodge the issue, she thought.

She replied resignedly: 'Okay. If you make it.'

As she was preparing an invoice for the secretaire, a young man came into the showroom, went to the piano stool and opened the lid. Finding it empty, he said: 'My father was in here recently and saw a package of music sheets inside. What happened to them?'

'They are being investigated by an expert,' Gwen responded brightly. 'The piano stool is quite a bargain. It was made in Leipzig, Germany, circa eighteen-hundred.'

The young man shook his head.

'My dad thought that the sheet music might be of interest. Never mind.'

After he had gone, Gwen felt elated. It renewed her confidence that the contents of the piano stool would turn out to be valuable.

Tom went out that evening to investigate some furniture advertised in a local newspaper. When Carla came home, Gwen told her about her dinner with Beinmender and laughingly mentioned the 'agreement' she had signed.

Carla's indignant response surprised her.

'How insulting! I hope you didn't sign it.'

'It was just a bit of fun,' Gwen added with a grin: 'At least it'll give him an incentive to get on with researching the manuscripts.'

'Was he very hopeful?'

'No. The opposite, if anything.'

'I always thought of Bernard Beinmender as the perfect English gentleman,'

'If there were such an animal, who would want him?' Gwen declared, airily.

THIRTY-THREE

Beinmender's father, a piano salesman from Saxony, had met and married Bernard's mother, a music teacher, when he came to England on business. He died in a car accident in Germany when his son was three months old. Bernard, who was musically gifted, tried hard to fulfil his mother's ambition for him to become a concert pianist. But after a disappointing performance in a competition, decided on an academic career. As a child during the post-war period, when there was still a great deal of anti-German sentiment, he had been subject to bullying because of his German name.

Carla's youthful, lissom beauty had made a deep impression when she first appeared in one of his classes at the Royal College of Music. He had asked her out for lunch and on one occasion had taken her to the English National Opera to see The Marriage of Figaro. But because of the difference in their ages he made no further overtures.

Carla was standing by the bust of Prince Albert in the entrance hall of the college the day after he had dined with her mother. As he walked towards her across the black and white chequered floor of the entrance hall, she tossed her head of gleaming black hair and said pugnaciously: 'Bugger off! How dare you make indecent proposals to my mother. Don't you have any respect for anybody!'

Utterly dismayed, he held up his hands and protested: 'It was a joke, for God's sake.'

'You certainly have a strange sense of humour.'

'Yes, it's always getting me into trouble. I apologise unreservedly. You can't for a moment think that I meant it.'

'It was a disgusting thing to do.'

'I shall apologise to her. Please don't let it spoil things between us. Come and have a drink. I'll explain exactly what happened.'

After a show of reluctance, Carla agreed to accompany him to the Glover's Arms, a pub some distance from the college where they had had lunch before. Carla was flattered by Beinmender's attention, thought him incredibly good-looking and admired his erudition. They ordered sandwiches and sat at a small table by a window overlooking the tiny pub garden. Beinmender fetched an orange juice for Carla and a lager for himself.

'That's a particularly daft-looking gnome,' he commented, pointing to a gloomy-looking, bearded statue in the middle of the circular lawn.

'Not daft enough to have made such a proposal to my mother.' Carla replied, pointedly

'It was an appalling blunder. Is she very upset?'

'You upset her even more by pouring cold water on her hopes for the manuscripts.'

'They may yet turn out to be genuine.'

'Really!'Carla was so excited that she spilled a copious amount of orange juice on her shirt.

Beinmender's eyes were irresistibly drawn towards her breasts as she dabbed furiously at her soaked shirt with a tissue. Filled with longing. He said: 'I don't want to raise your mother's hopes unduly. But two of the people I spoke to today think it is just possible that Mozart may have appeared in another guise for some obscure and as yet unexplained reason. That doesn't, of course, explain why the documents are dated subsequent to his death.'

'It would really make an enormous difference to my parents, if they turned out to be valuable,' Carla exclaimed. 'My sister and I are very expensive to keep — Gloria is doing business studies at Manchester university. We had to move from our house into a small flat last year. I have to go to a friend's house to practise.'

'How about coming to my place — we could try out the Wunder violin concerto. My neighbours are quite used to my

189

piano-playing. It might give us some sense of whether it is truly Mozart.'

'If it wasn't, I certainly wouldn't tell my mother. She is completely obsessed with the notion that she's going to make a huge sum of money.'

'She seemed quite philosophical about it last night.'

'How did she react when you made that disgusting proposal?'

'We both knew it was just a joke,' Beinmender said, uncomfortably. 'I had had too much to drink.'

'You wouldn't have said it if you didn't find her sexy.'

'What a ridiculous thing to say!'

'But it's true.'

'She is a lovely woman, I agree. But I had no intention of making a pass at her.'

'She once had ambitions to be an opera singer. She still has a very good voice.'

'Yes, she told me. She'd make a good Carmen.'

'How would you cast me?'

'Micaela, perhaps?'

'Micaela is a sexless, naive creature.'

'She is kind, honourable good and virtuous. That is how I see you.'

'Then you don't in the least understand me.'

'I must get to know you better.'

'Offering to make love to my mother was hardly the best way to go about it.'

Beinmender gave a deep sigh.

'It was a joke in extremely bad taste. Do we have to go all over it again?'

'Suppose the manuscripts turned out to be genuine and she insists on honouring her side of the bargain.'

'I promise, in that case, I shall renege on the deal.'

'And if it turns out to be legally enforceable?'

'I'd rather go to prison. Carla, darling, you'd make a damned good lawyer.'

'And you, Bernard. You are extremely good at wriggling out of awkward questions.'

'I would never do anything to upset you. I love you too much.'

'Liar! Flatterer!'

Secretly delighted with his declaration, Carla finished her glass of orange juice and then said thoughtfully: 'My mother wonders why you never married.'

'My shrink probably has the answer.'

'You saw a psychiatrist!'

'It's not so terrible — Americans do it all the time. Someone suggested that I should see a shrink when I was having difficulty playing the piano.'

'And what did he say?'

'He said it might have something to do with the fact that I used to be taunted at school about my German name. My father was German — he died three months after I was born. I have German relatives in Saxony whom I have never met. The other boys used to call me a Nazi. I have — or should I say *had* — another problem — I always felt I had let my mother down terribly by not becoming a professional pianist.'

'You played beautifully when I last heard you.'

'I am almost back to my former level of mediocrity.'

'When shall we play that piece together.'

'Saturday night?'

'I won't tell my mother.'

'Why not?'

'She might be jealous.'

She shot him a mischievous grin.

Beinmender replied, with an intensely grave expression: 'I hope she'll have good reason to be.'

'Now what do you mean by that?

'Exactly what I said.'

'You wouldn't try to seduce me.'

'No, but it would be very nice if it happened the other way around.'

THIRTY-FOUR

Gwen's instinct about her husband had been correct. Tom Bateson did have a mistress — in London — not as she had thought in Birmingham. Her name was Bess; she was the wife of an MP. When Tom told Bess about Gwen's find, she asked him if he would obtain for her a copy of Johann Wunder's journal. The editor of a magazine had promised her she would do a feature on the art gallery Bess owned in South Moulton Street, in return for a good story. The discovery of hitherto unknown Mozart manuscripts seemed to fit the bill exactly.

With the intention of meeting Bess's request, Tom said to Gwen, as they sat watching television in the living-room of their flat: 'A lady journalist I met recently was very intrigued when I told her about the manuscripts. Is it all right to let her see the excerpt from Johann Wunder's journal?'

'What newspaper does she work for?'

'She's a freelance. I met her at the golf club. She's married to the guy who enquired about a Jacobean dining-table recently. I thought, in any case, a bit of publicity might help to get things moving.'

'But you keep casting doubts on the whole thing ... I suppose we could photocopy it,' Gwen added doubtfully.'

'I'll do it after you've gone to bed.'

The photocopier and a computer were in Gloria's bedroom. Gloria grumbled about the presence of these two items of business equipment in her room, even though she was rarely at home.

Gwen didn't answer. She seemed absorbed in the television programme.

Tom said: 'Well, is that okay?'

Gwen said: 'On second thoughts, no.'

'Perhaps you'll have the grace to tell me why.'

'I don't think the time is right. Anyway, the publicity should be done in some coordinated way, not piecemeal. Otherwise, when the story does break it will lack any impact. I'm definitely against dealing with the press until we know exactly how we stand.'

'When will that be?'

'When we have proof that the manuscripts are genuine.'

'Okay,' Tom said resignedly. 'Have it your way.'

He picked up the Daily Telegraph.

'Aren't you coming to bed?'

'Not just yet. I think I'll finish the crossword puzzle.'

He flourished the newspaper.

Gwen stood up and went into the bathroom.

Tom thought about secretly photocopying the journal but decided it would be too risky. There was no point in starting another row that would contribute to the break-up of his marriage — Bess had already made it very clear that she would not divorce her husband.

He tried to concentrate on the crossword but found it impossible. He was intensely irritated by Gwen's assumption that she would make all decisions in connection with the manuscripts. He was also fuming because she had entertained Beinmender in his absence. Her complaints never ceased these days. If he let her participate in the buying, they would have to employ an assistant, which would eat into their already sorely-stretched profit margins.

193

The drastic decline in their business fortunes and their subsequent move from the family house had been painful for the whole family. Because of complaints from the neighbours, he rarely had the opportunity these days of hearing Carla play the violin, one of the few compensations for keeping her at college. Nor could he afford any longer to keep for his own home some of the prize items of furniture he came across.

Bess and Tom had come to an arrangement under which Bess placed an advertisement in Tom's local newsagent which ran: "Cleaning lady has one free day available on…" The day specified was the day on which he was to telephone her. The ad hadn't appeared recently. Tom resented the increasingly long intervals between their love-making.

. Her request to see Beinmender's translation persuaded him that it was possible his wife had made a major find. He firmly believed that women had more intuition in these matters than men. It was Bess who had once recognised from his description of an obscure painting that it was valuable. When he told her about Gwen's purchase of the piano stool and its contents, she had suggested that he should reimburse Gwen for the credit card transaction at the auction, to ensure that in the event of any dispute he would have equal claim to ownership.

Carla had already left the house when, the following morning, he and Gwen sat down at the breakfast bar in their small kitchen.

'You slept badly,' he commented.

'So did you.'

'This Mozart thing is getting out of hand.'

'In what way?'

'All this fuss because I wanted to show the Wunder journal to someone. It's not exactly the Koh-I-Noor diamond.'

'It could turn out to be worth as much. Do you realise that universities from all over the world will be bidding for it.'

'If it's genuine — which I very much doubt. However, I'll give you a cheque today for what you laid out at the auction.'

'There's no hurry. The bill hasn't come in yet.'

'I'll pay you, anyway.'

'What's the point. It will only increase your business overdraft.'

'A few pounds this way or that won't make any difference.'

'Are you worried because I bought the manuscripts with my own money?'

'We're a married couple. What's mine is yours and vice versa.'

Gwen gave a slightly hysterical laugh, cracked her egg with a spoon and said: 'That makes a nice change from your usual attitude.'

After a pause, she continued: 'Why have you never made me a director of the Company?'

'What difference would it make? We share everything.'

'If that were really so, you would give me the opportunity to go out "treasure-hunting," as you call it, instead of shutting me up in the shop all day.'

'You didn't used to complain. Bringing up a family didn't allow you to gain the experience I have acquired. I'll be quite happy to share my knowledge with you. But you must admit that you have no talent at all for haggling. That's at least as important as the ability to recognise a good piece. How are we going to deal with that problem?'

'Don't bother,' Gwen said curtly. 'We'll come to an agreement. You keep the business and I'll hang onto the manuscripts.'

'And if they turn out to be worthless?'

'They won't.'

Tom got up from the table and said: 'You'd better open up the shop in time. I have to have a look at a bureau in Richmond. The guy said it was a large double-busted piece. Sounds a bit like Dolly Parton.'

Gwen, not deigning to answer, gave him a stony stare.

THIRTY-FIVE

einmender watched anxiously from the window of his mansion-block flat in St John's Wood. He was worried in case Carla had changed her mind about coming. Seeing a taxi draw up, he whistled with relief and hastened downstairs to greet her. He paid the driver and carried the violin-case upstairs to his flat. Carla followed him, glanced at the white walls and stylish modern Italian furniture in the living-room and commented cheerfully: 'Nice pad. I like your taste.' Privately, she thought that the black Blüthner baby-grand in one corner of the room ruined the general effect.

'I paid an interior designer,' Beinmender declared, 'I'm hopeless at that sort of thing.'

Noticing a painting by Klimt over the fireplace, Carla whispered in awe: 'Is it an original?'

'My mother bought it when his works were quite reasonably priced.'

'Whenever we get something nice at home, my father sells it.'

'He has to make a living.'

'I suppose so. But it annoys me — I grow to like a piece of furniture and   before I know what's happened it has disappeared. All he's concerned with is making money.'

'Just as well for you,' Beinmender said with a   smile. 'Here, come and look at this.' He beckoned her towards a portrait of Mozart by Barbara Kraft on the wall by the side of the piano. 'It's a reproduction, of course.'

Carla staring at the portrait, remarked: 'He looks quite severe, doesn't he.'

'He was probably trying to impress his boss, Hieronymus von Colloredo,. Here, let me take your coat.'

Carla handed him the duffel coat she had borrowed from her sister. Underneath, she was wearing a short black dress. When he returned from putting her coat in the hall cupboard, she had seated herself at the piano and was idly running her hands along the keys. Beinmender glanced appreciatively at her shapely legs and enquired: 'When did you decide to take up the violin?'

'My mother took me to a concert. David Oistrakh was playing the Max Bruch concerto. I was ten at the time. I didn't stop talking about it until Daddy bought me a violin and arranged for me to have lessons.'

'I'm glad he did. You played beautifully the last time I heard you. Do you want to start?' Beinmender glanced at the violin, still in its case, near the piano.

'May I see the rest of the flat first?'

'Sure. C'mon.'

He showed her a kitchen that had been modernised to a high standard and a book-lined study. A small bust of Beethoven stood on the desk. Carla picked it up idly and examined it

As she replaced the bust on the leather-topped desk, he said, straight-faced: 'Music has moved on since his day. I'm turning radar transmissions from Air Traffic Control into music.'

'What will it sound like?'

'The bat population will highly appreciate it. I'm only joking. Come on.'

He showed her a bedroom and then led her into his own. It was decorated in sombre brown. A black and white chequer-board duvet covered the bed. A music keyboard and a desktop computer stood on a table on the far side of the double bed.

Carla enquired: 'Why do you have your computer in your bedroom?'

'When I can't sleep I play on the keyboard. It can reproduce a full orchestra. I can even turn out a garbled opera. It's quite good fun. Do you want to hear an example?'

He went over to the computer and switched it on. When he turned round she was standing naked on the bed, with a small pile of clothing at her feet. Taken aback, he mumbled: 'Carla, my darling, you're so incredibly beautiful.' He fervently kissed her breasts, switched off the sound and made haste to cast off his own clothes.

*

'That was by far and away the nicest surprise I've ever had in my life,' he exclaimed afterwards, enthusiastically.

'Was I a good fuck?'

'Superb.'

'I saw the aurora borealis in technicolour.'

'Liar.'

'No, really.'

'I invited you here to make music not to make love.'

'We've just made music. Composers can only hint at the pleasure love-making gives.'

'Mozart came very close, don't you think?'

'Yes, he was a sexy man.'

'I want you all to myself from now on. I truly love you, Carla, my darling. I intend to marry you some day.'

Carla propped herself up on one elbow and said flatly: 'Marriage is a disgusting institution.'

'Are you saying that because I'm too old?'

'No, it's just what I believe.'

'Wouldn't you like to have children some day?'

'You don't have to marry to have children. Anyway, there are all kinds of things I want to do before then.'

'What do you want to do?'

'I shall travel all over the world and have lots of foreign lovers.'

'I can make love in several different languages.'

'Okay. Make love to me in German.'

'*Ich leibe dich.*'

'I mean *doing* it. I bet you don't know how. Let's pretend we're a couple of raunchy dachshunds.'

She crawled over him, biting his chest and shoulders and growling. He roared with laughter, until she suddenly stopped growling and they made love again.

*

Wrapped in a white towelling robe, matching the one Bernard was wearing, Carla sat at the kitchen table and waited for him to serve dinner. He placed a salmon paté before her. Afterwards, he served lasagne with a mixed salad, accompanied by a nineteen-eighty-one Chablis. This was followed by Neapolitan ice-cream and cherries. They drank coffee, after which he led her into the living-room and with a flourish placed photocopies of the two-hundred-year old violin concerto on a music-stand.

She exclaimed: 'To think that my mother owns Mozart manuscripts! It's incredible.'

'What about your father?'

'My mother says they're hers because she paid for them with her own money. They're always arguing. Which is one reason why I shall never marry.'

Beinmender sat at the piano and after playing some introductory bars, suggested that they should play the first movement.

Carla made some adjustments and announced that she was ready, Beinmender said: 'Okay, I'll be the orchestra. Let's go.'

Humming to aid his concentration, he softly played the introduction and then lifted his hand as a signal to start. Soon they were both engrossed in playing music of unearthly beauty, which, it seemed to both of them, only Mozart could have

199

composed. When they had finished, they looked at one another in awe.

Beinmender then murmured: 'Is it a brilliant pastiche? No, it couldn't be — it is genuine Mozart.'

'It couldn't be by anyone else.' Carla declared, emphatically.

'You played very well,' Beinmender commented.

'So did you.'

'I was already familiar with the score. I am convinced now that Mozart wrote it.'

'But how can one possibly be absolutely sure?'

'Every facet of his personality seems to issue from the music.'

'What were you thinking of while you were playing?'

'Do you really want to know?'

'Yes.'

'I was thinking of Mozart smiling, as he gently mocked my efforts to engage the affections of a very young, beautiful and highly spirited girl.'

Carla replied, smiling. 'That's not exactly how I saw it.'

'What did it sound like to you?'

'Idyllic lovemaking under the trees by a river on a beautiful summer's day.'

'Which just goes to show that we all interpret music in different ways. Incidentally, Peter Schafer in his play Amadeus hinted that a rival composer, Salieri, poisoned Mozart out of jealousy. Carl Barr's investigation showed that it is much more likely that he died of typhus, probably aggravated by a heart condition. But, of course, he may not have died on the day history has recorded. The journal — and indeed the music we have just played — calls that into question.'

Carla said: 'No wonder my mother thinks she has won the National Lottery.'

'I rather dampened her hopes when we were having dinner together. But I'm more than ever inclined now to believe that this is the real stuff.'

'Do you really think so!'

'Yes, it's undoubtedly Mozart pure and unalloyed.'

'And the opera?'

'The music is exciting but the libretto is a bit naff. The fugue, *Seiben*, is an extraordinarily complex piece. Could you come next Saturday and we'll play some excerpts from the opera?'

Carla nodded and then suddenly shivered.

'Are you cold?' Beinmender enquired.'

'A bit.'

'Something has gone wrong with the heating. Let's go back to bed.'

Huddled under the chequered duvet, Carla asked curiously: 'When did you decide to give up playing the piano professionally?'

'After I had performed dreadfully in a competition. I was twenty-one.'

'Everybody is entitled to an occasional bad performance.'

'I knew I'd never make it.'

'I think you play brilliantly.'

I missed the boat and that's it. Perhaps I should have played Mozart instead of Rach. Anyway, it's too late now. Mozart was a real firecracker, wasn't he. To me he is still alive, throwing off sparks that give comfort and pleasure to millions of people all over the world.'

'Perhaps what we have just played was written by his reincarnation.'

'Wunder could not be Mozart reincarnated. They were about the same age.'

'Whoever wrote it must have been possessed by Mozart's spirit.'

'Funny you should say that, because at one point in the journal Wunder considers the possibility that he has been taken over by a mischievous imp. Another time, he wonders if his music-making was acquired in the same way as animals pass on their capacity for performing complex actions such as nest-building and so on. Reincarnation, of course, is such an appealing notion that we all give it credence at some time during our lives. But I think it's sheer hocus pocus. Anyway, for what it's worth, I am slowly coming round to the view that the journal is genuine and that the date of Mozart's death was incorrectly recorded.'

He tried to caress her again. Carla drew away and said: 'Hang on a minute! Perhaps Mozart and this other guy who wrote the journal were two different people but shared the same genes. That would explain the similarity in the music.'

'The odds against two individuals having identical genes, would be billions to one. Even if they were identical twins, their music would not necessarily sound the same. Incidentally, you have great musical talent.'

'Thank you, kind professor. Please cease from what you are doing. We are engaged in a serious discussion. Oh, what was I going to say? Yes — you said that you can't believe Mozart is really dead because he keeps throwing off brilliant sparks into the future. Perhaps one of those immortal sparks entered Johann Wunder, turning him into Mozart, which enabled him to produce that brilliant music we have just played.'

'That's just the "possession" theory put in a different way.'

'Okay, well I do believe people send out vibes into the future. Johann Wunder may have picked bits of Mozart out of the air.'

'Doesn't sound at all plausible. You're very obstinate, aren't you.'

'The theory appeals to me because I sometimes feel that I'm just a radio that other people are tuning in to.'

'Perhaps you lack a strong sense of self.'

'Not really. But music can have strange effects. Perhaps Mozart was turned into a kind of radio transmitter. From what I have read he didn't have a proper childhood — his father, Leopold, drummed music into him and his sister, Nannerl, from the moment they were born.'

'What you have just said about him being a radio transmitter isn't scientifically possible. But there are so many fascinating facets to his character that it is impossible for any one person to appreciate all of them. Perhaps the solution to our problem is simply to accept his sheer brilliance exploding across Time, turning him into Johann Wunder.'

Carla, suddenly losing interest in the argument, ran her fingers lightly through the tangle of hairs on his chest.

Beinmender kissed her and said earnestly: 'I want you all for myself. And you want lots of lovers. I'll solve the problem by making love to you in so many ways that it will seem your wish has been granted.'

Carla exclaimed with an air of perfervid excitement, 'Okay, go ahead. Be an Italian racing driver!'

'I'll try in a moment.'

'Not in a moment — NOW!'

Beinmender protested: 'Hang on a minute. Even an Italian racing driver is allowed a pit stop!'

THIRTY-SIX

Carla was appalled to see a yellow sticky label on the college notice-board, which read: 'Professor Beinmender and Carla Bateson are having an affair.' She tore it down and thrust it into her trouser pocket. She telephoned Beinmender at his home that evening, to tell him about it.

'Who do you think is responsible?' he asked.

'Someone with a grudge. Probably someone who thinks he was marked unfairly in an exam.'

'A girl called Ailsa MacDonald complained the other day. But I don't think it's of the slightest importance.'

'It is to me. Will you see me in the Glovers' Arms tomorrow lunch time?'

He was there when she arrived. After kissing her, he enquired anxiously: 'Do you want to stop seeing me?'

'No, of course not. I just thought I ought to let you know.'

'Had you told anyone that we have been seeing each other?'

'No.'

He said gloomily: 'I'm too old for you.'

'I don't mind. Really.'

'Did you enjoy yourself on Saturday?'

'It was wonderful.'

'Which did you like best — playing Mozart, or making love?'

'They were both beautiful,' Carla declared, fervently.

When they had found a vacant table, he murmured thoughtfully: 'We could stop all this nonsense very simply.'

'How?'

'By getting married.'

Carla blew her nose and said: 'Damn this hay fever'. She continued in a slightly nasal tone, 'I may want to marry you some day. But not for a long time.'

'How about an open marriage?'

'Why bother!'

'Of course. You're quite right. I wasn't serious.'

They sat in silence for a while. Carla noticed a gray streak in his hair but he didn't seem old; occasionally he seemed like a naughty schoolboy. She was concerned, however, because he had consulted a psychiatrist, which hinted that there might be a darker side to his nature.

She said, 'You're not drinking your Guinness. We won't worry about that stupid business. I'll tell everyone that I have been busy consulting you about the manuscripts my mother found. That will quash any rumours.'

He drank some Guinness, then putting the glass down, said firmly: 'I don't believe there are any. It was just somebody being stupid. Will you come on Saturday?'

'Yes.

'We'll take a look at the opera, Cypriana, this time. It has some very intriguing features.'

'Such as?'

'Polyandry. All very sexy stuff.'

'Is it likely that Mozart would have written about it all those years ago?'

'Fornication, as someone once said, is a constant. He and his librettist da Ponte obviously had great fun writing *Die Entfhring aus dem Serail.* about a woman abducted from a harem... Nowadays, of course, it's men who are in danger of being abducted!'

She shot him a scornful look, from which he pretended to recoil in fear. He then took her hand and placing it to his lips, kissed each finger with grave and loving deliberation.

THIRTY-SEVEN

Tom Bateson wandered into Bess's art gallery and glanced around. There was no-one in sight. Leaning forward with his hands behind his back, he pretended to examine a stylised rendering of a square-rigged sailing ship.

Bess came from behind a pillar at the back of the gallery and asked, stony-faced: 'Does it appeal to you, sir?'

He replied with a cheeky grin: 'I'll buy it when my ship comes in.'

'No chance of that, if you don't assert your rights to the Mozart manuscripts?'

'Gwen insists they're hers.'

'You are an absolute fool, Tom Bateson. You're about to throw away the most exciting thing that ever happened to you.'

'Oh, come off it, Bess. How was I to know she would behave like this. I just don't know what's got into her.'

'Someone else, perhaps,' Bess remarked, acidly.

'For God's sake. Gwen isn't like that.'

'How about this man Beinmender?'

'He's our only contact in the music world. There's nothing going on between them.'

'Well, you have been warned.' She stared at him coldly for a moment and then said: 'Why didn't you get me a copy of the journal?'

'My wife wants to keep it under wraps.'

'You're very inconsiderate. You don't care in the least about my wishes.'

'I did try. But she has hidden it away somewhere.'

'You had better leave now. I am expecting my husband at any moment.'

'I called in because I was doing a little business in the West End. Why haven't I heard from you lately?'

He followed her gaze towards the street and noticed a very tall, hooknosed man with a sallow complexion about to enter the gallery He muttered: 'Goodbye,' and made a hasty exit.

After collecting his van from a car park at the rear of Oxford Street, he drove to his next appointment in Stoke D'Abernon, thinking that the affair was probably over and that maybe it was just as well. The sex had been good but he didn't really like her — it was nasty of her to suggest that there was something going on between Gwen and Beinmender. There was nothing to worry about there, although Gwen was certainly behaving in a very perverse manner.

Through the car windscreen, which suddenly became obscured by a downfall of rain, he saw a pedestrian scurrying across the road. The blurred image reminded him of some of the distorted images in Bess's gallery and it occurred to him that it was possible that his own perception of Gwen had become distorted. Perhaps her grievances were genuine. He would tell her that she could go out and about and do some buying.

Thinking about the extract from the Johann Wunder diary he had read, he wondered idly what birth-control method they had used in those far off days. Taking contraceptive precautions must have been very expensive. Not as expensive as having a baby, though. A lot of infants used to die — Queen Anne had how many babies? Seventeen — something like that — most of whom had died in infancy.

He made up his mind to take steps to repair his marriage. Bess had just been a temporary diversion. Good fun, though, while it lasted.

In Stoke D'Abernon he bought an armoire that needed a repair. He would do the job himself. He enjoyed working in the evenings in a back room of the shop. Repairing a piece of furniture, he reflected on his way home, was less risky than extra marital sex.

He stopped outside a florist's and bought carnations and roses. When he entered the kitchen, Gwen accepted the bouquet, kissed him on the cheek and said: 'What's come over you?'

'Just to show I love you.'

'I'm not changing my mind about the music sheets they're mine.'

'Okay. Don't let a few dreary old sheets of music come between us, darling.'

'I won't. Just as long as you don't think you can sweet-talk me into parting with them.'

'Forget it. Have you heard from Gloria?'

'She's coming home next weekend. You had better take the computer and the photocopier out of the bedroom.'

Tom grimaced irritably. There was no room for them in the flat, nor in the shop where he would shortly be working on the armoire. He abruptly changed the subject.

'Will Carla be home for dinner?'

'Yes. She discussed the latest developments with Bernard today. He has been in E-mail correspondence with people all over the world about the manuscripts. They're generating tremendous interest.'

'You still have the receipt he gave you.'

'Of course. Do you think I'm daft.'

'Perhaps you should ask the bank to keep it.'

'I have put it away somewhere safe.'

He left to hang his wet raincoat in the hall cupboard. When he returned to the kitchen, he said: 'I was thinking today about the guy who wrote the journal. Once he recovered from his illness, he acted like a right Don Juan, bonking women left, right and centre.'

'He was a single man.'

'He was already married.'

'He didn't *know* he was married. He had lost his memory. Anyway, what excuse do you have?

'What are you're talking about?'

'Who's Bess?'

'I don't know anyone called Bess.'

'Yes you do. She's the lady you sold that picture to a few years ago.'

'Oh, yes. I'd forgotten.'

'You've been seeing her.'

'What makes you say that?'

'She rang the shop recently and asked for you when you were away.'

'She probably thought I could supply another painting.'

'She has a gallery in South Moulton Street. I dialled the BT number to see who had been calling.'

'So what does that prove?'

'It proves you can't fool me any more. I rang our work room on two occasions in the evening when you were supposed to be there and I got no reply.'

'I had probably slipped over the road to the pub.'

'No, that's not like you. There have been lots of other signs that you were having an affair. A bunch of flowers isn't going to put it right.'

'Oh, come off it, Gwen. You know I love you.'

'You only say that so that you can lay claim to the manuscripts. To hell with it. It's all over between us.

THIRTY-EIGHT

Gwen telephoned Beinmender the following evening.
'Hello, Bernard. It's Gwen Bateson. Would you mind if I came over to see the music sheets. I just want to reassure myself that they really exist.'

'By all means. I told Carla today there's more encouraging news about them.'

'I'll be with you in half an hour.'

Beinmender decided not to tell Gwen about his relationship with her daughter. When to tell her parents about him was something for Carla to decide. It seemed natural that her mother should wish to take another look at the manuscripts. He took them from the cupboard in his study, laid them out on a table in the living-room and covered them with a protective cloth.

He put on a fresh sweater and tidied the flat.

Gwen said as he opened the front-door: 'Hi, Bernard. It was nice of you to see me at such short notice.'

'My pleasure. Let me take your raincoat.'

She was wearing a smart, green, short, button-through dress and he noted that, like her daughter, she had good legs.

A fragrant perfume filled the air, as he led her into the living-room. Pointing to the manuscripts, he said: 'I hope you've got them insured for a substantial sum of money. I have arranged temporary cover while they are in my apartment.'

She smiled and said: 'You really think that's necessary?'

'Of course.'

She lifted the white cloth covering the manuscripts and enquired: 'Have you circulated your translation of the journal to the other interested parties?'

'No. The universities to whom I sent copies are using their own translators. Don't be surprised if some differences emerge.'

'May I see them when they send them back to you?'

'Odd though it may sound, I'm not sure if I am allowed to show them to anybody. The agreements I signed are exclusively between the agent — that's me — and the university departments concerned. But don't worry — I'm sure they will come to the conclusion that the author was Mozart.'

'Are they taking it very seriously?'

'Extremely. The documents are generating a great deal of excitement in musical circles all over the world. The reason I expressed such strong reservations initially was that I didn't want you to be disappointed if things went badly. But letters, telephone calls and E-mail are flooding in from all kinds of interested parties. I had a telephone call from China a couple of days ago.'

'That's wonderful.'

'Have you briefed a lawyer to look after your interests.'

'No. It didn't seem necessary.' Suddenly looking forlorn, Gwen added: 'There's something I have to tell you.'

He wondered for a moment if Gwen had found out about his relationship with Carla.

'What is it?'

'My husband and I are going to divorce.'

'I'm very sorry to hear it. Do sit down. You look as though you could do with a drink.'

Gwen shook her head. He persuaded her to accept a glass of white wine.

When she was seated in an armchair, he enquired: 'Is there anything I can do to help?'

Gwen shook her head.

When did it happen?'

'Yesterday. Certain things that I had noticed all came together and I realised he had another woman.'

'Does Carla know?' he enquired.

'Not yet. She wasn't in when I left the house. Tom, no doubt, will tell her.'

Beinmender went back to the drinks cabinet, poured himself out a glass of wine and enquired solemnly: 'Is there any hope of a reconciliation?'

Gwen shook her head and drank all the wine.

He refilled her glass, sat opposite on a settee and said: 'It does seem a shame, especially now there's a prospect of your becoming quite well-to-do.'

'I have been unhappy for a long time.'

'It will be hard on your girls.'

'I'll use the money from the manuscripts to help them with their careers.'

'Should I keep Tom informed about what's happening?'

Gwen exclaimed fiercely: 'No! The manuscripts are nothing to do with him. I paid for them with my own money.'

Bernard remained judiciously silent, wondering how this latest development might affect his relationship with Carla.

He said: 'If and when a general consensus is reached that Johann Wunder was indeed Mozart, the auction houses will be clamouring for your custom. You should start thinking about how to handle them.'

'Should I sell the journal separately from the music?'

'That is a matter for the auctioneers. They may want to publish it in advance of the sale of the music to generate interest.'

'How will all this affect Mozart's reputation?'

'If the journal is accepted as genuine, it's bound to lead to a major reassessment. Nothing more dramatic could ever have happened. There will be many new books written about him as well as television programmes and so on.'

Gwen requested another drink.

As he filled her glass, she said musingly : 'Do you think Mozart's wife would have forgiven him his infidelities?'

'We don't know for sure whether he was ever unfaithful — I am referring to his first incarnation so to speak. His name is associated with several opera singers. But the relationships might have been innocent — nobody is immune from gossip. It was said that Constanze, his wife, was something of a flirt herself.'

'I'm not going to forgive Tom.'

Beinmender shrugged.

Gwen went on: 'There might have been some excuse for Mozart. He was separated from his wife for months at a time. All that creative tension needed an outlet.'

Beinmender agreed: 'You're right. He probably had more than his fair share of temptation.'

'You're in no position to criticise him after giving me that naughty paper to sign,' Gwen said, smiling.

'You will be delighted to know that I freely and of my own good will absolve you from your side of the agreement.'

'Don't you find me attractive?'

'Of course. Very attractive. You're a beautiful woman. Tom's an absolute fool.'

'Prove it — prove that you find me attractive.'

Gwen swayed seductively towards Beinmender, put her arms around him and whispered: 'Having signed the paper, I intend as an honourable woman to keep my word.'

She lifted her head and tried to kiss him.

Beinmender placed his hands on her shoulders and said pleadingly: 'Gwen, I said I have renounced the agreement. It was only meant as a joke. Look!'

He pulled out his wallet and showed her the crumpled piece of paper on which he had added to the original writing the words: 'If Mozart is Johann Wunder, I'm Paderewski.'

'Who the hell is Paderewski?'

'It doesn't really matter — he was a pianist who became Prime Minister of Poland. Look, I'm terribly sorry. There's

something I have got to tell you before we do anything silly —
I'm in love with your daughter.'

Gwen said with an incredulous expression: 'You're an utter
bastard, Bernard Beinmender. She's half your age. It is
absolutely disgusting. I shall have you removed from your
teaching post.'

'Be reasonable, Gwen. I love Carla. I want to marry her.'

She pushed past him in a fury, snatched her raincoat from the
hall cupboard and rushed out of the flat.

THIRTY-NINE

The sound of impassioned piano-playing usually greeted Beinmender's cleaning lady when she arrived at his flat on a Saturday morning — Beinmender invariably practised before going to the local supermarket to stock up with food for the week. This morning, however, as she mounted the stairs, all was silent. He opened the front door when she rang and said in a melancholy voice: 'Come in, Mrs Dee-Bee.'

Mrs Dexter-Brown, a thin, scrawny lady of sixty with a beaky nose, said as she entered the flat, 'You're looking under the weather this morning, Mr Beinmender. All that business with Mozart must be giving you problems.'

'Not really. It's attracting a great deal of interest.'

'I bet the people who found the manuscripts are pleased to hear that. Mind you, having too much money can be a burden. Are they paying you for your trouble, Mr Beinmender?'

'I'm doing it out of friendship.'

'I'd insist on a share, if I were you. You are a musical professor after all.'

'The fact is, Mrs Dee-Bee, I have fallen for one of the daughters of the family.'

He told her about Gwen's visit.

Flattered at being taken into his confidence, Mrs Dexter-Brown declared: 'You behaved very properly in the circumstances, Mr Beinmender, if I may say so. If you had acted otherwise, you might have caused a permanent rift between mother and daughter.'

'Whatever chance I stood with Carla will probably vanish when she finds out what happened last night. Not that she takes me at all seriously.'

'None of the youngsters take anything seriously these days. The new generation just believe in living for the day and being kind to one another.'

'Carla isn't all that kind to me.'

'Perhaps because you used to be her teacher.'

'You're probably right. I'm going out to do some shopping. She's coming for dinner this evening.'

'Give her a good talking to, Mr Beinmender, She won't find another gentleman as nice as you.'

The hum of the vacuum cleaner from the living-room ceased soon after he returned from his shopping expedition. Mrs Dexter-Brown followed him into the kitchen. As he placed food into the refrigerator, she announced: 'I've thought over your little problem, Mr. Beinmender, and I think I have found an answer. You just tell Carla's mother that if she tries to stop her daughter going out with you, you'll stop working on those manuscripts. And tell her that you're entitled to something for your trouble.'

Beinmender went on stocking the fridge.

He answered politely: 'You may be right. Thanks for your advice.'

He went into his bedroom to avoid further discussion and switched on the computer. He had prepared a synopsis of the Cypriana libretto, which he intended to show Carla when she came that evening.

*

It was obvious to Beinmender from Carla's cheerful demeanour when she arrived that her mother had said nothing about the previous night's embarrassing incident. Feeling relieved, he showed Carla the synopsis of Wunder's opera buffa. She sprawled out on a settee and began reading.

Cypriana: An Opera in Four Acts

Act One opens with Alexander, the mayor of the town of Karium, declaring to Irene, his wife, that he has to go on an important mission to the capital city, Kurdos, to seek relief from the burdensome taxes demanded by the King of Cyprus. She recalls that the King had once tried to seduce her and assures Alexander that her virtue matters more to her than life itself.

Alexander sets out for Kurdos with his manservant, Gotches. They stop by a large boundary stone hallowed by the goddess Mnemosyne, who emerges from behind it and announces that she has quarrelled with her lover. As an act of revenge, she has decreed that any mortal who sleeps in its shadow for more than one hour will lose his memory. Alexander, overcome by tiredness, falls asleep. When he wakes up he tells Gotches that his mind has become a blank. But he dreamed while he was asleep that he would fall in love with a young woman of surpassing beauty. As they walk towards Kurdos, Alexander and Gotches enumerate the different qualities their womenfolk should possess. A beautiful maiden, Rosanna, appears in the distance and beckons him. I think she has all the necessary qualities plus a few more, breathes Alexander as he hastens towards her.

Act Two

Rosanna is watering flowers as Alexander confesses his love for her. He says he came from a town where life is very dull and everyone is over-taxed. Asked about his marital state, he swears that he is single.

Rosanna's maid servant, Limonda, questions Gotches about his master. He declares that everything his master says is true. Suspecting Alexander of deceit, she asks if he is willing to drink a potion that will force him to tell the truth. Gotches persuades Alexander to submit but drinks the magic potion himself and gives Alexander a harmless substitute.

After Alexander again declares that he is unmarried, Gotches is questioned. Confused by the potion he has drunk, Gotches swears that his master never tells a lie except, he adds, when the Gods tell him he is telling the truth. How can we find out what the Gods are telling him, Limonda enquires. To ascertain that you must sleep for more than an hour in the shadow of the boundary stone, Gotches cunningly tells her.

Act Three

The King hears Alexander's appeal for a reduction of taxes and is surprised when Alexander says he can't remember the name of his home town. How, he asks, in that case, can he remember the amount of tax that is due. Alexander replies. Get rid of all taxes and the shock will enable me to remember the name. If my people don't experience the pain of paying taxes, they certainly won't remember me, says the King. They will always remember with kindness someone who lightens the burden of taxes, Alexander assures him.

The King then says he had once been rebuffed by a beautiful woman called Irene. She will assuredly repent her unkindness, Alexander tells him, if you woo her with lower taxes.

Alexander then promises to be eternally faithful to Rosanna. Not sure whether to believe him, she sends Limonda on an errand to sleep behind the boundary stone. She tells him that if Limonda comes back with the right message she will believe him. However, when she returns Rosanna has lost her memory and can neither remember what the Gods have told her, or even who she is. Rosanna gives Alexander the benefit of the doubt. They sing a duet called "Memory is both a Blessing and a Curse" and then fall into an embrace.

Act Four

218

Disguised as a horse salesman, the King goes to visit Irene. He catalogues all the cunning tricks that horse salesmen employ but assures Irene that he only cheats in order to make enough money to pay the King's taxes. They sing a duet about making sacrifices for the common good. She accompanies him to the boundary stone. He tells her to rest. After singing an aria in praise of virtue, she yawns. The King leads her behind the boundary stone. When they reappear the King promises to reduce all taxes in his kingdom because she has so generously sacrificed her virtue to the common good. Unable to remember who she is, Irene follows the King to Kurdos.

Gotches is trying to persuade Limonda to submit to his embraces. He sings an aria, which declares that the poor need more love than the rich because they suffer greater hardship. Limonda tells Gotches that to win her love he must find her a fruit that everyone in the world can enjoy. They dance round a tree singing a duet extolling the apple of love, "whose roundness reflects the world." Alexander appears and plucks an apple off the tree. When Irene appears they fail to recognise one another but he praises her beauty.

They share the apple.

The curtain falls briefly. When it opens again the whole cast are asleep in the shade of the boundary stone.

Irene wakes up and declares to Alexander that she cannot remember what happened the previous night. But she is most pleased to see him safe home after his journey.

Alexander boasts to Irene of his successful tax-reducing mission

The King promises to make Rosanna his queen and they sing a duet about their joyful reunion.

Limonda and Gotches sing an aria praising the apple which, by tempting Eve has brought more children into the world than all the other fruits put together.

The Goddess Mnemosyne comes forward and announces that she and her lover are united once again. She tells the audience that to show her gratitude, she will become the true guardian of morality and make sure that in future every person will remember his or her past.. She urges the audience to go home, sleep the sleep of the just and forget the scandalous events they have seen unfold on the island of Cypriana

*

'So what do you think?' Bernard enquired, when Carla had finished reading.

'This business of them all losing their memories seems a lot to swallow.'

'Anything can happen in opera. Try to imagine the setting — a sub-tropical paradise and the lovely music. The music is marvellous. But you must remember that Mozart wasn't a professional librettist.'

'There's a great deal of sleeping around.'

'The magic boundary-stone is a dramatic device that allows both hero and heroine to stray while being viewed sympathetically by the audience. You must see it in its eighteenth-century context. Mozart — or was it Wunder? — needed to draw in the crowd but he also needed to avoid antagonizing those in authority. He comes out in the end on the side of virtue, with the Goddess of Memory making a parting injunction to the audience to be good. Incidentally, do you remember last week we discussed how different aspects of Mozart's personality showed in his work. This opera is a good example of his diversity.'

'Does it help in any way to settle the question of whether Wunder was Mozart?'

'The music is utterly and completely Mozartian.'

'Perhaps Johann Wunder alias Mozart invented a libretto to justify his own extra marital affairs. That would make him a terrible humbug,'

'That's a bit much coming from someone who says she wants lots of lovers. I see it as just an amusing entertainment that exposes ordinary people and their weaknesses.'

'Have you had lots of affairs?'

'A few.'

'I intend to catch up with you before I settle down.'

'Then hurry up, because I want you all to myself.'

Carla fanned herself with the synopsis, put it down on the coffee table and said challengingly, 'Do you honestly believe in marriage?'

'It works for a lot of people.'

'Not for my parents. They're getting divorced.'

'Why should that bother you, if you don't believe in marriage?'

'I had always thought they were blissfully happy. I'm sad because I was mistaken.'

'They had many good years together. Anyway, it may all blow over.'

'Not if the manuscripts turn out to be valuable. My mother is determined to start up in her own business.'

'Carla, my dearest girl, let's get married. I promise always to put your career ahead of mine. I'll be very happy to act as your manager.'

Carla frowned heavily and said: 'That's a load of shit!'

'Why?' Beinmender said, looking hurt.

'Firstly because I don't intend to get married. And secondly, if anybody needs their career managing, it's you. Why have you never tried to get bookings as a concert pianist.'

'Because I'm way past it. I gave all that up nineteen years ago.'

'Everyone who hears you play thinks you're the greatest.' Carla added mischievously, 'Especially Ailsa Macdonald.'

Beinmender grimaced and said: 'That's enough of that. Let's play some of the music from Cypriana.'

'The libretto is a lot of crap.'

'The music puts a magic gloss on everything.'

While Beinmender played the piano and hummed and sang, Carla, looking over his shoulder at the score, played some of the vocal pieces on her violin. When they had finished, Carla threw herself onto his lap, crying: 'Marvellous. Beautiful. How did you manage to transcribe it for the piano?'

'I just played key parts on the electronic keyboard and the computer wrote out the music score. It's definitely Mozartian, isn't it.'

'It's splendid. And you have a great voice.'

'I took lessons. My tutor said it lacked timbre. You played with great sympathy on the violin. I've recorded it.'

He pointed to a microphone half hidden behind a standard lamp. 'It's wired into the computer. We can play it in bed later on.'

'Who says we're going to bed?'

'No rumpy-pumpy, no dinner.'

'I would rather starve,' Carla announced with maidenly primness. 'And then almost pleadingly: 'But we do make a good partnership, don't we.'

'Fantastic! Heloise and Abelard — but I beg leave to keep my balls.'

'Keep them with pleasure, kind sir — for my pleasure.'

'Caesar and Cleopatra.'

'The age difference is approximately the same.'

'Did you have to remind me?

'Figaro and Susanna'

'Back to Mozart. Now do you believe Wunder and Mozart are one and the same person?'

Carla pondered with a slightly anxious expression for a moment and then said: 'If they were, and Mozart subsequently wrote Cypriana, I'm sure he did so because he felt guilty for screwing all those women.'

Beinmender shook his head.

'I disagree. He was genuinely suffering from amnesia. If he wasn't, why would he have paid all that money to be treated by Dr Freulich?'

'You'll probably forget me in a day or two.'

'Never. I swear it.'

'In that case you shall have your reward.'

She gave him a playful peck on the cheek but when he attempted to kiss her, she pulled away and said: 'Promise me that if my mother makes a pile of money from the manuscripts you'll never again mention that dreadful bargain you made with her.'

'God! why bring up that awful business. I was stoned out of my head at the time.'

'How do I know *you* won't have a convenient lapse of memory? I would really hate and detest you if you screwed my mother.'

'There isn't the slightest possibility.'

As Carla took his hand and silently led him into his bedroom, Beinmender wondered if he should tell her about her mother's visit to his flat. However, since nothing untoward had happened, it didn't seem necessary.

Carla made an elaborate pretence at shyness as he undressed her. They invented a playful game during which they imitated two out-of-control space-ships, tumbling and rolling wildly until they grew closer together and finally docked.

Later, he switched on the computer beside the bed and played the arias from the opera he had recorded.

She murmured: 'It is beautiful. It is Mozart even though the libretto is clumsy.'

'He didn't have his regiular script writers, da Ponte or Emmanuel Schikaneder, to help him. Remember, also that he had been through the mill. It is possible that his harsh experiences had coarsened him.'

'Don't you ever become coarsened, Herr Beinmender.'

'My finer sensibilities will always be exclusively reserved for you.'

'Which part of me do you like best.'

'Your breasts, your legs, your beautiful ass. But if I had to choose, it would be none of those — I would choose your violin playing.'

'And if I had to choose, I would choose your cock.'

'Not my piano-playing?'

'That as well.'

Later, when they were eating the meal he had prepared, he enquired a little anxiously: 'Why did you call me *Herr* Beinmender when we were in bed?'

'You said your father was German.'

'Yes.' He added, with an agonised expression.' And I wish like hell I could be absolutely sure that he wasn't a Nazi.'

FORTY

Gwen was furious with Beinmender. She considered reporting him to the principal of the College but soon realised that it was doubtful if an accusation of wrongdoing would succeed. Taking such a drastic step would, in any case, alienate Carla, whose support she was going to need during her forthcoming divorce battle. Her hopes for getting the manuscripts authenticated and obtaining financial independence rested heavily on the professor. She decided that she would have to swallow her pride.

Tom was still living in the flat — he slept now in Gloria's room and made his own meals. Conversation between them was limited to business matters. In desperate need of a confidante, Gwen telephoned an old school friend, Alexis, who worked for Frazers, a firm of auctioneers with whom she had had some dealings. They arranged to meet for lunch in Fortnum and Masons.

As soon as they sat down, Gwen told Alexis about her impending divorce and her problems with Carla. She also mentioned the Mozart documents and her determination to keep them for herself. Alexis seemed much more interested in the manuscripts than in her marital problems After describing how she had found them, Gwen managed to turn the conversation round to Carla's relationship with Beinmender, omitting to mention her own recent humiliating experience. She asked what she should do.

Alexis said: 'Is it so terrible?'

'He's much too old for her.'

'Have you spoken to Carla about it?'

'Not yet.'

The waitress appeared. They ordered omelettes, a side salad and coffee.

225

When the waitress had gone, Alexis commented: 'It doesn't appear to be in your interest to quarrel with Beinmender. Let him continue handling the manuscripts. In the meantime try to find out from Carla how she feels about him.'

'You're quite right, Alexis. If Tom hadn't upset me so much I'm sure I would have found out sooner that they were having an affair.'

'Beinmender is a strange name.'

'His father was German. He died when Bernard was young. Bernard studied German as part of his musical studies. He has translated the journal. It makes fascinating reading. Have any original musical manuscripts come up for sale with Frazers?'

.Gwen was disappointed when informed of the paltry sums they had fetched at auction. But she cheered up on being assured that Mozart manuscripts were in an entirely different league.

'What kind of a man is Bernard Beinmender?' Alexis enquired.

'Tall, handsome, charming. He's also a fine pianist.'

'It's no wonder then that your daughter has fallen for him.'

'He's much too old for her.'

'Just right for you, perhaps.'

'Alexis, what are you saying!'

Alexis smiled and said: 'Just fooling.'

'You're not suggesting ...'

'I'm not suggesting anything. But I can see it's not an easy situation for you, since he holds the whip hand. Would you consider handing the documents over to an auction house — my own — for example. We have lots of contacts in the musical world and could set up our own enquiries.'

Gwen wrinkled her brow.

'Not really. Beinmender is an acknowledged expert. It would be a shame to have to start all over again.'

'You'll just have to sit tight then. Incidentally, don't think you are the only one who has a problem with her daughter. My daughter went to live with a middle-aged Pop musician who hadn't a penny to his name.'

'That's terrible.'

'It seemed so at the time. But recently he got a recording contract and she's expecting a baby.'

'Oh, Alexis, I'm so pleased. I have been telling you all my problems and we haven't discussed yours.'

'Did I tell you that I've had a mastectomy?'

On her way home, Gwen decided that her own problems faded into insignificance when compared with those of her friend. She realised that her situation might have been worse if she had slept with Beinmender. She would let him continue working on the manuscripts. Alexis's opinion of their worth encouraged her to believe that she would soon be both rich and independent.

FORTY-ONE

A brief note from Carla to Beinmender, scribbled on a sheet of paper read: 'Sorry, Bernard. Jacko has invited me to stay with him. Our friendship is over. I enjoyed it while it lasted.'

Jacko Barnes was Carla's former boyfriend, a brilliant, quite mad, violinist, who had left college early without any qualifications after cutting a swathe through the female students. He earned a living busking on the Underground, together with his Jack Russell terrier. The dog and Jacko's demonic violin music proved irresistible to the travelling public. It was rumoured that he earned more money than some contemporaries now playing in orchestras — a good deal more than the few trying to win recognition as soloists.

Beinmender fell into a deep depression. He felt like a fish who has been caught and then thrown back into muddy waters. He slept little, lost his appetite and ignored the deluge of E-mail, letters and urgent enquiries relating to the Mozart manuscripts that kept arriving in his apartment. He also ignored frantic messages left by Gwen Bateson on his answer-phone.

The reactions to the Wunder manuscripts from musicologists and handwriting experts in Oxford, Yale, Cleveland, Brandeis and other universities had been encouraging. Several handwriting experts had declared unequivocally that the handwriting in the documents exactly mirrored Mozart's hand. They pointed to the typical variations in the letter 'S'— a feature long accepted as one of Mozart's characteristics. The same easy rhythm, typical of Mozart's quick intelligence, ran through Wunder's untidy scrawl. Beinmender himself had already noted these remarkable similarities when comparing them with photographed copies of Mozart's works in the library of the Royal College of Music.

228

Most of his colleagues agreed that the two concerti and the opera bore an uncanny resemblance to the other six-hundred-and twenty-six of Mozart's works listed in the Ludvig von Köchel catalogue. The fugue was so different from anything he had written before that it seemed almost to have come from another mind. But such a display of versatility could be considered typical of Mozart's creative genius. Before, however, the new works could be admitted to the Mozart canon further tests and analyses of the most rigorous kind would be demanded.

Psychiatrists on both sides of the Atlantic had been asked to identity the nature of the amnesia from which Johann Wunder claimed to have suffered. Linguistic experts were using the latest methods of computer analysis to compare Mozart's literary style with that of Wunder. History supported the account of Wunder's time in Galicia. References in historical documents pointed to the existence of a Bear Inn in the town of Korlyshev during the eighteenth century. A Count Poceski had owned much of the surrounding land The town no longer existed, having been completely destroyed during the Nazi invasion of Poland.

Beinmender's unhappiness was intensified by this discovery. Anti-German feeling had been rife during the immediate post-war period when he was growing up. His mother rarely referred to his dead father. The taunts and bullying he had received at school for possessing a German name had left such a deep impression that at one stage he believed that his dead father bore entire responsibility for the criminal actions of the Nazis. He had reasoned himself out of these absurd ideas as he grew older. But now, in his present dark mood, it seemed to him that his father might have been personally responsible for the war-time destruction of Korlyshev.

His alarm clock woke him up. He had been drinking heavily the night before. Bright sunshine hurt his eyes. He reached over to the computer and turned on the music he and Carla had played together. The familiar sounds seemed to bring her within reach. Quite sure that he would never see her again, he groaned out loud. Soon, he fell back into a deep sleep. He dreamed that he was being interviewed by Adolf Hitler.

'You realise, Colonel Mozart, that some aspects of your music are intolerable — especially those celebrating Freemasonry — a corrupt and degrading organization controlled by Jews.'

'I apologise, *mein Führer,* if my music has offended you.'

'The German people find that kind of music repugnant.'

Pointing to corpses dangling from meathooks on wires strung between white brick walls, Hitler declaimed: 'You see those traitors, Colonel Mozart. They are hanging from violin strings. Cat gut your tongue, Mozart?'

'No, *mein Führer.*'

'You apprehend my little joke?'

'I think so.'

'You think so!'

The *Führer,* his eyes bulging under his darkened brow, gave vent to a thunderous harangue: 'The nation-state should be at the centre of your emotions. A human being who fails in this regard is no better than an ant. True Aryans experience their greatest pleasure by wiping out inferior races. Such emotions must be expressed in music, Colonel Mozart. Your work must embody the clinical ruthlessness of our mighty, all-conquering, purifying Nazi philosophy. Those traitors hanging there have paid the penalty for their neglect. If you follow their example, you, too, will end up one day strung up on violin strings. Is that understood?'

'Yes, *mein Fuhrer.*'

'You are dismissed.'

'Heil Hitler.'

Beinmender waking from his dream, looked at his watch. He had overslept. He telephoned the college secretary and told her that he had flu. He considered committing suicide by jumping in front of an Underground train. He scribbled a note: 'To my darling Carla. I can't live without you. Ask Jacko to play

230

Mozart's Third violin concerto at my funeral. Your devoted Bernard.'

He put on a pair of light gray trousers and a long-sleeved, red and white striped shirt, placed the suicide note in the top pocket, then walked to St. John's Wood Underground station. After searching for Jacko in every station on the way to Baker Street, he continued his search on the Piccadilly line.

During his journey he came across other buskers — a mouth-organist, a group playing Vivaldi's The Four Seasons, a girl with long pigtails playing a Reggae tune on a steel drum, and an oboeist of exceptional quality playing something he couldn't quite identify by Dvorak. By three in the afternoon, thoroughly tired and disgruntled, but by now less suicidal, he left the Underground at Charing Cross and walked over to the National Gallery.

In the restaurant, he surreptitiously glanced at his suicide note; it sounded absurdly melodramatic. How stupid he had been to think that he could compete for a girl's affection with a young musical genius who could hypnotise crowds with his demonic violin-playing. He tore the suicide note into shreds and stuffed it into his trouser pocket.

The dream involving the *Fuhrer* returned to him and with it a dread of experiencing a nervous breakdown similar to one he had suffered in his youth. He used his mobile to put through an urgent call for help to the psychiatrist who had helped him through his previous illness.

*

Sitting in Dr Robert O'Hara's waiting-room in Wimpole Street, he studied the bright, modern paintings on the walls, obviously chosen to dispel the heavy atmosphere of the old building. He wondered whether the psychiatrist would remember him.

A pert young receptionist directed him into a small office.

'Hello, Bernard. How are ye?' The psychiatrist with a creased face and tousled fair hair greeted him with an outstretched hand. Dr O'Hara had aged. But his slightly wary, blue eyes remained the same.

'Not too well, I'm afraid.'

'Sit down. You're depressed again, I gather. I've glanced through your case notes. You used to worry because you thought your father might have been a Nazi.'

'It hasn't bothered me for years. But this morning I dreamed that I was being interviewed by Hitler. I felt like killing myself.'

He told Dr O'Hara about the dream, about the Mozart documents and his relationship with Carla and the Batesons. Finally, he said: 'You would think that I would have more sense than to fall in love with a young girl nearly half my age.'

'The French say that love, like lightning, can strike anyone anywhere.'

'It's absurd when it happens to someone of my age.'

'Are you married?'

'No.'

'Think how difficult it would be if you were. We must try to find out why you have taken your rejection so badly. The mating game is pretty rough — more like rugby than tennis. We all get hurt in the scrum. You were quite devoted to your mother, were you not. Is she still alive?'

'She died five years ago.'

'Have you had many girl friends?'

'Three what you might call relationships.'

'Did you contemplate marriage at any time?'

'With two. One went back to her husband. The other one insisted on a pre-nuptial agreement, which I refused.'

'You didn't love her enough to agree to it?'

'I guess that was it.'

'But with this girl it's head-over-heels stuff.'

'Oh absolutely. I'd do anything for her — I'd part with my life just for a smile.'

'That's interesting,'

Robert O'Hara glanced down at the paper on which he had taken some notes. 'What are you going to do about the supposed Mozartian documents on which you have been working?'

'I feel under an obligation to continue my efforts. Carla's mother is convinced they are going to make her a fortune. She and her husband are about to divorce. I have been so upset recently I haven't even answered her telephone calls.'

The psychiatrist stared at him from under unruly eyebrows.

'Do you think the fact that the documents are written in German may have triggered these guilty feelings.'

'It's possible.'

'Is there some particular event or episode in the documents that might have started it all off?'

'Not that I can think of. A minor pogrom occurs in the diary. That may have something to do with it.'

'Well, we mustn't attach too much significance to an isolated dream. We don't know yet if it is important. But if it is, we should be able to solve the problem. I am going to think about what you have told me. In the meantime I am going to prescribe medication which will stabilize your mood — stop you feeling so badly about your broken love affair. Is there any hope of healing the breach?'

'She has gone off with someone very much younger.'

'Mmm. Take the pills as prescribed. You must keep on with them until I say otherwise. Telephone me if you feel you can't cope. See my secretary on your way out. She will make another appointment for you to see me.'

Robert O'Hara stood up.

They shook hands.

Beinmender went back home on the Underground, feeling better. O'Hara, instead of condemning his foolish infatuation, had enquired instead whether there was any hope of a reconciliation. Which suggested that he was a normal human being. He resolved to go to work the following day.

233

He collected his prescription from the pharmacy and when he arrived home placed them in a kitchen cupboard. He listened to the messages on his answering machine, made some notes and telephoned Gwen Bateson.

'Gwen, this is Bernard. I have a lot of explaining to do. I haven't been well but I am prepared to continue to work on your Mozart documents, if that's what you want.'

'Yes, it is. I have spoken to Carla. What happened between us was not entirely your fault.'

'I take the full blame. I am still deeply in love with her.'

'Did you know she's living with someone else?'

'Yes. How is Tom?'

'He's furious about everything. I am going ahead with the divorce.'

'I'm sorry to hear it.'

'It makes it all the more important for me to make some money. Please do whatever you can to help me put the documents up for auction.'

'Of course.' Beinmender, suddenly remembering his cleaning lady's advice, said: 'I wondered if you had considered compensating me for the work I'm doing.'

Gwen answered quickly: 'Of course, Bernard. I should have brought up the question before. I'll get my solicitor to draw up an agreement under which you will receive ten percent of whatever the documents realise at auction.'

'Thank you. That's agreed. I'll be in touch.'

Bernard smiled as he put down the telephone, feeling grateful towards Mrs Dexter-Brown.

He decided to go through his E-mail correspondence before taking a pill. When he had finished, he sat back in his chair and tried to take a balanced view of the information that had come in. A division seemed to be opening up between fervent believers in the Mozartian origin of the manuscripts and the doubters. For the moment, the believers were in the ascendancy, mainly because of the evidence of the handwriting experts. Some of the sceptics insisted that the sexual behaviour of Johann Wunder was uncharacteristic of Mozart, a man of noble principles. Beinmender reckoned their argument was not strong — there had always been speculation about Mozart's relationship with some of the divas who sang in his operas. Johann Wunder's sexual activities could be considered perfectly normal for the circumstances in which he found himself.

He was so taken up with these thoughts that he forgot to take his pill.

One particular item on his E-mail list caught his attention. A professor who taught music history at the Julliard School of Music in New York wrote:

Dear Prof Beinmender,

I must confess to a passionate interest in the extraordinary documents that have come into your hands. I have always been an aficionado of Amadeus.
I shall be in Poland and Germany soon visiting Auschwitz where my parents died. I'll make a detour to take a look at some of the places mentioned in Wunder's diary. Will let you know if I find anything of interest.
Sincerely

Joseph Schwartz.

Beinmender hastened to acknowledge the message,

FORTY-TWO

The following evening, as Beinmender entered Kensington Underground station, he heard a Berlioz violin sonata being played with extraordinary panache. He immediately recognised the performer and hurried down the escalator. Thoughts of suicide were now replaced by a savage animosity towards his former pupil, who was standing at the foot of the elevator, totally absorbed in his fiery rendition. Jacko Barnes was tall, skinny and swarthy and had a large hooked nose. He wore designer jeans and a black Calvin Klein shirt. A lock of dank hair hung over his brow. The violin case at his feet was brimful of coins.

He looked up as Beinmender came down the escalator, and mumbled: 'Hi, Prof.'

'I need to speak to you,' Beinmender said.

'I'm busy.'

'This is urgent.'

'Meet me in the pub upstairs at eight o'clock — The Lion Lays Down with the Lamb.'

Jacko's eyes closed as he concentrated on the music.

'Where is it?'

'Near the station. Fuck it, you're ruining my performance.'

Beinmender returned to the surface, found the pub Jacko had mentioned and ordered a sandwich and a pint of beer. At nine-fifteen, just as he had given up hope, Jacko, arrived, wearing a smart beige linen suit with a pink shirt and an orange tie. Beinmender took comfort from the fact that he had changed from his working clothes; it suggested that Jacko was taking him seriously.

236

Beinmender stood up and enquired in a surly voice: 'How's Carla?'

'She's all right. Can I buy you a pint of beer?'

'I'll have a whiskey. Judging from the money in your violin case, you could afford to buy me champagne.'

'I don't do so badly. I'm hoping to get some concerts soon.'

'Very good. Is Carla living with you?'

'Sort of. She's not very happy at home. Her parents are splitting up.'

'So I heard.'

They sat down at a nearby table. Beinmender gulped down his whiskey. Unsure how to tackle the situation, he went to the bar and ordered another one. Restraining an impulse to hit Jacko, he returned with his drink and said: 'Does Carla talk about me at all?'

'Yeah. She thinks you're a great guy.'

'What are your feelings towards her?'

Jacko looked slightly ruffled.

'She's all right.'

'Is that all?' Beinmender said, sarcastically.

'What do you want me to say?'

'I'm concerned about her happiness.'

'She's worried about her career. Says she lacks the vital spark.'

'Unlike you,' Beinmender said, derisively.

'You're damned right. My audience think I'm God's gift from Heaven.'

'You don't exactly suffer from an overdose of modesty, do you.'

'Having a touch of genius is something one has to live with. But it has its problems.'

'Such as?'

'Sometimes I think I'm Pagannini. You once told us, incidentally, that he made an incredible amount of money. I could make more than I am now in the long term by doing concert tours. But I am trying to work things out for myself.'

'What is there to work out'

Jacko's eyes closed.

'I can't decide whether to go out in a blaze of glory like some fucking rock musician or play the long game.'

'The long game?'

'Growing old and all that shit.'

'The Rolling Stones have successfully played the long game.'

'Rock grandfathers are a joke.'

'So where does Carla come into all this?'

'Carla?'

'Yes, if you make her unhappy, I'll punch your face in.'

Jacko smiled.

'Professor, you're a laugh. You're the one who's making her unhappy. I've given Carla a bed in my flat, that's all.'

'Why did she run out on me?'

'She has some idea that you slept with her mother. It upset her. So I gave her a bed. Is that wrong?'

'I didn't sleep with her mother.'

'She thinks you did. Not that I can see anything against it. I've had a few mothers and daughters.'

Beinmender began to feel more cheerful.

Jacko went on: 'She's a good kid. If I was the marrying kind I'd marry her myself. I'm going to get another beer.'

When he returned, carrying a pint of beer and a glass of whiskey for Beinmender, he handed him his glass and said: 'Carla believes in love, the family and all that crap.'

'That's not the impression I got.'

Jacko gave him an odd look.

'She has to fight you — you're a kind of parent substitute. But underneath she's just a soft pussy-cat.'

'I don't think so.'

'Well, who knows. Incidentally, I'd rather go out comparatively young like Mozart. Carla told me all about that crappy story that Mozart was rescued from the grave by an old pedlar.'

'You don't believe it?'

238

Jacko lit a cigarette, inhaled and went on: 'It sounds bizarre. But I'm prepared to swallow it, if only for the reason that most people will scoff at it. It's best not to follow the herd, which almost always gets things wrong.' He gave a big grin. 'For example, everyone used to believe that cigarettes were good for you.'

He gave a short, rasping cough.

'Why are you smoking, then?' Beinmender enquired.

Jacko smiled.

'Because I have a death wish.'

'Carla obviously has discussed the Mozart documents with you.'

'Yes. She thinks you'll have to get more proof before they're accepted. But I believe Mozart wrote the journal. Nobody else could have. It's as simple as that.'

Jacko lit another cigarette and said: 'You haven't asked me yet if I'm sleeping with Carla.'

'I'm sure you are. But it's none of my damned business.'

'Well, I'm not. I have another girl who happens to be extremely jealous.'

Beinmender tried to hide a blinding sense of relief. He said after a moment: 'Could I come up to your place and see her?'

'In a minute. Wait till I've finished this cigarette. Incidentally, has it occurred to you that somebody might have written the journal at the dictation of Mozart's ghost? Pagannini sometimes sits on my shoulder when I'm playing. I break out in a cold sweat.'

'You've become obsessed through reading his biography, or perhaps seeing a movie about him.'

'No, he haunts me all the time. He's as addictive as smoking. C'mon. Let's go see if Carla is in.'

FORTY-THREE

Beinmender followed Jacko up several flights of dark stairs to the top of a dingy, three-storey Edwardian house in Cricklewood. He stood on a landing next to an ancient gas cooker and a grimy sink, while Jacko opened the door. The sound of furious scratching and excited barking came from within.

'Quiet, Limbo!' Jacko shouted. A Jack Russell terrier threw himself excitedly at Jacko, as he entered the room and then sniffed curiously at Beinmender's trouser legs.

The sitting-room contained a scratched wooden table, a garish yellow sofa and some mauve beanbags. The light-fitting consisted of a Daily Telegraph front page rolled into a cone. Piles of coins and a few bank notes on the table spoke of a day's successful busking.

'Tax free,' Jacko boasted, as he followed Beinmender's gaze. 'I reckon I made about two-hundred today.'

Pointing to a single divan bed under the window, Jacko announced with a wicked grin: 'That's where Carla sleeps.'

He commanded: 'Sit down. Sit down, ' and added would you like a cup of coffee.'

Beinmender shook his head and sat on the sagging sofa. He was still finding it difficult to adjust to the idea that Jacko was not his enemy. But, why, he wondered, had Carla not asked him about his relationship with her mother.

He noticed a violin case on the divan bed.

'Would you like a joint? — it'll cool you down. You're looking ragged.'

Beinmender shook his head.

'What time will she be back?' he asked.

'Who knows. She's practising at her friend Nathalie's house. They probably go in for girlie talk afterwards.'

'Isn't that her violin case? '

'No, it's mine.'

Beinmender, conscious of the dog watching him alertly, reached out and patted his head.

'Why do you call him Limbo?' he enquired.

'Cos that's the situation he's in. The old guy across the road who owned him died. I took him in because no one else seemed to want him. He still goes back every few days and stands outside the house. I reckon he'll do the same when I leave here. The name suits him, don't you think.'

'Have you got any proper work lined up?'

Jacko's expression darkened.

'I think I may be booked for a couple of concerts soon. This agent of mine comes up with a different story every week. It doesn't bother me, though. I'm making a good living.'

'Time you got yourself a new agent. I know a good one.'

'Do you?' Jacko's face brightened.

'I'll tell him about you.'

'That would be great.'

Beinmender gazed down at the dog.

'Does Limbo appreciate music?' he asked.

'He likes Rap.' Jacko replied with a laugh. 'Quite sensible, really, when you come to think of it. Pagannini would probably have been into it, if he were around today.'

'Why do you play classical music in the Underground?'

'The punters love it; it makes them feel cultured.'

There was a knock on the door. Jacko opened it. Carla came into the room. Jacko said: 'There's an old friend of yours here.'

Carla said coldly to Beinmender: 'What the hell are you doing here?'

'I came here to explain.'

'I never want to see you again.'

'You said in your note that you had enjoyed our friendship.'

'I didn't know then that you had fucked my mother.'

'What rubbish!'

'And she says you don't answer her letters and phone calls.'

'Only because I have been so upset at losing you. I rang her up yesterday.'

'I suppose it amused you to sleep with both of us, you bastard.'

'Who told you that?'

'You told her I had slept with you.'

'Only because?'

'Because what?'

Beinmender didn't answer.

Jacko, who had been listening to this with an amused expression, suddenly said: 'This is obviously a private conversation. I'm off to bed,' and went into the adjoining room.

Carla hissed: 'Did you tell her before or after you had slept with her?'

'I DIDN'T sleep with her, for God's sake. That's the whole point. Your mother came to see me because she wanted to see the manuscripts. She wanted me to destroy the piece of paper involving her in that ridiculous bargain, which I did. I told her about us because I wanted to let her know that I love you. I'm still madly in love with you. I've been through hell since you left me.'

Carla seemed mollified by his explanation.

'It hasn't been exactly a picnic for me recently,' she said, defiantly. He put his arms round her and said: 'I'm very sorry. I appreciate this divorce business is very painful for you. But believe me I never ...'

She reached up, put her finger over his lips and said: 'Shall we agree never to mention that subject again.'

'Okay.

He held her tight.

After a while, he said: 'Would you like to move your things into my place?'

'No, I'm not ready for anything like that. Incidentally, my mother is still very worried that the Wunder journal may be a fake.'

'Tell her not to worry. It's going to be okay.'

'Is there anything in it which gives you grounds for doubt?'

'Not really. But acceptance of its authenticity will depend upon a whole lot of other people.'

Carla sat down on the sofa.

After a pause, she said: 'Why should they have doubts, if you don't?'

Beinmender frowned and scratched his head.

'There are statements in the journal that can be interpreted in many different ways.'

'Then you do have doubts.'

'It's always prudent to have doubts. If I swallowed everything uncritically, I wouldn't be doing my job properly. Incidentally, your mother has promised me a commission on the sale when they go up for auction.'

'So what is it that is causing you to have doubts?'

'I would rather not say at the moment.'

'I am certainly not going to live with you if you don't trust me.'

'I do trust you.'

'I haven't been sleeping with Jacko.'

'So I believe.'

'I slept with him before. But not recently.'

'I'm not complaining.'

'Don't you care?'

'Of course I care. But there's nothing I can do about it. I want you all to myself. But I'm prepared to wait.'

Carla suddenly said fretfully: 'I wish my mother had never bought that wretched piano stool. If she didn't think she was going to make her fortune, she wouldn't have started divorce proceedings.'

'Darling, your parents obviously don't get on. They would probably have decided to divorce anyway.'

243

'You must tell me about these doubts you're having.'

'I'm not sure that they mean anything at all. Will you come home with me now?'

'I'm too tired.'

'I'll meet you at Glover's pub for lunch and we'll sort things out.'

'Okay. Give me a bell on my mobile.'

She wouldn't allow him to kiss her. Nevertheless, he walked home to his flat in St. John's Wood, feeling elated.

FORTY-FOUR

Walking home through the dark streets of Kilburn, Beinmender remembered the phenomenon of false memories alluded to by Johann Wunder in his journal. It occurred to him that the bullying he had experienced at school might have planted in his mind a false belief that his father had been a Nazi war criminal. Dr O'Hara had once explained that his mother's reluctance to talk about his father probably had more to do with problems in their marriage than with his father's war record. He was rehearsing how he would explain this to Carla, when a voice said: 'Let's have your watch and your wallet, mate. No fuckin'around!'

A vicious-looking knife blade was shining in the lamplight. The face of the person holding it was masked by a balaclava. Beinmender carefully and deliberately took his wallet from his back pocket, handed it over and said ingratiatingly: 'Hang on a moment, my watch has a new strap. It's rather difficult to get off.'

Pretending to struggle with it, he suddenly lifted both hands in a powerful move that knocked the knife out of the man's hand. He then gave him a furious punch that felled him and for good measure kicked him in the groin. His assailant ran off, leaving the wallet and the knife behind. Beinmender bent down, picked up both articles from the pavement and continued his journey home, jauntily whistling Mozart's horn concerto.

Back in his flat, he poured himself out a large whiskey and savoured his moment of triumph. He felt on top of the world, a match for Jacko, or anybody else for that matter in future who might try to steal his girl.

He corrected some examination papers and then played the recording of the duet he and Carla had made from Cypriana. Soothed by the sounds, he logged onto the Internet and deleted some junk mail. A message from Professor Schwartz remained on the screen. It read:

Hi, Professor Beinmender

I promised I would get it touch with you if I came across anything useful. One always has to bear in mind that negative results can be as significant as positive ones.

I am in Leipzig at the moment.

Recently, when I was in Vienna, I checked up on the letter Wunder wrote about the garment he was wearing at the time he was rescued. The handwriting certainly resembles that in the other photo-copied documents you sent to us.

Mozart, in his first incarnation, played several concerts here in Leipzig. Incidentally, I noticed while trawling through the telephone directory that the name Beinmender is quite common in this part of the world.

On my way to Poland, I visited Brno, now in the Czech republic. But I found no trace of a Doctor Freulich. Perhaps this isn't surprising. He probably had to close down his practice, because the Establishment was so hostile towards his methods.

Deutero-Mozart is an elusive fellow.

This comes to you via my versatile notebook computer. Would hate to be without it.

Best wishes

Joseph Schwartz

FORTY-FIVE

Entering their shop, Tom found his wife wiping a French buhl clock. He growled at her angrily: 'What's all this business about giving Beinmender ten-per-cent. I've just seen a letter from our solicitor.'

Gwen replied coolly: 'If you want anybody to do a good job, you have to pay them.'

'He's a professor. He is well off enough as it is.'

'Don't be stupid. I want him to have an incentive to get the manuscripts recognised as soon as possible.'

'You'll reward someone who's seduced our daughter and at the same time deny me my rightful share. There's a sign outside that says Bateson's Antiques That means both of us. My solicitor says that no way can you get away with it. A partnership means exactly what it says: A fifty-fifty split.'

'Marriage is also a partnership. You broke those rules, so I can break business rules.'

'That's where you're wrong. I shall fight tooth and nail to prevent it. So don't forget — you're in no position to give Beinmender a commission without first clearing it with me.'

'You'll find out in due course that I can. And what is more, if you had the slightest amount of commonsense, you would know that it was the right thing to do.'

'If he's living with Carla, I'll have him sacked from his post.'

'She's not living with him — she's been staying with Jacko Barnes for the past few days.'

'That gypsy scoundrel!'

'He's a brilliant musician. She's staying with him because she is so upset with us.'

'So when will she be coming home?'

'Tonight. She has apparently made it up with Beinmender, although she still has some reservations about him.'

'I'm pleased to hear she's coming home. Perhaps she's getting some sense at last.'

'She told me that she and Bernard played some music from Cypriana — the opera in the music stool. Carla says it's very beautiful.'

'So what are these doubts Carla has about Beinmender?'

'I don't know. She just told me over the phone that she has made it up with him but wants time to think it over. Your daughter can be very sensible at times.'

'She doesn't take after her mother.'

He paused, and then looking downcast, mumbled: 'How would you feel about seeing a marriage counsellor?'

'That's the last thing I want.'

Tom's expression darkened. He took some documents from a desk at the back of the shop and left without saying another word.

FORTY-SIX

Because of a dental problem, Carla cancelled the lunch appointment she had made with Bernard and arranged to meet him instead that evening at a Chinese restaurant near his flat.

Beinmender examined the knife he had captured when he arrived home from work. It was a fearsome weapon. He had acted extremely rashly but didn't regret his action.

Checking his E-mail, he found a message from an American academic, who strongly challenged the authenticity of the manuscripts. He pointed out that Mozart, having at one time been a personal friend of Dr Anton Mesmer, would have known that Mesmer's ideas had been condemned and would not have agreed to be treated by his method. He conveniently ignored the grievous loss of memory from which Johann Wunder, Mozart's alter ego, had suffered. Beinmender set about composing a suitable rebuttal. He became so engrossed in his task that he was late for his appointment with Carla.

Carla was waiting patiently in the foyer, as he rushed through the door of the restaurant. He apologised, kissed her and asked how she had fared with the dentist. She touched a slightly swollen cheek and declared it bearable. A diminutive Chinese waitress led them to their table in a recess.

After ordering drinks, Beinmender told Carla about his clash with the American professor. He went on: 'I can see what he is getting at. Anton Mesmer commissioned an opera from Mozart- it was called Bastien and Bastienne. But this guy — he's from Harvard — has entirely ignored the fact that Johann Wunder, having lost his memory, would not have remembered having met Mesmer. Nor does he seem to appreciate that although the magnets Mesmer and Freulich used were in themselves useless, Dr Mesmer's technique produced results very similar to that of modern hypnotherapy.'

Carla enquired: 'In that case, why was everybody down on Dr Mesmer?'

'A committee that was set up in Paris by Louis the Sixteenth, condemned his method of treatment, because there was no proof of the existence of "Mesmeric fluid," on which Mesmer's theory was based. But it doesn't make any sense to try to discredit the whole Wunder-Mozart thesis on that account. Nor, for that matter, Dr Freulich's treatment.'

Carla furrowed her brow.

'You mean Mesmer's method actually worked.'

'To some degree, yes. In any case, he can't be blamed too much for his belief in "Mesmeric fluid". Scientists in the last century fell into a similar trap by positing the existence of something in space called Ether, which we now know doesn't exist. His work certainly advanced our knowledge of the human mind. He wasn't a complete nutter. I still have to examine some other niggling doubts this guy has raised.'

There was a pause as the waitress placed drinks on the table.

Carla then said: 'I'm trying to persuade my parents to get together again. But it seems hopeless. They won't even talk to each other.'

'Since you can do nothing about it, why not come and live with me?'

'No, I'm determined to stay at home for the time being.'

'I'm quietly confident that your mother will make a tidy sum eventually from the sale of the manuscripts.'

'I'm sorry she found them.'

Beinmender ordered the meal and then said with a sigh: 'It doesn't seem right that we have to be kept apart just because your parents can't be sensible.'

'That isn't the only reason.'

'What other reason is there?'

'I would rather not talk about it.'

'Please tell me — we must be honest with each other.'

'Okay, if you insist. I find this business of your worrying in case your father was a Nazi quite weird. Nobody cares about that old stuff any more.'

'I was discussing it with my psychiatrist recently. Nazi-ism has never entirely gone away. But that's beside the point. I was ragged rotten about my German name when I was a boy.'

'Why didn't you change it?.'

'Because it's the name I was born with.'

'We're all Europeans now. All that old-fashioned nationalism has long since gone.'

'If you had lost your family in a concentration camp, would you be able to forgive the Germans?'

'People do terrible things in war time. We bombed Germany to smithereens. I just don't see how we can be happy together, if you're still worrying about what your father may have done in the distant past. Consulting a psychiatrist seems quite bizarre.'

'I consulted him last week because I was knocked sideways when you walked out on me.'

'How else should I have behaved when I had the impression you were screwing my mother. Sorry — we're not supposed to mention that again. Anyway, forget I said it and now tell me why you are still confident that the manuscripts will turn out to be genuine.'

Beinmender said patiently: 'I am not a hundred-per-cent confident- only ninety-per cent. Some of the objections are quite frivolous. Others need to be taken seriously. By the way, an American scholar on holiday in Europe has taken it upon himself to do some investigation while he is over here. He tells me that the handwriting on the letter that Wunder addressed to a gentleman's outfitter in Vienna strongly resembles Mozart's. So that's a plus. But a great deal more work will be required before we can declare to the world with absolute confidence that Mozart lived on after the official date of his reported death.'

251

'Is there any other good news?'

'Although the libretto of Cypriana is very weak, everyone agrees that the music has that celestial Mozartian touch.'

He leaned over the table and pleaded: 'When can we get together again?

'I'm going to live at home for a while. I want to try to persuade my parents to be sensible. It doesn't make sense for them to divorce.'

'If there is anything I can do to help, please let me know.'

'I certainly will.'

But when he told her of the attempted mugging the previous night, instead of applauding his action, she said angrily: 'You could have been killed! How can I have confidence in someone who behaves like a complete prat!'

Beinmender hung his head in pretended shame.

FORTY-SEVEN

Beinmender was confident that Robert O'Hara would agree with his own conclusion that Wunder and Mozart were one and the same person. He invited Carla to dinner, saying he would like to go over the Wunder journal with her. At first she refused, reminding him of her determination to spend as much time at home.

'I know things are very difficult for you. But this is important. Please make an exception and come for lunch on Saturday?'

After a show of reluctance, Carla agreed.

Beinmender went shopping on Saturday morning, selecting wine and ingredients for an Italian meal He was busy cooking when the doorbell rang. Rushing to the door, he was disappointed to find Mrs Dexter-Brown standing outside. She had left her handbag in the flat. After a search, she found it by his computer in the bedroom.

She said, as she was about to leave: 'You must be having company, Mr Beinmender — I can smell all that lovely cooking. Is it mother or daughter this time?'

'Daughter.'

She gave him an encouraging smile.

A minute later, the doorbell rang again. Carla stood there wearing a yellow silk shirt, a long black skirt and an intoxicating perfume.

'You were obviously looking forward to seeing me,' she said, smiling. Momentarily confused, Beinmender glanced down and wondered if his passion had become evident. She explained:

'Your cleaning lady — I passed her on the stairs — said you were cooking madly.'

'Not madly — methodically. Hang on a minute, I forgot to take the wine out of the fridge.'

When he arrived in the sitting-room, she was reading his translation of the Wunder journal.

'So you've found it.'

'It's fascinating,' she replied, without looking up.

'Reading old-fashioned German gave me a feel for the period. It made me feel a little better about having a German father. '

'Why should that worry you?'

'You were lucky — you knew both your parents.'

'Who'd want to know them! They won't even talk to each other.'

'I wish you'd marry me. You are the only person in the world I want to be with always. I'll make you so happy you'll never want to leave me.'

'My father obviously said exactly the same thing to my mother.'

'We can learn from their mistakes.'

'Grow up, Bernard!'

'That's interesting, coming from someone who is years my junior.'

'That didn't stop you from seducing me at the first opportunity?'

'You took your kit off — what was I supposed to think?'

'I was just testing your powers of resistance.'

Beinmender ran his hands gently over her face and whispered: 'Test me again.'

She shook her head and said: 'No. I have given that up until my parents make it up.'

'Why let their mistakes spoil your life?'

'I don't know. I just don't want them to get divorced. Let me get on with reading the journal.'

After a while, Carla looked up and said to Beinmender: 'It's a great story. So what can you do to persuade people that it's a true account of what happened?'

'I'm going to Leipzig where the story ends next weekend. We still don't know whether it was written by a miraculously reborn Wolfgang, or by some desperately frustrated musician trying to exploit Mozart's name. I had an E-mail from Professor Schwartz this morning. He's in Leipzig at the moment doing some research on J S Bach. I have arranged to meet him in the Bach museum on Saturday morning for a discussion. Incidentally, the piano we had at home in my youth came from the factory in Saxony for which my father worked. It's not very far from Leipzig. I'll see if I can find out more about him while I'm there. My psychiatrist says it might help me to get rid of my hang-up.'

Carla, her legs dangling over the side of an armchair in his sitting-room, gave him a sceptical look.

'Supposing you discover that your father had been commander of a concentration camp. Wouldn't that depress you even further.'

'I need to know the truth.'

'Bernard,' Carla said impatiently, 'What difference does it make now what you father did or didn't do. It was a different world then. It has nothing to do with you now. You can't inherit Nazi propensities.'

'Goebbels killed all his six children after Germany had been defeated before committing suicide. He knew they would bear an intolerable stigma, if he let them live.'

'But you know nothing about your father.'

'I know he served in the Wehrmacht.'

'He died soon after you were born. What he did before you were born simply has no relevance.'

'Perhaps my father's spirit has affected me, as you once suggested Wunder was possessed by Mozart's spirit.'

'You were quick enough to shoot down that idea. Anyway you weren't even brought up by your father, so his influence over you has been absolutely nil.'

'Nevertheless, those ghastly pictures from the concentration camps haunt me whenever I see them.'

'The Germans are as peace-loving and democratic as we are now — perhaps more so. Mozart was German — Austrian — it amounts to the same thing. You used to lecture us about the wonderful literature and music Germany has given to the world.'

'Leaving that aside for the moment, can you believe that Mozart survived his last illness?'

'Does it matter? Surely the important thing is that two splendid concerti, a fugue and an opera have been added to the world's stock of classical music and will soon be played in concert halls all over the world.'

'The manuscripts won't fetch much if we fail to prove their Mozart attribution.'

'It'll serve my mother right for being greedy.'

'Anyway, as I've said, I am going to discuss the whole thing with Professor Schwartz in Leipzig. I am leaving on Friday..'

Trying very hard to appear casual, he added: 'I don't suppose you'd care to come with me — at my expense, of course.'

Carla looking very surprised, considered for a moment and then said 'Okay, but separate bedrooms.'

'Agreed.'

He gave her a delighted grin.

*

When Beinmender had entered Dr O'Hara's office for what he hoped would be his final appointment, the psychiatrist had looked up and said: 'I regret to have to tell you that my secretary has just informed me that your private medical insurance doesn't cover psychiatric treatment.'

'I'll pay for it myself. My main reason, anyway, for coming to see you is to sound out your opinion of the Wunder journal. Have you formed any thoughts about it?'

After a pause, Dr O'Hara stroked his chin and said: 'People sometimes come into my consulting room and swear to having had experiences which I know are false. Nevertheless, I have to accept that they sincerely believe that they are telling the truth. One has to be sceptical of Johann Wunder's story. He was unconscious at the time he was found, so he could not possibly have known for certain what happened to him. The rumour he mentions that his benefactor found him lying unconscious in a brothel sounds on the whole a good deal more credible.'

Dr O'Hara added, smiling, 'By the same token one should also be sceptical about his account of his sexual adventures. It's natural in the male to boast of easy conquests. But down to the real issue, cases of complete amnesia are well recorded in psychiatric literature, although they are comparatively rare. It is possible — just possible — that he woke up after a period of unconsciousness with no recollection whatsoever of his previous life.'

'But isn't the fact that he remembers names of musicians and other famous people inconsistent with his inability to remember details of his personal life?'

'No. It seems that personal and internal memories are recorded in different parts of the brain. You could compare the phenomenon with the different types of memory in a computer, although that is not an exact parallel.'

'What do you think of his experiences at the hands of Dr Freulich and his daughter, Bella?'

'I would say that his swift seduction of the blue-stocking Bella is the most convincing proof of all that Wunder was the brilliant, all-conquering musician Wolfgang Amadeus Mozart. Seriously, though, the description of his experience with the magnets is consistent with known facts. Mozart knew all about Mesmer's magnets — there is a mocking reference to them in his opera Cosi Fan Tutti.'

'But Wunder's account in the journal suggests he had only a faint recollection of Dr Anton Mesmer.'

'His difficulty in remembering Mesmer is consistent with amnesia. His experiences under the care of Dr Freulich fit in with the known medical facts. Freulich was using more or less the same hypnotic techniques that are in use today — but he and Mesmer didn't realise that the magnets were superfluous. Incidentally, Mesmer's belief in the therapeutic powers of magnetism wasn't as reprehensible an error as, say, Lysenko's in the field of genetics a hundred and fifty years later.'

'What about the incident with the parrot?'

'That may well have reminded Wunder of *Die Zauberflöte.* '

'But that is no proof that the person remembering it was Mozart.'

'I agree.'

'Is it possible that Bella was on the right track when she suggested that Wunder's amnesia might have been caused by something other than cerebral injury?'

'Surprisingly, she seems to have had an insight into the condition we call "psychogenic fugue," which occurs when, under severe psychosocial stress, someone runs away from a dangerous or disturbing situation. The word "fugue" in French means flight. One can speculate that Mozart became a fugitive from his previous life after waking up in the old pedlar's wagon. He had been very ill, was heavily in debt and had been under enormous pressure to complete his famous Requiem.

'The journal also offers some evidence that Mozart's childhood was overshadowed by the rigid regime his father imposed on him. From an early age he and his sister, Nannerl, were under extreme pressure to develop their musical talents. The stress could have been a predisposing element in the dissociative amnesia I have suggested he suffered from when he was writing the journal. His references to "a lion" obviously derives from a suppressed fear of his father — Leo the lion — Leopold. It all tends to confirm that Mozart was the true author of the journal. But on the other hand, it may still have been the invention of some unscrupulous person trying to make money by using Mozart's name.'

'It hardly seems likely, does it, that an eighteenth-century musician would have guessed at the existence of pysyochgenic fugue.'

'It's not impossible. There is an old medical axiom which tells us that symptoms always remain the same. The only changes are in diagnosis and therapy.'

'He would have known, of course, that Mozart had been buried in St. Mark's graveyard when he made up the story.'

'One cannot declare with absolute confidence that the journal was written by someone else. It is quite easy to visualise a scenario in which a solitary gravedigger, having been instructed to bury a corpse, suddenly sees signs of life. Wouldn't it be an entirely normal reaction for the man to run away in horror, leaving the corpse half-buried? It would be equally understandable if he then drank himself senseless in the nearest tavern. If Mozart was subsequently revived by an old pedlarman, then his amnesia could be explained by psychogenic fugue, possibly with cerebral injury as a contributory factor.'

'Thank you very much. Would you care to put your opinion in writing. Mrs Bateson, the legal owner of the documents, would be happy to pay you.'

O'Hara wrinkled his nose thoughtfully and said: 'I'll have to think about it for a while. Jumping to conclusions can damage a doctor's reputation. Dr Mesmer himself offers a salutary example.'

'I take your point. Incidentally, does the account of Johann Wunder's behaviour under hypnosis stand up to scrutiny?

'That part is quite convincing. Talking of hypnosis, would you consider allowing yourself to be hypnotised when you next come to see me?'

'You said you weren't sure if I am a suitable subject.'

'We could try to find out, using a simple test.'

259

'I'll think about it. I am going to fly to Leipzig this weekend, to try to get confirmation that Johann Wunder lived there. I may do a little research on my family background at the same time.'

'That sounds an excellent idea. Make an appointment to see me when you come back.'

Dr O'Hara glancing up at the clock on the wall, added: 'I think this is the right moment to end this session.'

FORTY-EIGHT

Bernard Beinmender followed Carla into WH Smiths at Heathrow Airport. She bought a romantic novel — he chose a music magazine with a CD attached, to fill a gap in his collection. After they were airborne, Bernard stared out of the cabin window, thinking about his relationship with the girl by his side. Carla was totally absorbed in her paperback. It was painfully obvious that, even apart from the difference in their ages, he and Carla were incompatible. Even their taste in popular music differed — Carla, a passionate devotee of Hip-Hop and Heavy Metal, deplored his addiction to jazz On one occasion when he had complained mildly about some jangling cacophonies to which she was listening she had called him an intolerant prat. Oddly, the recollection of this angry outburst gave him a certain wry pleasure.

Admiring her silky, dark hair and fine features, as she bent over the novel, he told himself that it was her youthful spirit that had completely captivated him. Since it seemed likely that this was the only trip they would ever take together, he must do his best to make it memorable.

But as the aircraft broke though the cloud and sunshine poured into the aircraft, he became more optimistic and thought — we have patched up our quarrels before. Things may not be quite as bad as they seem.

*

The Glenischer hotel had a nineteenth-century air of decadent luxury left over from the communist era. Artificial palm trees abounded in the foyer and the soft furnishings were in dark red plush velvet. However, it was efficiently run. The two adjoining rooms were comfortable, with en-suite bathrooms and were equipped with television. The refrigerators were stocked with liquor.

When he had showered and changed, he knocked on Carla's door. She was wearing a short, rose-coloured frock. Clothes were spread all over the bed. An enticing perfume filled the air.

Looking down, she enquired: 'What do you think of this dress?'

'You'll knock Professor's Schwartz's eye out. We're meeting him at the Bach museum at ten o'clock tomorrow morning. Unless, that is, you'd prefer to explore the town by yourself?'

'No, I'd like to meet him. Do you attach much importance to his views?'

'His views and that of other American academics will be crucial. Oh, by the way, I bought a little gift for you.'

He handed her a small violin-shaped golden clasp he had bought in Tiffany's.

She gave him a shy smile.

'It's lovely.'

'It'll remind you to keep practising.'

Later, glancing around the opulent dining-room, Carla mused:

'Isn't it amazing that we're here just because my mother happened to bid for an old piano stool.'

'Small events can bring about big ones. When the news finally breaks that new Mozart works have been discovered, it will send waves all round the world.'

When Carla had finished consulting the menu he said: 'I gather your mother checked the provenance of the music stool.'

'Yes, it came from this part of Germany.'

I sent Professor Schwartz scanned images of the manuscripts through the wires. He sounds quite an amusing guy.'

'Has he come all the way just to investigate the Wunder documents?'

'He has other fish to fry. But he is a real Mozart buff.'

'My mother is only interested in how much money the documents fetch.'

'Nothing wrong with that.'

Carla suddenly laughed.

'I have just remembered — there was a funny passage in the Wunder journal when the old pedlarman buys a fake Rubens and his horse treads on it. It will serve my mother right if the manuscripts also turn out to be fakes.'

'Why are you so hard on her. She told me she intends to spend some of the money on you and your sister.'

Carla grimaced. 'It doesn't seem right for her to divorce my father for a momentary weakness.'

'Wouldn't you divorce me if I was unfaithful?'

'I don't intend to marry,'

'That was a hypothetical question.'

'They should forgive each other and start again.'

I had the impression that you were against open marriages.'

Carla examined the food which had just been placed before her and said: 'I don't think we should be having this conversation.'

'Why not?'

'It's liable to fuck up our own relationship.'

'Do we have one'

'I think so. It's not perfect.... But that's your fault.'

'In what way?'

Carla examined the food on her plate carefully, before answering.

'For allowing yourself to get so screwed up about your father. Seeing a psychiatrist has probably made it worse. Why not put the whole thing out of your mind.'

'It's easy for you to say that. You know all about your father.'

'He was unfaithful — I don't need to see a psychiatrist about that.'

'There's a lot of difference between being unfaithful and committing mass murder.'

'For goodness sake, Bernard — the chances are that your father was just an ordinary foot soldier.'

'I hope to find out more about him while I'm here. He was born in Magdeburg only about fifty miles away. I intend to drive there tomorrow and see if anybody remembers him.'

'Why don't you put the whole thing out of your mind and just get on with living.'

'It's something I must settle while I'm here.'

Beinmender ordered another bottle of wine, as Carla, looking fretful, devoured strudel and ice-cream, After drinking two more glasses, he pleaded: 'Darling, let's just enjoy ourselves.'

'Okay. No more talk of war and the Nazis. We'll concentrate on the local culture.'

'Which reminds me — Goering is reputed to have said: "Whenever I hear people talking about culture I reach for my revolver."'

Carla gave him a withering look, took her handbag and stood up.'

He grabbed her arm and whispered hastily: 'I'm sorry. I was only kidding. It won't happen again.'

'Promise.'

'I sincerely and honestly promise.'

*

Joseph Schwartz was a tall man with a gray goatee beard. He wore a knee-length camel-hair coat and a velvet fedora. Looking admiringly at Carla, he congratulated Beinmender on having such a beautiful daughter. Bernard replied stiffly: 'Carla is my girlfriend.'

Joseph Schwartz said with an apologetic air: 'I have an absolute genius for putting my foot in it. I must say you're a lucky man. I'll buy coffee to make amends.'

As they made their way towards a restaurant, he pointed to a nearby church, observing that Johann Sebastian Bach had been the organist there for many years.

264

After ordering coffee and pastries, he remarked: 'Mozart studied J S Bach's manuscripts while he was here in seventeen-eight-nine. He was a great friend of one of Bach's sons.'

Beinmender responded: 'But can we believe that he eventually made his home here? Has Carla's mother made the most remarkable musical find of the century? Or is it all a gigantic hoax?'

Joseph Schwartz sampled a pastry piled with fruit and thick cream, gave an appreciative 'Hmm' and said   reflectively: 'Let's first discuss an important theory of mine; namely that there is an intimate connection between high cholesterol and good music. The Germans are excellent at producing both.'

'I also like their beer,' Beinmender commented.

'Again, a close connection. The beer gives them the extra wind to play in their oom-pa-oom-pa bands.'

Carla leaned forward and used a tissue to remove a fleck of cream that had appeared on Beinmender's upper lip.

Joseph Schwartz commented with a serious expression: 'It is clear to me now, Carla, that it is you who are the parent, not as I so foolishly assumed, the other way around.'

'If you buy me another delicious pastry, I'll mother you as well.'

'In which case you can have the whole bakery! Talking of bakeries, do you recall, Bernard, the burning down of the bakery in Korlyshev, recorded in the journal? I was unable to find out much about it when I was in Poland. The town had been wiped out by the Nazis.'

'Do you think it sounds plausible?' Beinmender enquired.

Joseph wiped his mouth with a napkin and said: 'That type of factional and religious strife was all too common in those days. Unfortunately, it still happens today — in Northern Ireland, for example.' He then enquired politely: 'What do you think, Carla?'

She mused: 'Whether the journal is plausible or not, the real miracle that everyone ignores is that my mother has found some really brilliant music.'

Joseph exclaimed: 'You're absolutely right, Carla. Bernard — you've got yourself a real treasure here. But going back to Bernard's original question about your mother making the find of the century, one always has to be ultra cautious. If we accepted attributions too easily, hundreds of Beethoven's Tenth Symphonies would arrive every day along with dozens of undiscovered operas by Guiseppe Verdi. There are some serious obstacles to be overcome. One of my colleagues back home, for whose opinion I have some respect, believes that the musical style of the concerti resembles more Pasquale Anfossi than Mozart. Since, anyway, it is accepted in some quarters that Mozart may have unconsciously plagiarised from Anfossi, the resemblance isn't altogether surprising. Incidentally, some interesting questions arise out of the opera, Cypriana.'

'What are they?'

'The whole plot hinges on the Magic Milestone, which blots out the memory of the protagonists, allowing them to pursue their various sexual adventures. One could hardly say that it is more absurd than the plot of, say, Cosi Fan Tutti. But — but here's the rub — Wunder must surely have been aware of his own memory problem while he was working on the plot. Which raises the question of whether he was faking his loss of memory. A highly intelligent man like Mozart, even supposing he experienced the events described in the journal, would surely have remembered whether he had a wife and family.'

Beinmender replied eagerly: 'Not necessarily. A psychiatrist I was talking to last week suggested that Mozart was suffering from "psychogenic fugue," which occurs when someone flies from a dangerous or disturbing situation. It chimes in with the conclusion Bella, Dr Freulich's daughter, came to two- hundred years ago. It raises another interesting point — if the author of the journal, as you suggest, *knew* he was Mozart and not Johann

Wunder, then in that case the manuscripts must be genuine. How's that for a clincher!'

'The odds are that this particular mystery will run for at least as long as the controversy over the Turin Shroud. Of one thing we can be sure — this is going to give birth to a whole new series of books about Mozart. I might write one myself,' he added, puckishly.'

Beinmender said earnestly to Carla: 'I agree with Joseph's verdict. And I think in all fairness you should let your mother know it's going to take a long, long time before she can count on making any money.'

'I shall be pleased to put her out of her misery.'

Turning to Joseph Schwartz, she said: 'You music boffins are certainly very hard to convince.'

'True,' Joseph Schwartz conceded. 'But there is yet another angle: how can you trust a story written by someone who admits he is brain-damaged?'

'That's not fair!' Carla protested.

'It will carry weight among people unwilling to change their views.'

'What do you personally believe?' Beinmender enquired.

'I have a hunch that the manuscripts are genuine. But as Carla has suggested, it could take a very long time before people will be prepared to acknowledge that Mozart was somehow miraculously transformed into Johann Wunder.'

'You think the music will eventually enter the Mozart canon,' Beinmender said.

In the very long term, yes.'

Carla intervened: 'But why should it take so long, when the music sounds so much like Mozart?'

'Because we have to make absolutely sure. Academics by their nature are a very conservative lot.'

'You're absolutely right, of course,' Beinmender agreed.

'Look on the bright side. It has given you a nice trip to Leipzig with this lovely young girl.'

Carla said with a smile: 'That is what I keep telling him.'

Beinmender was silent as a waiter refilled his coffee cup. He muttered: 'Wunder was not actually brain-damaged in the strict sense of the word. One can tell from the journal that his mind was functioning perfectly.'

Joseph Schwartz replied: 'Yes, but if he was unable to recall his own wife, in what sense can it be said that he was Wolfgang Mozart? It is probably closer to the truth to say that the music in the manuscripts was composed by a man who had once been Mozart.'

'That's splitting hairs?' Carla said, impatiently.'

'Splitting personalities,' Joseph Schwartz replied, twitching his eyebrows, humorously.

'If it could be shown that his memory had subsequently returned, wouldn't that change the whole picture?' Carla enquired.

'Yes. But that's very unlikely. The journal is the sole record. And it ends with him changing his name.'

*

Later, while they were examining the musical score of the Goldberg Variations in the Bach museum, Joseph Schwartz whispered to Beinmender: 'You're not going to believe this. You may be Mozart's descendant.'

'What do you mean?'

'Do you remember the journal records that Johann Wunder chose a new name to live under?'

'Yes.'

'It says that he chose a name he saw on a shop front.'

'So what is significant about that?'

'The name he chose was — wait for it — Beinmender!'

'You're kidding,' Beinmender responded.

'No, I examined the City records and a family consisting of Johann, Leah and Daniel Beinmender lived in the Jewish quarter at that time.'

Joseph Schwartz then added, whispering mischievously into Beinmender's ear, 'So if you marry that girl another Mozart may spring from your loins.'

'*Wunderbar!*' Beinmender declared enthusiastically.

'*Wunderbar!*' Joseph Schwartz echoed .

'What are you talking about?' Carla enquired.

'Nothing imporant,' Joseph said. Both men assumed an air of innocence.. Carla chose that moment to pour out to Joseph Schwartz her concern about Beinmender's obsession with his supposed Nazi ancestry.

'Well, if it's any consolation, there's a remote possibility that he may be part-Jewish himself.' He told her how Johann Wunder and family had lived under the name Beinmender, adding: 'But, of course, there are hundreds of Beinmenders in Saxony.'

'Does it lend weight to the possibility that the account is genuine?'

Joseph Schwartz replied. 'Not really. I was so excited when I found this in the records that I telephoned my opposite number at Yale. He shot me down by pointing out that the author of the "fake diary," as he called it, may have looked up the records and then constructed his story in this manner simply to give it an appearance of authenticity.'

'So how long do you think it might be before my mother makes any money?' Carla asked.

Joseph Schwartz said with a grin: 'Two hundred years, wouldn't you say, Bernard?'

'Plus or minus fifty,' Beinmender replied, solemnly.

They spent some time examining the Johann Sebastian Bach memorabilia and manuscripts. Joseph Schwartz was soon totally absorbed in making notes on the life and works of the great contrapuntist. He looked up and smiled absently as Carla and Bernard bade him goodbye. They walked out of the museum and caught a bus back to the hotel.

FORTY-NINE

As they waited to be served in the hotel dining-room, Carla said consolingly: 'Don't look so downhearted — Joseph may be quite wrong in his estimate. He probably meant five or ten years not a hundred.'

Beinmender replied: 'I'm not at all downhearted.' He paused as the waiter put bowls of soup in front of them. 'In fact, I am very pleased at the way everything has turned out.'

'You think his colleagues in America will eventually accept the manuscripts as genuine?'

'Yes. But, of course, it will be a long process. I think in all fairness you should put your mother in the picture.'

'I'll go and phone her now. But why are you pleased?'

'I'll tell you when you've made your phone call.'

'What did your mother say?' he enquired when she returned.

'She sounded quite resigned. You were going to tell me why you're pleased.'

'Joseph told me that it was absurd to consider that I had any links with Nazi Germany.'

'That's exactly what I have been telling you all along.'

Carla drank her potato soup with relish.

'Yes, but he put it more cogently.'

After a while, she said: 'But do you still want to go to Magdeburg to check on your father?'

Beinmender smiled and said: 'It doesn't seem quite so urgent now.'

Carla said, thoughtfully: 'I can see one of the points Joseph made: namely, that Wunder, without any memory of Mozart, could not in one sense *be* Mozart. But surely if he experienced Mozart's early conditioning and his musical training, you could say he possessed Mozart's soul, in the same way as you used to

tell us in your lectures that the real soul of Germany was
represented by Bach, Mozart, Schubert and Beethoven.'

'Full marks for being an attentive student. And now tell me
why I should go to Magdeburg?'

'To wipe the slate clean.'

'You're quite right. You understand me better than I
understand myself.'

*

Beinmender was putting on his jacket, in readiness to start
their journey, when Carla burst into the room, flung her arms
around him and said: 'It's happened. Everything is okay.'

'What exactly has happened?'

'My mother has just rung back to say she forgot to tell me
that she has called off the divorce proceedings.'

'Well, that's great.'

'Take off your jacket?'

'We're supposed to be going out.'

Carla removed his tie, She then made love to him with
extraordinary abandon. They rested and then, with her soft
breasts pressed against his chest, she whispered urgently:
'You've had your pit stop, Bernard Beinmender. Now be a
German racing driver.'

*

Afterwards, lying with his hands behind his head on the pillow,
Beinmender said reflectively: 'Funny name, Beinmender. Some
of my students used to call me Mindbender. Minds are strange
things. Shakespeare's Seven Ages of Man suggests that our
lives are divided into periods that make our previous selves
almost unrecognisable. Mozart in his new persona of Johann
Wunder seems to have written that beautiful fugue in order to
show that in passing from one stage to another, we end up with
only a hazy recollection of our former selves. His fugue

271

celebrates the loss of his previous identity and the acquisition of a new one. A similar process goes on with all of us — we scarcely remember our babyhood. Even childhood seems impossibly remote. But I can assure you of one thing — whether I am Beinmender or Mindbender, in youth, middle, or old age I shall always love you. Does that please you, *meine Liebe*? '

Carla didn't answer. She was fast asleep, dreaming that she was Wolfgang Amadeus Mozart.